MW00399487

Millionaires Row

Aaron's Descent

Author: Shi ONeill

This book is dedicated to my wonderful husband who wouldn't let me stop until this work was published; and to my friend Jacque and my sister Sue who generously gave of their time to help me edit the final manuscript.

1

Chapter 1

Hamilton, Ohio - 1894

It was one of those nights, the kind that makes your skin crawl. The air was barely warm from the day and the earth hadn't quite shaken the cold of winter. A cool fog formed that silently blanketed the few who still walked the streets. Jackson felt anxious as the little knot in his stomach tightened. He wondered what lurked in the mist past the limit of his vision, waiting for him. Muffled sounds beyond the muted veil of twilight only heightened his anxiety.

The steady pulse of the city eased into the languid rhythm of nightfall as he walked along the Fifth Street Canal. In the water blood-red streaks mirrored the sunset of early spring. Ribbons of red accented the stillness of the four-foot depth that carried barges from Cincinnati to Cleveland. A pair of rusty railroad tracks meandered alongside the canal until they disappeared into the dusky countryside. Trains often helped the barges and Jon Boats laden with local corn, barley and livestock make their way north as they navigated the narrow waterway.

Kicking up dust on the dirt road that followed the tracks, a sweaty brown gelding erratically pulled a classic Columbia Town Buggy. The reins listlessly dragged the ground and it was obvious that the horse was in control. Slumped over on the leather seat of the posh black carriage, tilting slightly left as if watching the canal, sat a thin disheveled old man. His morning coat was buttoned only at the top. It pushed his waistcoat and collar up around his neck in a way that made his face look like a wrinkled leather pouch. His bowler, covered with mud and God knows what else, could be seen lazily dancing down the tracks carried by gentle puffs of wind.

In the dimming light Jackson and his buddy Duffy walked home from the brewery on Court Street and nearly passed the spectacle without noticing.

"That's just crazy ole Bill. I see the old man messed up like this all da time." Duffy slurred, his tongue thickened from his earlier good fortune at the old man's Malt House. "He was buying rounds at his place all afternoon. Looks like he's passed-out drunk again."

"Good thing that horse knows his way home." Jackson muttered.

"I'm telling ya Jack, I'm not sure I'd put my

life in the hands of that old nag. Last week I had to pull the buggy off the tracks because it got stuck between the rails. Took the old man home; he only lives a couple blocks from here. Guess I'd better make sure he gets home OK, I'm going over and see what's up."

Duffy headed over to the buggy calling old Bill's name in an attempt to stir him from his drunken slumber. As he reached out to set him straight in the seat he noticed the old man was cold to the touch. Not natural for the kind of May evening that requires little more than shirtsleeves. Waving his friend over Duffy leaned his head down to the motionless chest, hoping to hear a heartbeat. His own heart jumped as sobriety quickly returned to help him handle the situation. And a situation it was, because beneath his quivering ear was the wealthiest man in this small town. Seemingly a little daft of late, but if a man owns most of the county a man could afford to be any way he wants.

"Holy Jesus, Jack, I think he's dead. Stay with him while I run to get help. If Aaron comes by on his way home from the ice-house, explain how I went for help. Maybe we'll get a reward for our good deed." Duffy shakily loped down the lane and crossed the small bridge that led to the west side of the canal, his bulky mass lumbering through the twilight toward the hospital and help

4

for the body that was losing heat as fast as the sky was losing light. As his wild heartbeat settled in his ears he thought, *"Don't let him be dead, don't let him be dead. Gettin' drunk ain't gonna kill a man. I gotta change my ways if a drunk can kill you; definitely changin' my ways – yep, tomorrow, definitely changin'. I saw him leave the saloon; he was fine except maybe for a little buzz."*

Duffy's internal dialogue looped through his confused mind as he shuffled through the darkening streets at his top speed. He wheezed as he ran, straining for a good breath of air - a guy his size just wasn't cut out for a jog like this. He soon rounded the corner to the hospital, a mere three blocks from the canal, and tried to speak when he finally pushed through the double doors. He gulped for several seconds before enough oxygen filled his lungs to allow only a slight breathy whisper.

Meanwhile, Jackson stood guard over the old man and his buggy. It was a creepy feeling spending time with a stiff in what was now full-blown dark. He jiggled around nervously, switching from one foot to the other, looking all around while waiting for the lamplighter to get to Canal Street. Black night descended quickly accompanied by a growing chorus of cicadas and winking fireflies. The smell of death with a hint of whiskey, enhanced by the stench of standing water wafting across the tracks, involuntarily

5

filled his throat with bile. Jackson wished they had just walked on by. Let someone else take care of this. Good deed, indeed! Facing Aaron when it comes to any matter concerning his father was something Jackson just did NOT want to do; *not for no amount of money, for NO reason.*

"He's deader'n a damn doornail for Chrissakes. Duffy's a crazy ole' bastard thinking we'll get a reward. Somehow this is going to end up being our fault. And I gotta pee, what am I supposed to do? If he doesn't get back soon, I'm just leavin'."

Jackson relieved himself in the canal and dutifully walked back to his charge.

Chapter 2

Hamilton, Ohio – 1994

I have never believed in ghosts, but then it
wasn't anything I thought about much. I definitely
never encountered one in my entire life, that I know
of, not until moving to Millionaire's Row. What
started out to be a curiosity grew into an obsession,
a compulsion, an immutable *need* to find out who
else lived in our house - beyond the veil so to speak.
It led me down paths I never dreamed I would
travel, treading cautiously with fear and
apprehension. I couldn't help myself, my curiosity
stronger than my fear of the unknown.

My journey began on a sunny day in early June.
My husband dragged me along on a trip around town with a
realtor. We were looking for a suitable replacement for our
high rent space on the West Side. It was an intense search
for something a bit larger and a lot cheaper. The broker
showed us three or four properties near town, none of

which grabbed us shouting *this is the place!*

We drove along the railroad tracks that used to front the old Fifth Street Canal, a narrow waterway that led to the Hydraulic in the early years of the city. We turned at Dayton Street, a popular shortcut to Erie Highway which is named for the famous Miami-Erie Canal. These two canals paralleled each other separated by six blocks of the finest homes built by industrial leaders of the city more than a century earlier. I know these things now, thanks to many hours of research; an examination of the past that made me aware of the lives imprinted on this neighborhood, the ether of those that still wander these streets, souls that cling to the tragedies that played out over a hundred years ago. But I get ahead of myself.

We cut across Dayton Street; the plan was to look at available houses in the suburbs. Dayton Street is lined with three-story brick mansions but I wasn't particularly paying attention, anxious to complete our search for the day. As I said, I was just along for the ride. Slowly driving down the street allowing for stopped traffic at the light I felt a tug, I don't know, just an unspoken pull causing me to look out the window to my left. There was an old Second-Empire French Mansard mansion vacant and with a For Sale sign in the yard. In fact, there were three old brick mansions for sale at the same intersection but it was this particular one that caught my eye. The realtor who was driving and my husband Aidan riding shotgun quickly looked then continued to ignore me when I asked if we could arrange a tour of the inside.

"It's not suitable, not at all what you're looking for. The price is right but it has been sitting vacant for over a decade," our guide said cruising along with his own agenda.

The day was spent investing way too much time looking at properties that held no interest whatsoever as far as I was concerned. I put my frustrations aside and made dinner for my husband and children, but I continued to be intrigued by the house on Dayton Street.

"Great meal, Hon, let me help you get the dishes," said Aidan.

"You know that house I asked about on Dayton Street? Do you think we could just drive by and take another look at it?"

"You heard what the realtor said, it doesn't fit our criteria and there must be a reason that it's been vacant for so long at that price. He said it doesn't have the proper zoning…"

"I know; I just want to take a closer look. We can worry about the zoning later. I don't know, something about it… well, I can't explain it." and I handed him a dish to dry.

With a sigh, he wrapped his arms around me.
"Yeah, all right - sure, let's take a ride," he consented.
"We can stop for ice cream – I'm sure the kids would be up
for that. There's no harm in taking a closer look I guess."
Aidan is a gentle man, always giving in to my whims. We
packed up the kids and went back to the abandoned house,
just to walk around and try to peek inside the over-sized
windows - to see what we could see.

We drove up and down Dayton Street two or three
times looking at every property with a FOR SALE sign in
the front lawn, to humor Aidan mostly, I already knew
what I wanted. The neighborhood was one that had been
allowed to decay over the years, a victim of absentee
landlords, but was now in the early stages of rehabilitation.
Young professionals were moving in, taking up residence
and making improvements. The area was designated as an
historic district so all renovations had to be appropriate for
the period the houses were constructed, which ranged from
1870 to 1910. Most, while historically accurate on the
outside, had been converted to apartments or legal offices
on the inside.

Aidan pulled our car into the driveway and around
back so no one would notice our clandestine snooping. We
parked and sat there for a minute, feeling like criminals

scouting a break-in.

"God Mom, do you think you're Morticia Addams or somethin'? It looks like the Addams family lived here. It's spooky, creepy and looks haunted."

"Logan, why not let me handle this," Aidan interjected. "How about the house next to it Erin, it's for sale. Or the house cattycorner, it's for sale too. They both look to be in much better shape than this one," he reasoned.

"I know, they look great; but there's just something about *this* house," I whined, the entire time trying to absorb every detail.

"Mom, you're nuts," Logan said. "It's old, it doesn't look like a house is supposed to; we can't live here. What's wrong with *our* house?"

Sara, our daughter, really had nothing to say. She came for the ice cream and her only problem with the house was that it stood between her and the Dairy Queen. She's very single-minded that little one.

"He's right you know. We're looking for a place that's homey; this would just require too much work to get to that point. People won't want to visit and believe me, I know you; you aren't going to want to have them over while the place looks like this. Let's think about it a little more and outline the pros and cons."

"Let's see if we can find a way in." I said

11

conspiratorially. "Where you've parked the car it can't be seen from the street. Come on, let's do it; we're already here." So we all piled out of the car and slowly walked the perimeter, peeking in windows and looking for an opening.

"Come here son, there's a window partly open behind this bush. I can give you a boost and maybe you can open the door for us." Logan reached for the window.

"Yuck, it's all covered with wet leaves, roly-polies and cobwebs. It's gonna cost you Dad."

"Not a problem, just get up here and let's get this over with."

It was a short drop to the floor for our lanky twelve-year old boy, who walked across the creaky floorboards of the foyer to the heavy wooden front door. With a little ingenuity, and a lot of pulling and pushing, the door inched open enough for us to get through.

"What's that smell Mom?" Logan asked, dramatically pinching his nose. "It's gaggin' me! Can't we just get out of here before we get caught? We're going to get arrested."

"It's just musty, it's been closed up a long time," I said, walking towards the open staircase. There was something dripping down the wall and cascading like a waterfall from the first landing. "I wonder what's going on here."

"Looks to me like a leaky roof," Aidan said in a low voice, "not really something I want to get into. If the roof's bad there's probably a lot of structural damage, Honey. I think this is more work than we can handle right now."

There was a noise outside the window we jimmied open and we all jumped at the sound.

"Please Mom, let's get out of here," both kids begged. Locking the door behind us we could see a game of flag football taking place in the extra lot. We sneaked around the other side of the building and back to our car before anyone noticed we were there, or so I hoped.

"Sorry, Babe, this house isn't for us. If we have to spend a lot of money on repairs it's not cheaper - we may as well stay where we are," Aidan argued.

"I vote we stay where we are, I don't want…"

"You don't get a vote young man," Aidan snapped, "now get in the car, all of you, before we end up in jail for trespassing."

"You know that's not going to happen, don't scare the kids," I said. "OK, it's time for ice cream! Let's go guys!" and to avoid any trouble we sneaked out the back alley and into the street.

Regardless of what my husband or kids thought, I was drawn to this house for a reason; I had a feeling of belonging.

The next several weeks found me driving by that old house every chance I got. I convinced Aiden to take an official look inside with the realtor, which led to a property inspection. As the clock ticked on the lease we were trying to escape he became more willing to discuss the possibilities. The asking price was well below market, definitely reasonable, since it sat vacant for the last ten years. It came with a huge double lot, which is rare in the city. I agreed to petition the review board to change the zoning to residential. For thirty years the building served as a church on the first floor while the top two floors housed the pastor and his family. It later became a medical center for children with special needs, and in rapid succession a variety of small businesses before the building became vacant.

In less than a week we moved everything from our small but expensive west-side apartment (yes, I got my way) to the three-story specter that consumed my thoughts. The house became a part of me in a way I can't explain.

In three short weeks we sorted through and boxed our accumulated clothes, dishes, toys and just plain junk that might "come in handy someday." During the transition of waiting for the apartment lease to run out, we made an all-out effort to make the dilapidated old mansion look like a real home. It's amazing what a coat of paint, some carpet and a little landscaping will do.

That was the beginning of my adventure. We spent the next three years turning the grand old lady into a fully-functional house with a kitchen, bathrooms and more space than we knew what to do with. During that period of rebirth, the house drew me in. We took it back one room at a time after officially moving into the expansive mysterious manse. Finally, today, the house is a home, and it is totally ours. Ours and Aaron's.

Chapter 3

Hamilton, Ohio - 1894

The courtroom was packed with curious spectators anxious to get a glimpse of Aaron Cavanaugh, one of the most controversial men around. The Cavanaugh family was worth millions, owning most the county. They rubbed elbows with important dignitaries in the state and federal governments; Aaron's cousin was even a countess in some European country. Airing the family's dirty laundry in court is not something Aaron found appealing, but he is his father's son and never walked away from a fight, public or otherwise.

Preliminary arguments had been stretching into weeks and this was the first day Aaron was required to attend. No one had a problem picking him out of the crowd. A fastidious man, he arrived in court in an expensive blue suit, a bleached white dress shirt with a stiffly starched collar and sporting a paisley silk cravat. It wasn't common dress on the streets of Hamilton, a working class city supported by the breweries and paper mills.

Aaron checked his buttons and smoothed his thick

brown hair to a perfect wedge in the back before taking the stand and facing his accusers. Aaron's brother-in-law was prosecutor and counsel for his bastard nephew who was trying to get his hands on the family fortune. Aaron would fight them with his dying breath; he wouldn't allow any of these parasites to enjoy even a cent of father's estate, not his nephew Edgar or either of his good-for-nothing sisters.

Aaron walked with a confident air around the polished walnut table and up the aisle to the witness box. Holding up his neatly manicured left hand while placing the right on the Bible, Aaron took an oath to speak nothing but the truth.

Taking a deep breath, he sat down on the hard wooden chair with the hope that all this foolishness would soon be over.

Chapter 4

The brochure for the May Promenade read, "Take a trip back in time and bite into a slice of Victoriana at the Dayton Lane Historic Area May Promenade, complete with house tours, carriage rides and old-time music."

"How quaint, I must be out of my mind."

Lucky us, our first year living in the district and we were asked to place our home in the Promenade, an event to showcase the neighborhood and its homes. Since our house sat vacant for such a long time they felt it would be a unique opportunity to add a property not previously shown on the tour. Of course my first response was *no, absolutely not, no way, how else can I put it for you; we haven't been here long enough to restore anything; it doesn't compare to the other homes, either inside or out.* I was embarrassed to show ours along with the homes that were quite opulent by comparison. My husband, however, didn't stand as firm on these matters as I did and he acquiesced, naturally. So our home was on the tour in spite of my protest.

We did what we could and opened our home to four

or five hundred strangers who didn't seem to mind that it was far less than grand.

The morning of the event could not have been more spectacular. The sun was shining, the birds singing and the neighborhood never looked better. Every lawn was manicured and brightly colored flower beds adorned each yard like vibrant petal rainbows of yellow, orange, red and purple. It was going to be loads of fun and I was getting into the spirit of things.

The area was closed to traffic so horse-drawn carriages and high-wheel bicyclers could mix with visitors as they strolled through streets, happily meandering from one house to the next. Bands were playing and residents wore turn-of-the-century garb, intermingling with the guests who turned out on this perfectly lovely day.

I waited at our garden gate punching tickets as friendly people moved chattily through our home. An elderly lady who appeared to be late seventies walked up to me on her way out and inquired, "Dear, do you live in this house?"

"Yes, I do. We moved in earlier this year and haven't really had much chance to renovate. It's something we could work on for the rest of our lives and not completely restore." I said.

"Don't worry; it looks beautiful to everyone else.

Only you can see the flaws. My name is Sally; I just wanted to introduce myself because I used to be the cook in this house many years ago before it was converted to a church."

"It's my pleasure, Sally. My name is Erin O'Reilly, that's my husband Aidan inside. You say it used to be a church?" I asked.

"Yes, that's why all the walls have been torn down on the first floor… such a shame, it was so beautiful. When I was cook here, three families lived in this house; they were all related. They owned the mercantile in town and were very well-to-do." Sally said that like it was a reflection on her own status, that she should be their cook. "At that time there was a spirit, a lady I would sometimes see on the stairs. Not every day, mind you, but frequent enough. Do you ever see her?"

"No, I've never seen anything like that here. Oh, we have the usual noises that come with older houses; you know, settling noises. But I've never *seen* anything."

"Well, you look for her Dearie. She's here," Sally's voice trailed off in her own thoughts. I thanked her and she gave me her phone number, in case I ever wanted to chat.

Unusual lady, I thought and put it out of my mind because the line had backed up while we were talking. I quickly began checking and punching tickets again to move the line along. The day continued in a festive mood; there were so many people that the afternoon seemed to fly by; people kept us busy the entire time. Towards the end of the day as the tour was winding down, a small group of women, all wearing red hats, stopped me in the parlor to ask a few questions.

"We used to go to church here when it was the Chapel of Love," one of them said.

"Chapel of Love! I like that," I replied. "It suits us."

"Yes, that was the name, it was a great church. We were just young girls then, not quite teenagers. Sometimes at the evening service a few of us would see a lady on the stairs heading up to the pastor's house. She was a gray mist from the waist down, so…"

"No, no – not a real lady, of course not, a gray mist like she said," another broke in.

"We called her a lady because she looked like a lady, yes she did; and it seemed romantic – a lady sneaking up to the pastor's rooms."

"He was a fine looking man, very handsome indeed," another of the ladies interrupted.

"She would move down the stairs, and then back up again. But she never moved off the steps."

"Well, you might be right about the mist being a woman," I said. "I spoke to someone earlier who came through the house and *she* said there was the ghost of a lady on the stairs when she was here many years ago."

"Did she go to our church?" one of the women asked.

"No, she used to be a cook in the house before it became a church, when it was still just someone's home." I said.

"We thought we would give you that little story, we've been anxious to come back in the church building again, it's been so many years now. It really hasn't changed that much, brings backs lots of memories," one of them said and the women graciously shook my hand and moved along.

At last – days end! I could look for Aidan and start closing up. His job was to escort the guests through the house while I punched tickets, and I hadn't caught a glimpse of him all day. I couldn't wait to tell him my news about "the lady".

After he worked with the other neighbors to clean up the streets so they could be opened to traffic again, Aidan came back and joined me in the gazebo.

"Let me tell you what *I* learned today," I said excitedly.

"Does it involve a ghost in the house?" he

22

interrupted.

"What? Shut Up! Did you talk to the church ladies? Wait, me first!" then I told him with as much detail as I could remember about Sally and the ladies that went to church here.

"Perfect," he said. "I met someone who used to be a secretary here when one of the businesses leased the building. Her desk sat in the parlor facing the stairway. *SHE* saw a lady on the stairs! That makes three unrelated sources describing the same thing. Now how do you explain that?"

"I can't," I was pumped, this was intriguing! "I'm going to look into this. You know there must be something to it if in one day that many people have the same story."

"And I think you should; you should get to the bottom of this mystery." Aidan said, maybe a little patronizingly. I didn't care.

"Did you get to see any of the other houses today?" he asked.

"Not at all, I was too busy." I replied.

"That's what the others said too. Everyone who worked the Promenade is going to take a private tour through the homes tomorrow night while their houses are still clean. I'd like to see the other homes, wouldn't you?"

"Sure," I said, pretending to listen. He slipped his

arms around my waist, nuzzling my neck, but my mind was racing in an entirely different direction.

The following night Logan hitched a ride to baseball practice with his coach and Sara decided to spend the night with friends. Neither had an interest in taking the home tour. So Aidan and I went from house to house, "*sans* kids", enjoying the beautiful homes on the tour that we missed the day before. Neighbors greeted us with glasses of wine, cheese and canapés. I was glad we didn't get a chance to take the tour on Sunday, this was much better. At the end of the evening we gathered around our neighbor's fire pit and talked about the event, how successful it was and how much fun we had on our own private tour. This turned into the first of many regular neighborhood parties where we walked to different homes for drinks and snacks and just good company. Before dousing the fire and heading our separate ways, the *Neighborhood Sashay* was born.

Chapter 5

Hamilton, Ohio - 1894

Aaron couldn't wait to get out of that stuffy courtroom and into the fresh air. He crossed the verdant green lawn, his pace a bit faster than his normal gait, trying his best to avoid the journalists covering the case that lined the sidewalks. And he almost made it out of the fray before passing Duffy, a man he avoided at all cost but luck just wasn't with him today.

"Hey there Mr. Cavanaugh!"

"Hello Duff."

"I was hoping I'd run into you today," Duffy replied hurriedly, "they asked me to testify tomorrow, what should I say?"

Aaron continued to briskly walk as he talked, forcing Duffy to change his direction. He followed behind him looking comically like a little puppy wanting a treat.

"Just answer their questions honestly," quipped Aaron. "You know my father wasn't out of his mind, drunk sometimes, but not crazy. Just tell them the truth."

"Yessir, you're right. I'll just…" but Aaron was

already out of earshot having dismissed the issue and doing his best to outpace old Duffy.

It was a warm day and Aaron decided to walk to the icehouse to sign the paychecks and review the next day's business before heading home. As he passed the newsstand on the corner, the headlines jumped out at him. ***TRIAL OF THE CENTURY CONTINUES*** *AS THE PROSECUTION PREPARES TO CALL AARON CAVANAUGH TO THE STAND*

"Hell will freeze over and I'll build an icehouse on it before they get one red cent of Dad's money," Aaron grumbled, spitting the sour taste from his mouth. He didn't have time for this nonsense. A few short minutes later he pushed through the familiar oak doors and into the sanctuary of his office. He was in charge here and had been for years. He alone was responsible for the Cavanaugh fortune, and no one would take it from him.

Chapter 6

Hamilton, Ohio – 1994

The library looked different when I walked in, the research room was no longer to the left of the door. In fact, I didn't see it anywhere.

"The library looks great, I like your renovations. I don't know where anything is now, though. Can you tell me where to find the Cummins room?" I asked the young clerk behind the new service desk.

"Sure, take the elevator to the second floor, and turn right when you get off. You'll need a key to get in to the reference stacks though," she retrieved a key labeled *Ref.* from the drawer and handed it to me. "Take this one and just drop it off on your way out."

"Thanks, I appreciate it."

With all the time I've spent in this building, I didn't even know the library *had* an elevator! But I found it quickly enough *and* the local history section on the second floor.

I began my research on the Dayton Street house by carefully examining the pages of city directories from 1892 forward. The rag pages were so old they crumbled at my touch. It felt wrong handling historical documents without cotton gloves, *but* the books were there for my use. I turned the pages with extreme caution while looking for clues to the invisible inhabitants of my home. I meticulously recorded every occupant for my address, and then cross-checked by name in those volumes that were organized by name instead of address. I generated several hand-written pages of names, occupations and servants for those who dwelled in the same rooms I now call home. OK, I had the names but they were just words on a page. What were their stories?

I went day after day to the library to search the books in the local history room, checking and cross-checking information. I engaged in the tedious task of searching the archived newspapers on microfilm, more days than not with little success. After months of pouring through rolls of microfilm I finally hit pay-dirt.

THE COMMON
PLEAS

**Still Engaged in
The Trial of the
Century**
Reported in full for
Republican Readers

Edgar   C.
Byron, his step-mother
Ella Cavanaugh Byron
and his Aunt Lelia
Cavanaugh claim Aaron
Longstreet   Schlager
Cavanaugh induced his
father to give money,
checks, and securities,
etc. to him and that no
account was ever made
or service rendered.
Sensational allegations
made.

The   plaintiff,
who is a grandchild of
the deceased, is the only
heir-at-law of Mary M.
Byron who was the
eldest daughter of
William   H.   H.
Cavanaugh, and who
died intestate in 1867.

Aaron   L.   S.
Cavanaugh is charged
with having acquired
large sums due to his
influence over his
father, managed his
business until his death
and dictated his will.
Deceased acquired a
large personal estate
and in addition to this

was in receipt of a large income, which fell into the hands of Aaron Cavanaugh. In all the eight causes of action in the petition it is alleged that Aaron L. S. Cavanaugh procured all the benefits from this estate, and in addition that he induced his father to sign and deliver to him checks and income in the amount of $58,063.54.

"Honey," I called to Aiden, "you aren't going to believe what I found! Look at all the articles I have about Aaron." On the table I arranged several copies I had made at the library of newspaper articles dating from 1894. "Wait until you read them! When Aaron's father died - he was a millionaire or something - his sisters and nephew sued Aaron for everything in his father's estate. These are so revealing; all kinds of information about their personal lives, you have to read them."

"I know you're excited, but for now, why don't you just tell me what you know while I put some supper on," Aidan said.

"There's nothing in here about what happened to

Aaron but it does say he had a sister that died, Fannie, and two sisters and a nephew that sued him for everything. Then blah, blah, blah - there's a lot of boring detail about the assets. I can't figure out how Fannie died, her story isn't in here. Only that she married, Aaron committed her to an insane asylum in Oxford, and after she died their father started drinking heavily. There's so much more than that in these articles, though, this trial went on for over a year. I don't know…"

"Take a breath, Honey. You're hyper-ventilating," he interrupted, stirring the stew as we talked.

"I'm going to research the United States Census starting tomorrow. I need to find out who all these people are. This just opens up so many doors."

"Sounds like a good idea. Are you thinking that Fannie is the lady on the stairs?"

"I don't know," I said easing into a chair, ready for some of Aiden's famous Irish Stew, "but it's a clue isn't it? A start?"

WILD is an acronym for "wake-initiated-lucid-dream", and a lucid dream is one that occurs when a person is awake but at the same time is in a dream state; the dreamer is still conscious. WILD is a better descriptor than I could *ever* come up with for my experience in the sweltering parlor one summer night.

When the temperature at midnight is over eighty and the humidity an Amazon rainforest, sleep doesn't come easily to an insomniac. My only hope for a few hours rest was the parlor couch and the open French doors to the pub. I knew the undersized air-conditioner in the pub window would be grunting and grinding, doing its best against the intolerable heat, but the noise was a trade-off I could deal with.

Sweat was rolling off my face and trickling down my neck as I slipped out of bed with my pillow and made my way down the steps. Bright lights from the street streamed through the nine-foot windows to illuminate the hall. With sweat-soaked pillow and clean sheet in hand I made my way down to the parlor, absolutely wide-awake.

I turned the couch into a make-shift bed and opened the antique stained glass doors that led to the pub. I had to prop them open with a plant since they stayed open only when they had a mind to. I lay down, closed my eyes and tried focusing on the weak puffs of cool air coming from the next room.

Our house hasn't changed much in the last one-hundred years. It would be easy for a weary person to be confused about just what year it was based solely on these surroundings. Flat on my back, my eyes closed I could hear the hum of the air conditioner in the adjoining room. Time was dragging. My over-active mind was a shuffling dialogue of the day's events, my research, irrelevant minutia; my thoughts were unsettled.

I decided to go back to bed and wait for the eventual alarm. I tried to get off the couch but my arms and legs refused to move; they had gone to sleep without me.

Feeling drugged, I slowly opened my eyes looking for the lyre table, the shabby chic lamp, and the baby grand piano. Everything seemed in order.

Very sluggishly I rolled off the couch and seemed to float across the wooden inlaid floor. I was conscious enough to walk carefully, remembering the time I jammed a rotten shard through the arch of my foot. But on this night I don't remember touching the floor. I floated gently across the parlor noting the snags in the decorative hardwood pattern.

I tried to focus, looking around. "Impossible," I thought. I could see but not see if that makes sense. Was I sleep-walking? The sooner I got to bed the better. Trying not to panic I made it to the foyer, then started a weary climb to the second floor and my bed, hoping to get some sleep.

"You know, I really do love this wallpaper; large mauve roses on a beige background. It goes perfectly in here," I thought to myself. But then there was something not quite right about the wallpaper, something seemed out of place. Didn't I just paint these rough plaster walls a navy blue last winter?

I reminded myself that I've had lucid dreams before. I knew how to wake myself up.

"Start over, start from the beginning, from the couch. Talk so you can hear it; touch something and feel it."

I focused on the couch and I was there. My WILD night was a foreshadowing of things to come.

Fannie

Chapter 7

Hamilton, Ohio – 1891

To Aaron, the old man looked like he had one foot in the grave himself. Since they received the telegram from the Palmer House in Chicago his father had been lethargic, un-talkative and more unkempt than Aaron had ever remembered seeing him – even after a long day on the farm when his dad smelled of pigswill and horse manure. How could he ever turn the old guy down? Now Aaron had to prepare for the long trip to Illinois to pick up his sister's remains.

"Why didn't I *make* her stay home?" he thought, "She was so fragile when that son-of-a-bitch stole her from the sanitarium. I don't understand why the courts allowed him to take her, *he* didn't take care of her, Father did – it was Father who gave her money so she could live *properly* among Chicago society. If only that no-good husband of hers had left her alone, eventually she would have forgotten him. What did she see in that bastard? He's a worthless drunken letch, his debauchery legendary and widely known, except to her. The only reason he married her was for Father's money, like he would ever see a penny of the family fortune. Not while I have a breath in my body, by God."

He thought back to just a few months ago when he had to take the train to Philadelphia to bring his sister home after a scandalous scene she made in the Colonnade Hotel. Fannie accused her husband of being unfaithful and giving her the pox, which resulted in Fred giving her a sound beating before storming out. She only followed him to beg him to come back to her. But there, well, something happened causing her mind to descend to the dark depths of Hell. Aaron sauntered into the famed luxurious hotel and found a forlorn Fannie waiting in the lounge. She was wearing a sparkling long gown, elbow-length satin gloves and a matching satin and lace confection embellished with tulle and feathers that elegantly restrained her wild curls. Good God she was beautiful! She resembled a graceful little bird with lustrous plumage masking tiny delicate bones.

The evidence of the night's scuffle was hidden in shadow, the dimness of the room hiding all but her beautiful profile. On closer inspection Aaron could see bruising and swelling on Fannie's face and purple-blue

36

marks on her arms and neck. Fred! Aaron wanted to find and kill that man, but his first priority was to get Fannie to a doctor then immediately home.

He didn't have time to think about that fiasco now, Aaron needed several days' worth of suits for his Chicago trip. There would be a memorial service at the First Chicago Unitarian Church in just two days and he would be the only family there. Besides he just enjoyed looking his best, not like some dirty farmer. He *wasn't* a farmer; he was a man of means, a stockman trading only the finest thoroughbreds; a businessman making a fortune in *icehouses*. Stylish hair and mustache were important to him - he never lacked style, most everyone would agree. But in this small Midwest town they wouldn't recognize style if it walked up and bit them in the ass. *Dandy*, that's what they called him, people who have never in their lives traveled in the high-class circles of Chicago and New York. If they had, they would recognize his status, show him more respect. He'll fit right in stepping off the train in Chicago.

Aaron was worried about the old man though. Fannie's death had aged him 20 years and he just wasn't coping well. He hoped his brother Willie would be able to handle Father's fits of depression until Aaron could get back with their sister. Aaron wrestled with the injustice of her death; thirty is just too young to have eternal dirt thrown in your face. That whoremonger Fred is going to pay for this! His anger escalating, Aaron closed his eyes and breathed deeply to regain control.

He placed two black suits and a tweed traveling suit in his valise, and enough shirts and personal linens to keep him fresh for the next four days. He didn't have time to get his hair trimmed before leaving, but he should be able to visit a barber in Chicago before the service. After all, Fannie was well connected, and Aaron wanted to show them all that the Cavanaugh family was as *genteel* as the aristocracy of America's "Second City". Surely the social elite will pay their respects at Fannie's service, and Aaron would be ready for them. They would see that Fannie had no reason to be ashamed of her small-town roots.

Closing the lid to his luggage and snapping the brass fittings into place Aaron heard his driver come up the staircase and tap lightly at his door. He cleared the frog in his throat and muttered, "I'll be right out, Stuart." With that, Aaron ran his unsteady hands down the front of his wool double-breasted frock coat, fingering the silk buttons, making sure they were secure. He would never admit he had a case of nerves as he readied to gather Fannie's frail little body and bring her home where she really belonged. *No, the button covers really could be pesky and Aaron was*

38

just being his detailed self. Opening the door, he motioned for Stuart to take the new leather valise. "I'll be down in a few minutes," he muttered. "Go ahead and get the buggy ready. Give me five more minutes."

Aaron hurried down the hallway to the front of the house to check on his father.

Tapping on the door lightly Aaron's words came out in a voice he didn't recognize, conciliatory and weak, not his style. "Pa? I need to leave now. Can I come in?" No answer came through the chamber door so Aaron quietly slipped into the room in case his father had fallen asleep. Aaron's heart ached for the old man; he would do anything to lift this hurt from him. The shrunken form before him wasn't sleeping, he was staring into the dimly-lit room without a blink and barely breathing. His thinning white hair wildly framed his face, gray stubble filling the cracks of its ever-deepening furrows.

Aaron leaned over the bed and said "Pa, I'm leaving. I'll be back in three or four days. Willie's staying here at the house to take care of you. Katie – you remember Cousin Katie, you like her – Katie said she would stop by every day to make your favorite dishes. Are you going to be alright?" Giving his father a gentle rub on his back, Aaron could smell the sourness of liquor on his breath. He'll tell Willie to limit the old man's drinking.

39

Not that Aaron blamed him for drowning his sorrows but the next several days will be hard enough on him without suffering through the meanness of a hangover.

"I'll be back before you know it." Aaron declared, backing out of the bedroom, locking the door behind him. He placed the key on the hall clock outside the door where everyone knew to find it. Can't have the old man stumbling around the house, not until Willie gets here. He frightens the servants, especially when he's drunk. Aaron wasn't concerned about locking the door, it was a routine only occasionally practiced, and the entire house staff was familiar with his situation. Sometimes Father would sleepwalk and it was *he* who feared falling down the stairwell located directly outside his bedroom door. Father had a brass button by his bed that chimed the bell in the parlor and kitchen if he wanted out or needed the staff.

Aaron smoothed his mustache and spit, wiping a small smudge off his highly polished shoes. He liked the way the gaslight mirrored on the shiny black leather. Reaching for his top hat from the hall tree he waltzed with a sense of purpose out the front door to the porch. The sun had set. Stuart, Aaron's loyal manservant, was waiting patiently at the side gate. It was an early May evening and Aaron would have preferred to walk the short distance to the train station, but he had luggage to deal with. He climbed into the buggy, his carefully packed bag on the seat next to Stuart. As much as he tried to fight it, Aaron couldn't shake the sense of dread as he prepared to bring his dead sister back to the family mausoleum. "Take the side streets, Stuart." he insisted. "I really don't want to see anybody; I'm not in the mood to explain Fannie's death to the idiots in this town."

"Yes sir." Stuart responded, pulling the surrey out onto the wide dusty road.

The train, belching steam, was waiting at the station as Aaron entered the new brick terminal building. He purchased his ticket while Stuart carefully placed Aaron's handsome valise on the flatbed wagon outside the long single-story structure. Stuart was thinking it wouldn't be hard for Mr. Cavanaugh to recognize his luggage among the shabby bags and cases on the landing. Aaron walked out with ticket in hand.

"Thanks Stuart. I'll meet you back here Friday at 7pm. Bring the buckboard; we'll be taking the body back to the homestead. Make sure my father and Willie get back to the farm Friday morning. And whatever you do, don't bring them along to the station. I don't want a scene. Just leave them at Evergreen while you pick me up."

"Yes sir." Stuart wanted to say more, but didn't

know how. The whole family was as intimidating as hell. "I'm sorry about Ms. Fannie sir," he said, eyes downcast.

Now why was that so hard, Stuart thought?

Without a word, Aaron mounted the steps of the club car as the steam engine abruptly jolted forward. The uniformed conductor in front of the short passenger train gave a wave to the engineer and jumped on the lead car as it slowly screeched along the tracks. The baleful sound of the brass whistle filled the night air. It seemed a mournful cry for Fannie. Aaron sidled through the narrow aisle of the club car, settling into a plush red velvet divan near the bartender. He craved a shot of whiskey to settle his nerves and ordered a double scotch from the mustachioed man behind the bar.

Chapter 8

Hamilton, Ohio - Labor Day 1994

Glowing embers took flight from the aged timber in the fire-pit, gradually ascending into an ever darkening sky. It was Sunday night before the Labor Day holiday, marking the unofficial end of summer. The warm breezes were a teasing reminder of warmer days. It was cause for celebration; mainly because any excuse for a party in the neighborhood was reason enough to get together. Stars blinked on as familiar faces gathered around a crackling fire, not seeking warmth - but rather the ambiance of a mesmerizing flame.

As one who lacked social skills, I waited for a lull in the constant simultaneous banter.

"Remember the stories about the spirit on the stairs in our house?" Anxious to relay what I found at the library but reluctant at the same time, I tested the water. If anyone showed interest I would share the scandalous personal stories I uncovered concerning the former occupants of my house.

Chatter, chatter, chatter, then a "Yeah, sure! I remember. Ooh, nothing's better than a ghost story around a campfire."

"I have a few things to share about spirits – or something - in my house," someone else interjected.

Before I lost my chance I spoke up. "I've been going through old newspapers on microfiche at the library and ...."

"So you found out who the lady was?"

"Well, no," I added meekly, "I found out who lived here in the nineteenth century and scandalous articles about the family in the old papers."

And just that fast I was out of the conversation, as others were anxious to tell their own ghostly tales. Anecdotes flowed one after the other, it seemed *everyone* had strange things going on in their house. I must admit I didn't believe half of what I heard; but then, they may have been saying the same about the incidents in my house – and I know those really happened.

"Let's find a psychic, someone to go through our houses and we'll just see if he finds anything. I'd be willing to pay for someone to go through my house," a neighbor from down the street offered.

"Me too," said another, then another, until nearly everyone was in agreement to find someone to verify what we *thought* we saw, heard or felt.

I offered to look into it.

Long after midnight we broke up to go our separate ways. It was agreed to find a reputable psychic to walk through our homes; someone who could provide some insight into what could possibly be causing our anomalies. I had no doubt mine were real, I experienced them. I couldn't speak for my neighbors but I definitely wanted an investigation.

Labor Day turned out to be a mixed bag weather-wise. I worked in the garden in the morning until I was forced inside by approaching storm clouds. It was just as well, I wanted to work on the computer anyway. It's amazing how many websites can be found on the Internet for psychic mediums. I read the biographies of all local psychics searching for credible references, assuming that if they worked with the police or appeared on television that they were legitimate, but as my husband always reminds me, "Just because it's on the Internet doesn't make it true."

Then I found Kevin. Kevin wasn't famous, but he *was* published. Did that make him legitimate? I don't know, but he seemed to be the most renowned in our immediate vicinity. He hosted a sizeable psychic fair (a good way to check him out in advance I thought). That should count for something, right?

"I wonder where we buy our tickets."

"I don't know, up those stairs I guess."

Jackie, a neighbor also interested in meeting Kevin, drove with me to the Psychic Fair; both of us were out of our element. We climbed the open stairway of the Convention Center in search of the conference hall, having no idea what to expect. The smell of burning sage stung my nose as we made our way up the stairs. Someone passed us waving a pungent smudge bundle in every direction as he descended.

A line winding down the hall and snaking around the seating area near the restrooms awaited us.

"Excuse me ma'am, is this the line for tickets?" I asked incredulously.

"Unfortunately, yes; but it moves pretty fast," she answered.

"Wow," I whispered to Jackie, "what a crowd, I'm surprised."

"Well, at least we know where the Ladies room is."

With our entrance bracelet securely fastened on our right wrist we walked through a set of double doors and into a psychic Wonderland!

Beyond the doors lay a maze of booths hosted by psychic mediums and readers, Wiccans, and Reiki healers working their magic on paying customers who lay prone on padded tables. To the left a double-wide booth exploded with colorful fabrics, dresses, robes and shawls of all kinds glimmering with sequins, embroidery and tassels. The aisles were congested with believers and skeptics alike. Some were dressed in glorious garb we saw displayed in an exotic booth we passed, and some in regular street clothes, jeans and t-shirts.

Above the din of the crowd we could hear the melodic rhythms of Tibetan singing bowls played by saffron-robed monks who were so involved in their music they were unaware of the chaos in the room.

"Oh-ma-gosh, where do we go first!" Jackie blurted, already headed down the next aisle as I stopped at a booth of crystals and lapis stones.

"Wait for me," I yelled over the noise. I rushed to catch up and held her by the elbow before I lost her again. "I think we need to find Kevin first, and then we can browse."

"Well, let's get that done so we can move on. Ask someone. We don't even really know what he looks like. That picture on the web could be ten years old." Jackie was impatient to take in everything in the room, and admittedly

47

there were sights I had never seen nor heard before. I
wanted time to look and shop too.

We stopped someone who looked like a volunteer
and asked where we could find Kevin. She pointed to a
table by the entrance; we must have walked right by it
coming in.

Kevin was talking to a couple as we walked up, so
we waited politely until he was free before introducing
ourselves. I explained we lived in an historic district, many
of the houses well over a century old, and that we were
interested in finding out if any were haunted. Did he do
that kind of thing?

In his soft mild mannered voice he replied, "I could
do that, but I don't understand exactly. Do you want me to
cleanse them? Send the souls on their way?"

"Well, we're not sure what we want. We're just
curious to know if there's anything to it. Some
unexplained things happen sometimes." Jackie replied. She
asked him about the possibility of reading the houses and
about his fee.

"I'm sure we can come to an agreement on the fee,"
Kevin said, "Here's my card. Call me sometime next week
and we can talk about the details."

"Thank you so much," I said. I slipped the card into
my pocket and shook his hand before walking away. It was

48

obvious he was popular, there was already a line five deep forming behind me. Having accomplished our task, Jackie and I merged into the ocean of people and were swept along by the crowd.

After stopping at every booth and taking time for Jackie to get a psychic reading, we stepped back through the looking glass, leaving Wonderland behind to the haunting flute sounds of Native American artist Blue Feather.

The arrangements were made. And to document the process, so there was no risk of missing or forgetting anything, we decided to videotape the tours in their entirety for as many days as necessary to go through ten houses. I emailed the cadre of fire pit friends and of course they all wanted to participate. It was necessary to limit the spectators to only a few so Kevin would not be distracted from his task. One of us would videotape, one would follow closely with a tape recorder, and one would take notes in the event of mechanical failure.

After a month of agonizing preparation, the day for Kevin's investigation into the first three houses had arrived; I was fairly excited and a little anxious. I had never met a psychic before this little project of ours, my impressions formed by movie images of crystal-ball gypsies in shadowy rooms swathed in flowing scarves where palms were read

49

and fortunes told. Meeting Kevin the week before changed all that.

Kevin was a slender thirty-something, and when we met at the fair he was wearing a golf polo, brown corduroys and a pair of comfortable brown suede Hush Puppy loafers. He was easygoing and friendly, very approachable. He couldn't have been further from my idea of what psychics should look like.

On the first day of our house tours I waited impatiently in the parlor with my curious neighbors for a fashionably tardy Kevin.

"Did he say he would be here at two?" Jackie asked.

"He did," I replied, "but we should cut him a break since he really isn't familiar with the area."

"I don't want to just sit here," the other neighbor complained. "Maybe I'll just go home and you can call me when he gets here."

I didn't want anyone to leave because it would be more difficult to round them up again when he *did* arrive.

"He'll be here any minute, don't leave. We should make sure we know exactly what we want to accomplish when he does get here so we aren't wasting time figuring it out as we go. Who's going to videotape and who will record?" I asked.

It was decided that I would follow closely with a

tape recorder while Jackie videoed with her camcorder. Among the three of us we certainly should get most of his impressions, allowing us to sort through them later. Our objective was to first see if we even had compelling reasons to believe we were haunted.

We talked about the possibility of getting something out of this endeavor for the historic district. No one felt threatened in any way by the alleged hauntings; it's not that we wanted to get rid of our "houseguests". This informal conversation evolved into the idea of a Ghost Walk fundraiser that we would propose at the next historic board meeting, and our "hook" would be that a reputable psychic confirmed that our spirits truly existed. After researching the actual history of the houses, we could tie them to his documented findings.

Nearly an hour late, Kevin pulled up in front of my house in a racy little convertible. He walked to the front porch where we were already waiting for him.

"I am so sorry." Kevin apologized, "I couldn't get away from my previous engagement, and then I got off on the wrong exit evidently, because it took much longer than I expected. I'll have to find a better way to get here." He tried to apologize again and I cut him off.

"It's okay Kevin," I said, "we actually got a lot of preliminary work done while we were waiting, so we're better prepared to make good use of your time." He nodded and visually relaxed.

Finally we began our leisurely walk through the neighborhood, meandering through the park, occasionally stopping for impressions that Kevin would have in certain areas. At the end of the five-block park we turned towards Dayton Street and its three-story brick mansions. We walked along the tree-lined boulevard and toured two of the more magnificent buildings. Both had reports of strange aberrations and in fact Kevin had quite a bit to say about past residents in each house.

We returned to Kevin's car and my house, the last on the list for the day. I was more than ready by that time to find out about the "lady". He started by walking our third-story loft, carefully inspecting every room, then returned to the narrow stairwell with a puzzled look.

"I'm not sensing a single thing up here. Not even psychic impressions, and definitely not ghosts of any kind," Kevin said.

"This floor was added to the house in 1913. The house was originally built as a two-story Italianate some time before 1880, then remodeled as a Second Empire French Mansard with the third floor in the twentieth century," I offered, proud that I knew the history of my home. "Maybe the spirits are from a time before the third floor was added."

"Possibly," Kevin said. "If it didn't exist in their lifetime, they wouldn't realize it's here now."

We walked down to the second floor which consisted of two bedrooms, our dining room, living room, kitchen, and breakfast room. He walked through slowly, spending several minutes in each room.

Hesitating in the back bedroom he said, "I sense a very sad gentleman in this room. One that was very close to his mother and father, and in fact after his mother passed over he spent a lot of time trying to contact her through psychics and mediums. He had séances in this house." Kevin would pause after each statement, nodding his head as though he were listening to someone that wasn't there; looking around as though he saw something we didn't. "He has a connection to the military and loved Sousa marches." Pause. "Yes, he loved his mother very much and mourned her for the rest of his life. He never married because no one could measure up to his mother. He was a Spiritualist and believed he could make contact with his mother."

Kevin walked through the other rooms giving them as much attention as the back bedroom, but came up with nothing. We walked down the formal stairway into the foyer, and then down to the basement. There he talked about an "old curmudgeon" who spoke to him and told Kevin we should "get out!" Obediently, we immediately returned to the foyer where Kevin began his tour of the first floor. He strolled through the pub, the den and hallway then back to the foyer.

"No, I don't sense anything else," he said.

"What about a lady?" I quickly interjected. "A number of people have seen a lady on the stairs over the years. Based on the number of people who have commented, I feel certain *something* must be there since they don't even know each other - yet their description is the same." As much as I tried not to lead him I couldn't help myself; I was desperate for answers.

Kevin walked to the open stairway and pensively climbed halfway to the landing. He closed his eyes, then stepped back down. "I don't feel anything," he said, and walked down to the doorway. "Wait! She's here, right behind me. She's trying to tell me something but I don't understand. I can hear a female voice talking, but I can't make out the words."

We spoke for a few minutes about arranging a time when he could return for a follow-up. While we were just chatting he asked, "Why do you want to keep these spirits around? I mean, usually people call me to send their ghosts on to the light, to help them pass over. But you just want information about who's here and didn't once ask me to send them on. I don't understand."

"None of us feel threatened, Kevin. We aren't afraid and don't mind living with them. They never try to hurt us." I said.

"They never would," he offered. "Spirits can never hurt you, don't forget that. They can't cause physical harm."

"Well, our main goal is to research your findings and back them up with historical fact. Since the district is paying for this, we were considering a *Ghost Walk* as a fundraiser. At Halloween, it would be something different, something special."

"It's an interesting project; I'd be interested in knowing how your research goes and if it supports my impressions. I'll call you about the remaining houses when I get back and can check my schedule."

With that Kevin walked out to his little sports car and drove away, nearly four hours after arriving.

A second psychic event came to the area that winter. I wanted to get a personal reading, but knew I would be too self-conscious if anyone went with me. I was possessed, consumed, by the alleged *lady on the stairs*, and more than anything I hoped for some clues to her identity.

I needed more details than the vague information that Kevin shared; and it was out there, of that I was certain.

Alone and afraid of the unknown, I was ready to turn around and go back home. I gathered enough courage to walk into the small meeting room of the local hotel. This wasn't the colossal event that Kevin's psychic fair had been, it consisted solely of psychics and mediums; no vendors, no crystals, no Buddhist monks. I circled the room and noticed a woman who looked relatively normal; a petite woman with a curly perm, slightly greying and shoulder-length. She hunched over the hand of her supplicant, tracing the lines crisscrossing the woman's palm with a carefully manicured finger. The softened lines circling her dewy grey eyes revealed compassion. Overcoming my fear I approached the table. A large sign with her picture and name hung above her on the wall.

"Excuse me, I'd like to reserve a time with Reverend Joan," I said sheepishly, causing the casually dressed gentleman behind the table to look up from his paperwork.

"Oh, yes, sure. Let me get you to sign your name next to an appointment time – looks like her first available is about a half hour from now." He handed me a pen and turned the journal in my direction. "Just sign here, the charge will be twenty-five dollars for fifteen minutes. You can look through this scrapbook while you wait if you like. It shows some of her work and travels; the light orbs in the photos are spirits surrounding her."

He opened the book to a page showing Reverend Joan with several people on what looked like a farm. They posed in front of a small white frame house surrounded by an expanse of lawn dotted with a few outbuildings, also white.

"That's what we call *The Hill,* that's where we live in Pennsylvania. That's Joan," he pointed, "and that's me – I'm her husband. We travel around the country visiting people and working these psychic fairs. You can see all the spirit orbs surrounding her here in this picture… and this one."

I feigned interest, pretending to look through several pages.

"I'll come back in about fifteen minutes," I said politely, and stepped away.

In the hallway I found the restrooms and wasted five minutes in the Ladies room. With another ten minutes to kill I just took a seat in the lobby trying to *will* the minute hand on my watch to move a bit faster. It seemed I waited forever, but fifteen minutes mercifully passed and I made my way back to Reverend Joan's booth. She was still engaged with the other client, so I stood next to her husband and looked through the well-worn scrapbook again, looking but not really seeing. My anxiety wouldn't allow me to focus.

"My name is Reverend Joan, I'm a Spiritualist minister. Please - come join me at the table," she said softly as her husband made sure to collect my money before the session. "If you will take my hands, I'm going to begin with a prayer for protection, then we'll do your reading."

"Okay," I said nervously. This was a first for me and I had no idea what to expect. To put me at ease she told me everything she was about to do before doing it.

"I'm going to hold your hands now, turn them palms up please." She began to pray, "Dearest God, Creator of heaven and earth, protect all here present in flesh and in spirit with your pure white light of eternal love. Amen."

Her eyes were trained on the palms of my hands as she began to speak, "I can see that you are very sensitive, I use that term to mean that you yourself are psychic," looking up she added "although you are also a caring sensitive person."

"No, I don't think I'm psychic. At least I've never experienced powers like yours."

"You haven't developed yours yet, but it does sleep within you. You need to focus, listen to your inner voice and you'll be surprised by your abilities. I highly recommend you find a Spiritualist Church to help guide you in your journey."

"We used to have a Unitarian church in town but I'm pretty certain it's not there anymore."

"Unitarian churches are wonderful places to worship, but they aren't Spiritualist. Find a *Spiritualist* Church, no matter how far you must travel. Cultivate your psychic gifts. Now, I see two men standing behind you. One is a Native American and the other is a white-haired older man. Do you know your spirit guides?" she asked.

"No. Is the white-haired man my father?"

"No, dear, he's not. But your father sends blessings to you and says thank you for the poem you wrote for his funeral.

With that comment it was all I could do to hold back my tears. I could feel my face redden as I struggled to maintain my composure, all the while thinking, *How could she know these things?*

"I have your spirit guides here, is there a question you'd like to ask me?"

"Do you know my spirit guides' names?"

"They tell me that if you speak to them directly they will give you their names. They also tell me that they've been trying to communicate with you for a very long time and don't know why you haven't acknowledged or

59

answered them when they speak to you."

"I didn't know they were there."

"If you want to work with your guides I suggest you practice meditation; take a class in mediumship, you have the power within. Do you have another question for me?" She paused while I tried to think. "Why did you seek me out today?" Reverend Joan asked, again in a voice so soft I had to strain to hear.

"I'm trying to find out who the lady is on the stairs in my house. Do you know who the spirits in my house are? Do I even *have* spirits in my house?"

"You are sharing your home with souls that have passed over. I'm seeing a very large 'A' and a hard 'K' sound but it may not actually be a 'K'."

"That makes sense, but it wouldn't explain the lady," I replied.

"That's all I'm receiving, do you have anything else you'd like to ask?"

My time was running out and it didn't look like I was going to get what I wanted about the lady, in particular a name I could research.

"Thank you, I can't think of anything else." The timer buzzed indicating I had used my fifteen minutes.

"You're very welcome. Make sure you sign my guestbook and I'll include you in my mailings," she said as she gestured toward her husband before greeting the next patron.

Driving home I ran through the day in my mind. That very night I scanned the Internet for Spiritualist Churches and found one located only forty-five minutes from home. I also carefully examined their doctrine to understand a little more about what I was getting into. The Spiritualist church I found was a Christian church that believes we can communicate with souls after they pass over. I guessed I was okay with that; at least it was a Christian church.

Aidan is a skeptic who just tolerates my dabbling with the supernatural. Trying to be supportive he said he would take me when I was ready; he was willing to give it a try so I wouldn't have to go alone.

Chapter 9

Baltimore & Ohio Passenger Train – 1891

Click-clack, click-clack, click-clack. The sound of the train sliding along the tracks was hypnotic, and the whiskey warm and relaxing as it slipped down Aaron's tight throat. Before he finished his first drink his body released and his tense shoulders drooped to a more natural position. All the muscles in his body shed the stress of the days leading up to this moment.

Now Aaron was alone with only his thoughts, and they turned back to happier times: a time when Mother was alive and everyone lived in harmony on the farm.

"I miss her every day of my life," Aaron lamented. Lost in his reflections, the ornate club car faded from view. His mind darted from thought to thought then drifted back to the times he tried without success to conjure up his mother's spirit. He frequently attended the Spiritualist Church with the hope that he could bring her back, just for a moment. Mother understood him; she was probably the *only* one who understood him. He considered all the women he'd met and bedded, and there were many, yet none of them held a candle to her. No woman could fill that void, that feeling of warmth and security that only his mother could provide. Yes, times were good when Mother was alive and the Cavanaugh's lived like gentry at Evergreen, the family homestead; a time when Fannie was an innocent naive child, when Willie was in school and Aaron ran the icehouse while Father cared for the livestock. It was a life of privilege.

Aaron, engrossed in his thoughts, was barely aware of the bartender as he came by to refill his glass.

The house at Evergreen was immense, a three-story white frame with a wrap-around porch topped with an ornate cupola. It was large enough to accommodate the six Cavanaugh children, four girls and two boys living, and a distant cousin from Ireland who served as a domestic. When the children were small, that cupola was the home of many flights of fancy. You could see for miles around from that height. Aaron would watch the barges on the Erie Canal gliding their way to exotic places he could only imagine at that time in his life. Aaron remembered Fannie … little Fannie. He sipped a fresh whiskey as his mind wandered lazily in the fog of days past.

Evergreen 1871

"Fannie! Fannie, hurry down! I'm waiting for you out back," Lelia yelled like a lunatic. Lelia was only a few years older than Fannie but far more mature. A year or two at that age can make the difference between a girl and a woman. Lelia had more boyfriends than Fannie could comprehend. She often wondered what her sister could possibly be doing when they slipped into town.

Lelia rarely got home before the first light of dawn, when she would sneak into the house through the mudroom door in back. Fannie knew that Lelia counted on her to tend to that door, to unlock it after everyone had gone to bed. It felt downright uncomfortable, and Fannie was sure to get caught one day and have to face the wrath of her father. She didn't want to do it, but Lelia held some power over her. "What do they *do* all night?" Fannie wondered.

"Fannie, get down here!" That tone snapped her right out of her thoughts, and Fannie took the steps two at a time as she ran down to the first floor, out the front door and around the porch. Lelia was waiting for her behind the barn.

"What is it Lelia? What's so darned important that you have to yell at me like that?"

In a hushed whisper, Lelia told Fannie about her

64

new beau. "He's so handsome, I *must* see him tonight or I'll just die! I need you to take care of the back door for me. Please, Fannie, he's expecting me; if I don't meet him at Smith's Theater tonight he'll go with someone else. He's the *one* Fannie, I know he is; please do it just one more time, I'm begging you. I promise I'll never ask you again."

"Why can't I say no to her? I'll just say NO!" Fannie thought to herself, but instead, like always she said, "Sure Lelia, I'll unlock the door, you can count on me."

Innocent little Fannie, Aaron was thinking. I blame Lelia for all this. Lelia corrupted her, turned her into a sneaky accomplice; introduced Fannie to the man who ruined her life. As the bartender poured him another drink Aaron's focus returned to the end of that night so long ago. So much had happened in the years since that it hardly seemed real, more like the haze of a dream as you wake in the morning with the elusive fragments still floating around in your head. But no, it really happened. Lelia's stupidity set the course of events that affected so many lives.

Fannie sneaked downstairs and faithfully unlocked the mudroom door, but Lelia didn't come home that night – or the next morning. No, instead of Lelia a deputy rode on horseback up the tree-lined road, stopping in front of an angry Aaron standing on the front porch steps.

"Hello Aaron, how's your morning?" The deputy

was feeling him out, because he had news that he knew would make Aaron's temper flare, it didn't take much to do that anyway. This information was promising a burst blood vessel. "Aaron, I don't want you to worry about Lelia, we've got her at the station and we're taking real good care of her."

"What's going on Larry? What's she done?"

"Well, Aaron, I'm not one to point fingers at anybody, you know that. Glasshouses and rocks, you know what I mean. But we found her fornicating behind the courthouse, in full public view. We can't allow that, Aaron. Fornicating is, after all, against the law; but out in the street like that for the whole town to see? Well, we just couldn't let that pass, even for a Cavanaugh. We had to take her in. So... you'll have to come bail her out, that is, if you want to."

Aaron said nothing, but his face burned scarlet – starting at his open collar and moving up, until Fannie thought he would surely explode. Still, not a word from his mouth. Containing his rage Aaron jumped in his father's buggy. Vigorously using his crop on the startled horse like a demon possessed he set out for town in a cloud of flying dust.

Fannie had been peeking out from behind the front door. She just knew she was going to "get it" when Aaron

66

came home, and it was all Lelia's fault.

"I'm guilty by association! She made me do it, didn't she?" Fannie was beside herself with fear, what will her punishment be?

"I'll never get to do the things other girls do, I'll be a prisoner at Evergreen forever because of Lelia," she moaned. "I hope she *rots* in jail!"

Fannie ran out to the washroom and spent the rest of the morning hiding under dirty laundry, praying she would escape the wrath of her father and brothers.

"Mr. Cavanaugh, Mr. Cavanaugh, sir." Aaron was lost in his thoughts as he tried to control his anger before facing Lelia, and he imagined he heard the jailer calling his name.

"Mr. Cavanaugh, is everything okay? Can I get you anything before I close the bar for the night?" The jailer became the mustachioed bartender as the club car came into focus and Aaron realized he was in that place where dreams and reality intermingle. He must have dozed off without realizing it, his memories so powerful they followed him into sleep.

"Sir, can I get you anything? You're welcome to spend the night in the club car; I can get you a comforter."

"Thank you; very kind of you," Aaron mumbled, taking advantage of the liquor fog enveloping him like a cozy blanket, longing for a couple hours sleep; just a little sleep before facing the onerous task of taking his sister home for the very last time.

Chapter 10

Hamilton, Ohio – 1994

I came back from a long day at the library thinking there has to be a better way. Slowly and carefully scrolling through miles of microfilm hoping something would "jump out at me" was way too tedious. Certainly there must be a searchable database of these public records online somewhere. I was Googling on the computer in the den when Aidan wandered in after work to see what I was up to.

"Honey, take a look at this," I said, "look what I found at the library today."

"What've you got?" he asked, grabbing the barely readable photocopy from my hands.

"It's another article about the trial, but it includes some very enlightening information about Lelia. I'm having a terrible time finding anything at all on her. It's like after this trial she just dropped off the face of the earth!"

"Give me a chance to read it. Some of it is pretty

hard to make out. Hand me the magnifying glass? Maybe that will help."

AARON TOO LATE TO SAY GOODBYE

William H. Cavanaugh Died Alone After Long Illness

At the time of going to press yesterday afternoon Mary Montgomery was on the stand and continued to testify about her employment with the deceased and Aaron Cavanaugh. Witness sent for the rest of the family after Aaron and Willie returned from the hospital with Wm. H. Cavanaugh's body. Aaron had sat up with the deceased many nights during months of illness preceding death. According to hospital staff, the Cavanaugh brothers were devastated as they awaited final pronouncement of the coroner before taking possession of their father's remains. Aaron was unable to receive his father's final words having arrived too late to attend his passing.

This Afternoon's Session

Court convened this afternoon at 1:30 o'clock and continued with the cross examination of Mrs. Montgomery. Witness for the last sixteen years worked for the deceased then Aaron. Witness said that deceased said to Mrs. Foster "Lelia, I want you to take your little girl and go home and stay there. You say you are married, but I don't know whether you are or not." This was during a visit of Mrs. Foster at the Cavanaugh homestead during the funeral of Mrs. William

H.   H.   Cavanaugh. Witness remembered hiding the deceased's boots on more than one occasion to keep him indoors when he was sick.

M.T. Leonard Called to Stand

Mr.   Leonard   of Dayton took the stand and said deceased generally hitched his horse on Court Street near Third and that he often drank whiskey in his saloon and generally forgot where he hitched his horse.

"It sounds to me like Lelia had an illegitimate daughter, doesn't it?" Aidan said after perusing the new article. "Was her last name Foster or Cavanaugh? She's referred to as both in your trial clippings."

"I don't know. I can't find anything for a Lelia Foster online or in public records. I'll tell you, though, this is really great stuff," I replied. "I found an article with Aaron on the stand where he's asked about *his* three illegitimate children! It said something like "heated words were exchanged between Aaron and the prosecutor and the

72

defense attorney tried to get the questions thrown out." I haven't had any luck finding anything on Lelia's marriage, her daughter, or Aaron's children if he really had any. And there is nothing on Lelia or Aaron's death. I went by the public records building today but got absolutely nothing."

"What are you doing now?" he asked.

"I'm trying to find online newspaper archives and genealogical sites that may have a searchable database. It just takes so long with the microfilm. It's tedious and I'm probably missing things, I know I am."

"I have dinner in the crock-pot if you're hungry. I'll be up in a minute, I have a few things I want to finish while they're fresh on my mind," I turned back to the monitor and my search.

Kevin mentioned that the young man in the back bedroom became a Spiritualist in an attempt to contact his mother; I had strong feelings that young man was Aaron. That piece of information from Kevin coupled with the comments made by Reverend Joan intrigued me, caused me to wrestle all winter with the idea of finding a Spiritualist Church. Like the trip to Reverend Joan it was something that I wanted but feared. What was I afraid of? I couldn't explain it, but I kept putting it off. I wanted to experience what Aaron experienced, then I might understand him better.

There's a tradition in our house on New Year's Eve; we write our resolutions on a piece of paper, fold it up and put our names on the outside. Each year we open our resolutions from the prior year to see how we did. On rare occasions we actually accomplished what we said we would, but more often than not, we rationalized why we didn't stick with our resolve.

"What's your resolution this year?" Aiden asked as I folded my white notepaper, his eyes sneaking a peek.

"Not fair, I'm not telling. I didn't ask you, it's private you know." I wrote my name on the bundle and for special measure sealed it with Scotch tape.

My resolution that year was to visit the Spiritualist Church and overcome my apprehension; it *was* a Christian Church after all. But just in case I didn't get up the nerve, I didn't want anyone, especially Aiden, teasing me about it. It took a couple of Sundays into the New Year, but I finally "bit the bullet" so to speak, and got up early one Sunday morning for a forty-five minute trip into the unknown. With Aidan by my side as he promised, we walked into a small four-room office in an industrial park. I had never been in a church like this, with no building – just an office.

We were greeted at the door by friendly "regular" people, teachers, artists, business men and women.

"I'm an idiot," I thought. I expected shamans and gypsies, but instead I found the friendliest group of everyday people I had ever met. How could I be so wrong?

I was put very much at ease when we walked into a small sanctuary with thirty or so chairs, only half of which were occupied. On the wall behind the lectern hung a framed print of Warner Sallman's famous *Head of Christ*. Aidan and I took our seats and read through the bulletin while waiting for the service to begin.

The organist played a song that was totally foreign to me, but it was rather simple and printed in the front of the songbook so I pretended to sing while the minister walked in from the back and opened with a prayer. The front row held four or five kids who were giggly and squirming in their seats as they waited anxiously for their children's story, a regular part of the service evidently. Then they were dismissed for the remainder of the time to a room, which according to our preacher catered to their special needs, loaded with games and children's bible stories and books that reinforced good moral behavior.

The remainder of the service proceeded like any other non-secular church except it was very interactive and what I would call "homey". Aidan appreciated the fact that it wasn't stuffy and judgmental, and no one was begging for tithes, which were the three main reasons he avoided church services. As we sang the doxology I felt a fool for putting this off for so long.

As I began collecting my coat and papers the minister said, "Now comes the part of the service that makes us different from every other."

Uh-oh, again I felt the crawly feeling in my stomach. But we were committed now and it would look too conspicuous if we stood up to leave at this point.

"Well, it won't kill me," I thought, "and I do have Aidan with me."

"Our first medium on the platform today will be Ruth, if you'll all rise and sing 'I've Got the Joy, Joy, Joy, Joy, Down in My Heart' found on page two-forty-three in your hymnal. Let's raise the vibration level by clapping while we sing! Remember, the higher the vibration the better the messages!" and the entire congregation stood and clapped enthusiastically to the song I learned in Sunday school as a child.

"Thank you, you may be seated," all closed their hymnals as Ruth looked over the room, seeing no one. "Today I'll be working with my joy guide Daisy and my Master Teacher guide Dr. Samuels. Spirit works on vibrations so if you hear a name that you think might apply to you speak up so Spirit can connect with your voice. The first name I'm getting is Joseph, does anyone have a

Joseph?" Three or four hands went up and I could hear several say "I have a Joseph."

Ruth gave readings for about fifteen minutes, each one continuing as the first. She would say a name and people from the congregation would speak up and get a reading. Ruth's readings were for the most part very general and could apply to anyone, but the individuals getting the reading were grateful and thanked her when she finished with them.

When Ruth took her seat the minister offered readings after a song that was a favorite to him. The congregation sang loudly and clapped to raise the vibration level. I must say that the readings from the minister were much more personal and specific. He seemed incredibly accurate based on the reaction from the congregation. Several times he mentioned names that might have been for me but other hands went up, so even though I could have spoken up a few times, I didn't. I was much too shy to have a reading; afraid that something personal would come out in front of all these strangers. Even though they treated us like family, I'm a very private person.

Aidan and I continued to attend every Sunday, getting to know the congregation and becoming more comfortable with them and the "Spiritualism factor" with each passing week. It was several months, though, before I was at ease during that portion of the service where mediums took the platform to give messages from those who were in spirit.

Reverend Ann was preaching one Sunday. She has a very different style and is without a doubt a phenomenal psychic medium. She came directly to me, not giving me a chance to decide if I wanted a message or not.

"I'm being directed to speak to you. Could you tell me your name please?"

"Me?" I asked as I looked around to see if she could be addressing someone behind me. She nodded in the affirmative and I replied, "Erin," choking on the frog I couldn't clear from my throat.

"Erin, have you been trying to contact someone who has passed over that occupies your house?" she asked me.

"Yes, I have."

"Is it a woman?"

"Yes," I said quietly, unsure of myself.

"Did you speak to her recently, like this past week? Did you ask her if she was there?"

"Yes!" I replied incredulously.

"She wants me to tell you something. She says you are right, that was her sobbing in the downstairs hallway. She wants me to tell you that she's harmless and you have nothing to worry about, she would never do anything to hurt you."

"Do you know her name?" I asked Reverend Ann.

"She isn't giving me a name, but she does tell me that she isn't the only one." She paused, then to some unseen person said "Yes, OK. (pause) Yes, I'll tell her."

"She wants you to know that there are a total of six spirits in the house. She said not to be afraid. When you think you sense her, she's there. Don't run off the next time, she said. She's fading away now."

"Thank you," she said to spirit then turned to me and said, "Thank you and God bless you." With that Reverend Ann moved on to another member of the audience on the other side of the room.

I was flabbergasted! I didn't hear a single word she said after that. On the way home from the service Aidan and I talked about the reading.

"She was dead-on, wouldn't you say?" asked Aidan.

"How does she do that?" I was still amazed, trying to rationalize what just happened. "It makes me believe, because she's good, but my mind tells me this can't be real."

"Honey, don't you think your mind tells you that because it has been filled with the doctrine forced down your throat growing up? You were never taught by the churches you've attended to investigate and find your own truth. That's why it seems outside the realm of possibility, because you've never been encouraged to think on your own. You have to have an open mind about these things."

"I know you're right, but it's hard to accept. I'll try to keep an open mind."

"Good," Aidan said as he pulled out into traffic.

"I think I'll look into a mediumship class. I accept things more if I can experience it first-hand."

"Do that, Honey. I think that's a good idea. Then maybe you can contact Aaron, or whoever the hell is in our house."

"Yep, that's what I'm going to do," I said.

Chapter 11

Baltimore & Ohio Passenger Train – 1891

"Next stop Gary Indiana! Gary, Indiana next stop!" The sound of the conductor's voice faded as he briskly walked to the back of the train.

Aaron stirred at the flurry of activity around him as passengers began gathering their belongings for de-boarding at Gary. He still had several stops to go, but it was best to prepare himself physically and mentally for what lay before him in Chicago. The taste of bile filled his mouth. He hated the morning-after taste of whiskey and would be sure to brush away the remnants from the night when he got his turn in the commode. It wouldn't do to have the sour smell of whiskey on his breath when he arrived at the Wexford Boarding House. He was looking forward to his shave and haircut in Chicago. When he looked good and smelled good he was an impressive man – and felt it! Yes, that was the first item on his agenda when settled in Chicago.

More than half the passengers got off the train in Gary, and only a few got on. Aaron took the opportunity to freshen up in the men's room. He would have time for a light breakfast in the dining car before arriving at his stop. He really couldn't handle much more than a little fruit and toast anyway with his nervous stomach.

"Grand Central Station, Grand Central in fifteen minutes..." warned the conductor as he walked through the dining car. Aaron gulped the last of his coffee and left more than half his breakfast on the table with enough money to cover the meal and then some. He was eager to collect his valises and line up a porter, not wanting to get stuck in the throng of people likely to board at Grand Central. He definitely wasn't in the mood to be slowed down by idiot people and long lines. His priority was to find a good barber and relax in the chair with a hot towel on his face. Pampering is what he needed now to shake the night and long trip from his stiff body.

Aaron was nearly the first to leave the train, having no trouble at all finding just the right porter to take care of his luggage and get him settled quickly in a hansom. Of course a little "greasing of the palm" always helps and Aaron spared no expense getting out of the terminal and on his way.

"Driver, I have arrangements at the Wexford Boarding House. Can you tell me if there might be a gentleman's club near there? I'm looking for a reputable barber close to my accommodations. Surely if there's a club in the area there must be a good barber nearby."

"Right, sir. I'm familiar with the Wexford and its neighborhood. The Mason's lodge is not far, but beyond walking distance. You'd have to arrange transportation again.

82

There is a decent barber you could walk to though, just a few blocks from where you'll be staying – located on Bayside Street not far from the park. It's far enough from the pier that the rowdy's don't frequent the place, as if they get a shave or cut anyway. An older Italian named Sam owns that place, a good fella but hard to understand at times."

"Thank you, I appreciate the information, I really do." Aaron had been thinking about that shave and cut since Gary, Indiana. It's just what he needed to smooth his rough edges. First he must settle into his room, but then he'll head straightway to Sam's barbershop. After a relaxing hour or so in the chair and a hot bath on his return he'll be his old self, and ready to face Chicago's best families at Fannie's memorial.

It was an uneventful ride to the boarding house and Aaron was grateful that the driver hadn't a penchant for conversation. Aaron slouched in his seat and took in the sights of downtown Chicago as the cab took the lake road heading north.

1880 Chicago was the busiest port in the United States. More ships called at the City's harbor than New York, San Francisco, New Orleans, Boston, Baltimore and Philadelphia combined. Because the population grew at such a phenomenal rate, the sewer system had to be extended to accommodate the overflowing population. It was well-known that Chicago's waste disposal system couldn't keep up and there was a growing fear of smallpox and the ravage of disease. On top of that, an increase in shipping brought with it hoards of longshoremen.

Now Aaron was not only concerned with stepping up his hygiene regimen but also the threat of criminal elements. His boarding house was too close to the docks for his liking. "I suppose that's the downside of living in a big city" he murmured, and made a mental note not to walk the streets after dark, to allow plenty of time for a safe return if necessary. Aaron was pleased when they pulled up in front of a clean white clapboard house.

The driver hitched the horses to an ornate brass hitching post, sporting a horse head with a ring through the nose, and positioned a wooden step in the dusty road on the house-side of the vehicle; it was a routine that he practiced thousands of times as he moved his clients from one side of the city to the other.

Aaron climbed the stairs to the boarding house and paid his attentive driver generously before walking through the screen door and into the parlor. The driver swiftly moved on to his next destination after the gentleman and his bags were safely deposited on the porch.

The Wexford House was a simple but well cared for clapboard house, a whitewashed Queen Anne with a wrap-around porch with pale blue dentil moldings. Two towers adorned with decorative trim and Tiffany transoms stood guard on each side of the central entrance. A neat wooden sign stood in front with the establishment's name painted in sky blue and lettering that stated: "Rooms for Gentlemen Only." A portly middle-aged woman led Aaron through a comfortable parlor. The lounges were plush and inviting. They passed several older gentlemen as she led him up the open stairs, across a small

84

landing, then up again to his room. Aaron nodded politely as they passed. His room was at the end of the hallway on the left, directly across from the washroom. Well, that was handy he thought, congratulating himself on his good fortune. Water closets were becoming ever more popular, but most homes had an outdoor facility or just a pot for night soil. The Wexford had a wonderful bathroom, just across the hall, with a commode and large claw foot tub. And he would be the first one to it in the mornings.

Aaron immediately unpacked his handsome new valise and hung his carefully chosen suits in the armoire. When all was in its proper place he walked hastily down the steps and out the door. Invigorated by the thought of his visit to the barber Aaron walked briskly, following the directions he was given by the carriage driver. He soon caught sight of the wooden pole with its familiar red and white stripe. Few people were aware that the barber pole originated when barbers also were known for bloodletting and would hang the blood-soaked bandages to dry on a wooden pole outside the door, making the familiar sight of red and white stripes as they flapped in the breeze. The round top was really a place to store leeches when that practice replaced cutting the veins. Aaron's head was full of these little known facts; he always considered himself a clever man.

The small building faced the park and looked to Aaron like it could hold only a few chairs. He walked through the door that was open to the street and paused, his anticipation mounting. Two gents were seated in elaborate, throne-like chairs; one getting a trim while the other was lathered for a shave. There was a small stove blackened from years of use, spewing curling wisps of smoke toward a tin ceiling. Next to it, on the floor, was a brass cuspidor already stained with a layer of brown. "Yes," Aaron thought, "sanctuary." This was a place where men could be men and not worry about offending the sensitivities of the ladies. Aaron could chew, spit or break wind on a whim; there was no need to put on airs in this haven of masculinity.

Aaron checked his cares at the door as Sam grinned a welcome.

"Saluto di benvenuto! Welcome friend!" Sam cried with an exuberance that was more than the situation called for. Behind Sam, positioned high on the wall for safety, was an ornately carved cabinet holding about thirty personalized, china shaving mugs with names of his patrons. Aaron agreed that having one's own mug was far more sanitary than sharing a communal one.

Below the cherry-wood cabinet hung an assortment of straight razors, with decorative ivory, celluloid or sterling silver handles and leather strops – Sam's tools of the trade. Lining the back bar were colorful ornate tonic bottles, some were milky opaline, some made with carnival glass. Arranged neatly below were shaving brushes, scissors, combs and clippers, talcum containers, sterilizers and manicuring implements. Each carefully lined up against the back wall and meticulously cleaned. This appealed to Aaron; without a doubt he was in the right place. Sam applied brilliantine to the scalp of one of the men and combing through it nodded to Aaron to take the empty chair. Aaron slipped into an upholstered leather barber's chair, ornately hand-carved. "Fancy" Aaron thought, propping his feet on an extended footstool, also carved with angelic cherubs and grapevines.

"I brought-a these chairs with me from the old country. Barbering is in my family for many generations, *in our souls!*"

"The time when I came over here, it was no style. The barbers, they have a great big clipper and put a bowl on the head, clip it around."

"Whatta happened, when they see me work, I build up a lotta customers," he said. "I have, what you say, all day long people waiting for me."

That's how Sam talked -- in a voice that dipped and rolled like a breeze from his native Tuscany. It was a comforting voice. It made you want to listen.

On the wall, next to the gilded mirror where Aaron admired his long straight nose, his black shiny hair and bushy mustache, was a hand-written sign that told Sam's patrons that a haircut, straight-blade shave and facial cost a buck. Right now, that would be the best-spent dollar in recent memory as far as Aaron was concerned.

The gentleman sporting a fresh hairstyle waved to Sam and wandered out the door. The second man was wrapped in a towel cocoon, a gentle rhythm to his breathing. Sam turned to Aaron after pocketing the haircut money.

"You new around here, I glad you picked the best barber in Chicago today!" Sam exclaimed in his robust booming voice.

87

The man with the towel on his face stirred, but didn't wake up. Outside, two men crossed the street from the park and sat on the wooden bench adjacent to the door. They were engaged in a conversation about what was fast becoming America's greatest pastime – baseball. The conversation soon escalated into an argument over whether Cap Anson, manager and first baseman for the Chicago Whitesox was in fact better in every aspect than lefty Abner Dalrymple, a very popular outfielder with 126 home runs this season. The men repeatedly cut each other short as one interrupted the other with yet another marvelous feat that could never be outdone. The voices, lively as they were, faded into a muffled dialogue that you can hear but can't quite make out the words.

"I'd like the works, everything." Aaron blurted out. He was tired, his nerves raw and he still suffered from the sour taste of last night's whiskey. "Trim my hair on the sides and back; groom the mustache and a shave please."

Sam went to work on the overwrought young man. There was a reason that his barber chairs were plush leather; it's hard to cut the hair or worse yet, shave a man who is so tense he can't sit still. The chairs, the scents, the hot towels were all instruments to relax the customer so Sam could work his magic. He rubbed a lightly scented cream into Aaron's cheeks as he massaged his face.

"Ohhh, this is heaven," Aaron groaned as he felt himself relax in spite of himself. He'd had facials before, but the massive hands of this northern Italian were something special.

The facial worked itself into a scalp massage and Aaron felt the world around him dissolve like butter in the summer sun. By the time the cedar-scented towel wound its way around his nose until it reached his ears Sam's voice sounded like it was miles away.

"Every morning he'd go to Gammage flower store, take one flower, put on lapel, every day a different color. He was what you call a distinguished man." Sam's voice drifted off as Aaron only half heard the words. The hot towel lightly scented, the burning cheeks, the lingering tingle of the massage; all these sensations had carried him to another world, a land void of cares and worry; a well-deserved limbo Aaron thought as he drifted into nothingness.

Evergreen 1870

Fannie was radiant as she knelt next to Mother's bed. A shaft of light broke through a small opening in the draperies and made its way across the darkened room, falling on the top of Fannie's bent head. Her wild hair caught the sunbeam and threw off a glow like a halo. Aaron stood in the doorway and wondered if that's what halos really were, just a sunbeam, nothing divine about it. But Fannie *was* divine; everyone's favorite; and spying on her now Aaron could see why. Fannie bent over her mother's hand, praying to a God who wasn't listening, praying that Mother would make it through the night.

Willie was down in the parlor with Father, who was indulging in a little too much whiskey, while Lelia prattled on

89

about herself, "Poor me, poor me," that inane drivel. These thoughts ran through Aaron's head in his own falsetto voice, and it just served to inflame his anger and hatred for Lelia. Lelia, who only two months before gave birth to that bastard child of hers conceived on the courthouse lawn for the world to see. What an idiot! And here was an angel, on bended knee praying for Aaron's saint of a mother – how could they come from the same womb?

That night the light was snuffed out from Aaron's world. That was the night Mother died.

Around two in the morning Aaron heard a slight peck at his bedroom door. It sounded like a branch tapping the window at first, so he barely stirred. He heard it again and shaking the sleep and confusion from his mind until he was firmly based in the here and now, he donned his silk robe and opened the door a crack.

"Aaron, she's gone," Fannie whimpered. "Mommy died, she just slipped off. I was watching her and she was sleeping deeply, then I heard a little gurgle and all the skin on her face fell like it wasn't attached to anything. It doesn't look like her, not at all."

"It's alright Fannie; she's in God's arms now. He's giving her a hug for you; she's happy and feels no more pain." Aaron didn't believe a word of what he was saying, but he wanted to make Fannie feel better.

"Aaron, she soiled herself," Fannie's words caught in her throat and she went from a whimper to a shoulder-shaking sob, "someone needs to help her, clean her."

"I'll take care of it Honey; I'll see that she's tended to."
Aaron slipped his arms gently around his little sister holding her
firmly to stop the shaking. This went on for what seemed like a
long time.

"Wait here in my room, I'll send Willie in to stay with
you. I need to tell Father, this is going to be really hard for him.
"

Ellen Cavanaugh, devoted wife and mother, died from a
severe case of influenza on a bone-chilling night in early
November. But it was more than the influenza in Aaron's mind.
She hadn't been the same since the scandal of Lelia giving birth
to her illegitimate daughter spread like a kerosene fire across the
county. In fact, Mother rarely left Evergreen after Lelia's fourth
month when her bulging stomach could no longer be hidden.
Even though Lelia was sent to live in another town the word
spread. The shame was more than Mother could bear. She was
already in a weakened and depressed state when the influenza
hit. She had no way of fighting back. It was everything Aaron
could do to contain his rage. He wanted to beat Lelia to a pulp
and leave her for the wild dogs that roamed the woods around
Evergreen. Now Mother was dead, and he blamed Lelia; and he
had to be the one to tell his father. As oldest son in the family, it
was his *duty* to tell him. More importantly, he promised Mother
he would take care of his father, so it was only right that he
break the news. And in Aaron's heart of hearts, he knew it was
also his duty to bury his mother. In his innermost thoughts,

Aaron wondered when it would be his turn to be taken care of. The only person in the world who had ever done that was lying in her bed, slowly stiffening as the life force drained from her withered body. There was no one in this world to lighten his burden, to make *him* feel loved.

The day of Mother's funeral there was a cold rain. The wind was just strong enough to make the icy drops sting as they pelted your flesh. Even though there were still red, gold and brown leaves on some trees it was obvious that winter was fast approaching. It was weather that heightened the sadness of such a loss. As numb as Aaron felt, the stinging rain was a constant reminder he was still alive, and Mother was not. It was a short ride by buckboard from Evergreen to Greenwood Cemetery. In fact, the cemetery had at one point been a part of the Cavanaugh estate. Father sold 1600 acres in a shrewd move several years ago and reinvested the money in yet another icehouse. Part of the cemetery deal provided a lovely hilltop for a family plot. Already his older sister and two of Mother's babies were buried there; and now the ground opened up to claim yet another Cavanaugh, his mother, his security, the only Cavanaugh that mattered.

After a respectable graveside service, the extended family returned to Evergreen, where the servants outdid themselves with a lavish meal that was too large to fit the dining area. They had to open the pocket doors so the whole ground floor was a maze of food, people, and idle chitchat about what a wonderful woman Ellen Cavanaugh had been.

Aaron could hear the last of the guests saying goodbye as the final buggy worked its way down the long road to town. He settled into his easy chair in the second parlor as the servants cleaned up the mess left by a hundred thoughtless guests. He'll admit that he had too much to drink that night, but never will he regret the things he said.

"Lelia, get the hell out of here – now!" Aaron exploded. Then, "whore" under his breath. "I can't stand the sight of you." It is true that Aaron said that, but he meant the parlor, he meant for that night, and Lelia thought he meant the house forever.

"Fine, Aaron, fine." Lelia snapped. "I'm depressed as it is, and I have this little baby to take care of. And HOW DARE you talk to me that way in front of my daughter!" she fired back, cupping the baby's ears.

"Lelia, she's two months old!" Aaron shouted. "She can't understand a word. The world doesn't revolve around you. No one cares that you're depressed. We buried our Mother today and you think only of yourself. You carouse, you get in a family way, Mother's shamed because of you, she dies and I blame you! Think of someone besides yourself for once!" There weren't enough horrid things to say to assuage Aaron's anger.

"Aaron!" Father boomed, entering the room.

"Sorry, Pa, I didn't know you were there." Aaron apologized.

"I can't stay in this house any longer Father. Either Aaron goes or I go!" Lelia whined. She had every right to be hurt by Aaron's bitter remarks.

"Lelia, don't make me choose because I'll choose Aaron every time."

Lelia stormed upstairs, packed her bags and searched for Stuart to take her into town. She didn't have to put up with Aaron's bad temper. She was a woman after all, a woman with a child. She would love that little girl like she herself had never been loved.

"Lelia, can I go with you?" Fannie was quietly sitting in the chair by the window in Lelia's bedroom. Fannie, the woman-child, was past her sobbing and felt numb. "There's no hope for me here now. If I don't leave with you I'll die an old maid at Evergreen. Please, can I go?" she pleaded.

"Of course, dear heart. It will be you, me, and baby. We'll take care of each other. We don't need those dirty old men. We'll give them a couple days to miss us, and then come back for money. They'll give us anything we ask for. That's the power women have over men in this world."

That was the beginning of the end, the ruination of Fannie. Aaron turned this thought over in his mind as he noticed laughter in the background. He actually wanted Lelia gone forever, but he never dreamed she would take Fannie. Once again, laughter pierced his reverie. The towel was gently unwound from his face as Sam said jokingly, "Oh yeah, this face is as pink and soft as a baby's butt now. It won't take much blade to shave this one." Peals of laughter filled the small barbershop. Evidently several of Sam's regulars came in while Aaron was traveling in his mind to a place he never wanted to

94

revisit.

Sam gave Aaron the cleanest shave he ever experienced, and did a respectable job on his hair too. A bit too European for his taste, but the Chicago elite would consider him a cosmopolitan. That was the important thing to Aaron, how the Cavanaugh family would be regarded at the service the next day.

Aaron paid Sam more than he should have and walked, deep in thought, out the door. His mind was still back at Evergreen. He stopped at a stall next to the barbershop, a flower store called Gammage. He bought one flower and slipped it in his lapel. He walked on with a bit of a strut in his stride, he felt like a distinguished gentleman.

Chapter 12

Chicago, Illinois – 1891

The birds woke Aaron long before the rising sun. The chirp of spring robins new to the nest outside the window was interrupted only by the occasional oCoo-OOH, ooo-ooo-oooo of the mourning dove. How appropriate, to be awakened by the lamenting song of the mourning dove, Aaron thought. He heard that mourning doves mate for life. The melancholy call of the dove outside his window sounded like she was separated from her love. She was trying to find him by throwing her familiar call high on the wind. That certainly hadn't been Fannie's problem; hers was a desperate cry for help, a cry that went unheard. Just days before her death, the divorce from her no-good scoundrel husband had become final. In Aaron's mind, it should have been a time of rejoicing. But, for some reason, to Fannie it was the end of her world. She looked on it with shame and humiliation. She would have stayed by his side forever, regardless of his philandering, but he dumped her. Her fragile sensibilities could never accept the fact that she gave herself to a man who didn't

love her; he probably never did. She felt flawed and
undeserving of the family she longed for. Fannie couldn't
have been further from the truth; the problem was Fred's.

It would be at least another forty-five minutes
before the full light of morning. Aaron, not the least bit
sleepy, would make use of the early hour to take his turn in
the bathroom. He planned to enjoy a leisurely soak in the
tub with plenty of time to make sure he looked perfect for
the day's events.

"It will take some time to figure out this new
haircut," he murmured under his breath as he flattened
down the sides with a little spittle.

By the time the sun was fully up and his housemates
stirring Aaron was dressed for the day, sitting in the
morning room with a cup of hot coffee, toast and scrambled
eggs. He was wearing a newly tailored black silk suit with
a bleached-white linen shirt sporting pleats down the front
and mother-of-pearl button covers. His gold tie pin
matched the new gold cufflinks that Kate gave him for
Christmas. No one quite understood his relationship with
his cousin Katie, and that suited Aaron just fine. She had
been widowed for a long time, since the beginning of the
Civil War. Occasionally she lived in Aaron's town house,
for those times she had to stay in the city. He took care of
her and she took care of him. It was a special friendship,

and what they did was no one's business but theirs. As Aaron sat eating his breakfast and reading the morning news he felt very dignified. Yes indeed.

On the Society page, there was a small article at the bottom right that spoke of the beautiful young Fannie MacKenzie, of her place in Chicago society and about the sadness of her untimely death. There was no mention of the manner of her demise or the divorce from her husband of just five short years. Separately on the obituary page was an even shorter article about the services that day at the First Chicago Unitarian Church. There were no personal comments in this one, only facts about the date and time of death and specifics of her memorial. It *did* include that a family member would be taking the body back to her hometown for burial, but no mention by name of Aaron or, in fact, of any immediate family.

Aaron took his last sip of coffee and indulged in a little idle chit-chat with the couple that joined his breakfast table. It was "Showtime" after all; time to impress Chicago with the civility and charm of the Cavanaugh family. Aaron was quite good at presenting an air of sophistication when the occasion called for it. After a little "social" practice on the couple to set the mood for the day Aaron called at the neighborhood livery to arrange for a carriage and driver for the rest of his stay. Fortunately they had a lovely Columbia model that suited his sense of style and a well-groomed silky-black Friesian to pull it. All that remained was to arrange for a driver.

By mid-morning Aaron was on his way to the church. The service was scheduled for 1 o'clock that afternoon, so there would be plenty of time to arrive, freshen up and prepare for the onslaught of Chicago's finest families. His stylish carriage retraced the path in reverse from the day before as it made its way south on Lake Shore, through the bustling downtown area to Michigan Avenue and 23rd Street where stood the majestic First Chicago Unitarian Church. Aaron didn't choose this church because the Cavanaugh's were, in fact, Unitarian as a family, but because it had the look of a stately European cathedral. Much research, or at least as much as time would allow, went into his selection of this venue. The church was very impressive, certainly greater than any to be found in Hamilton. Never in his life had he seen a church that could rival the magnificence of this building.

The minister was an English gentleman, Reverend Brooke Herford of Manchester, England. He was a well-bred and caring man that showed great interest in Fannie, learning of her heartaches in recent months from her friends in the congregation. He had met Fannie on several occasions and found her to be a well-mannered and demure young woman. Yes, he would prepare a poignant eulogy for her memorial, and yes, many of Chicago's aristocracy regularly attended his church.

Aaron's thoughts didn't wander as they had the day before, he was intent on how he would present himself (he must be in top form at all times) and what he would say about his precious Fannie. The time it took to get back into the city seemed far less than it did to travel out to the North Shore the day before and Aaron hardly felt prepared by the time they pulled up in front of the gothic facade. He took a few seconds to control his breathing toying with his mother-of-pearl buttons. Was he ready to see Fannie laid out in a coffin? He dreaded what was waiting for him inside, an innocent who was spoiled in childhood by the family that adored her, and spoiled in a completely different sense by a man who used women, disposing of them at will. Aaron hoped it was his precious little sister he would find draped in burial garments in this magnificent cathedral - not the broken dove cast aside by the ne'er-do-well Fred MacKenzie. Aaron smoothed his hair, checked his button covers once more, took a deep breath and stepped inside.

If a case of the nerves hadn't already taken Aaron's breath away the site of the main sanctuary would have. As the massive front doors slammed heavily behind him,

Aaron noticed first the damp coolness that enveloped him. A mixture of incense and mustiness filled his nostrils as he walked through the expanse of the chapel. In the central position high above the chancel was a stained glass window patterned after the Rose Window at Notre Dame Cathedral in Paris. Aaron was taken aback at the beauty of the transformed morning sun taking on the blues and purples of the glass as it silently passed through to the floor. The staccato clatter of his new shoes striking the marble floor echoed throughout as Aaron tried to walk quietly down the center aisle to Reverend Herford who waited patiently at the far end next to Fannie's casket.

"Mr. Cavanaugh?" the good reverend inquired.

"Yes, and you are Reverend Herford?" Aaron asked.

"Yes Sir. I hope you approve of the arrangements I've made. I tried to follow your requests as closely as possible; I only received your post two days ago. And with Sunday services, well, you understand."

Reverend Hereford slowly opened the heavy lid of the polished cherry casket. Inside slept a dainty little angel wrapped in a gossamer ivory gown, with tiny blue ribbons pinning her wild golden locks in place. Fannie always did have trouble keeping those silken wisps under control; they were constantly hanging down in her eyes as a girl.

"Lovely, Reverend, just lovely…" Aaron whispered. "She looks beautiful." His words were barely audible as though spoken only to himself. Aaron stood quietly for several minutes immersed in the vision of his little sister. Even in death she was the most exquisite creature he had ever seen. Maybe it was the air of mystery shrouding the church or the intensity of the moment, but Aaron could smell his mother, the scent of lavender soap and skin that was unique to her. He felt his mother there with him, helping him get through Fannie's memorial. For a fleeting second as Aaron looked up to continue his conversation with the reverend his eyes caught something in the periphery, a luminescence. Aaron had a feeling they were here together, his mother and his sister Fannie – they had come to help him through this. He wouldn't be the only Cavanaugh here, the three would get through this heartrending service as a family, and Aaron was comforted by the thought. He labored to get a good breath; he just couldn't seem to fill his lungs.

"She's breathtaking, isn't she Reverend?"

"Yes, son, she is. You mustn't be sad, her life doesn't end here."

Aaron replied with a positive nod and unintelligible sound. As much as he wanted it to be true, secretly he believed that life-everlasting was invented by ignorant fools. When you die it's over, done, you're gone forever never to be heard from again. Isn't that true? If it were otherwise wouldn't he have contacted Mother by now? Admonishing himself, he felt his sense of Mother and Fannie had been a moment of weakness, maybe wishful thinking. Aaron didn't know what to think. One thing he knew for certain, he had to be strong for the crowd of Fannie's friends that he had to face in just a very short time.

Chapter 13

Hamilton, Ohio – 2002

Aidan was winding down from a long workday in his customary fashion with a cold beer and a home-improvement cable show. I just finished the dinner dishes and walked out of the kitchen into the unlit second-floor hallway. Instinctively I paused, feeling a little peculiar; a slight buzz in my ears and butterflies in my stomach. I sensed someone was there, but in the dark I could see no one. Aidan and I were the only people in the house and Aidan was in the living room. I could faintly hear him commenting to *If Walls Could Talk* from the other end of the hall, so I knew he was watching TV. Hesitating I searched the shadows in the hallway, half-expecting to see something and hoping to God I didn't. The hall was empty. A few steps more towards the living room and I was overcome by a powerful smell - roses. I stopped halfway down the poorly lit hallway and inhaling deeply. I wanted to find an explanation for the fragrance, an actual source, so my imagination didn't run wild and fabricate an otherworldly reason for the heady scent. The aroma lingered. Aware of my shallow breathing, goose-bumps formed on my arms. I wasn't afraid though, I didn't feel I was in danger, only that I wasn't alone in the hallway.

"Aidan come here," I called. "I need you… hurry." He didn't come right away. It took a minute or two for him to pull away from Grant Goodeve's story about an old Indiana farmhouse, but he eventually joined me in the hall. "Do you notice anything unusual in the hallway?" I asked, grabbing his arm.

"The cold draft? This house is always drafty Hon." A wrinkle of his nose and a second later, "Do you mean the flower smell?"

"Yes! You smell it? It's so strong; it completely masks the old-house smell."

"It's strange, no doubt about it," he admitted.

I looked at him, he looked at me.

"Done here? Can I get back to my show?" Dismissed, he swiftly returned to his well-worn spot on the couch and settled in before the commercial was over.

In the weeks to come I often noticed the overpowering smell of roses, not only in the second floor hallway but also in the downstairs hall, and each time I added an entry to my ever-expanding journal.

I stared at my reflection in the window, lost in my

thoughts. The darkness on the other side of the glass, a harbinger of the late hour, transformed the ordinary glass into a mirror. Sundown in summer comes at nine or later, so it must have been fairly late in the evening. Aidan's meeting, running longer than expected, gave me the opportunity to continue my research in the quiet of our cozy den just off the parlor. Sitting at my desk the only noise was the drone of the CPU fan on the computer, the only light the desk lamp and the glow from the monitor. Otherwise it was pitch-dark and eerily quiet; the comforting white-noise lulled me into my creative zone. I was absorbed in my research on the history of our house, searching public records and making notes. There was some reason I was drawn to this house, and I was hooked on the idea of learning the personal stories of every single person that ever lived here.

Engrossed in my work I gradually became aware of a female voice softly sobbing, crying and sniffling. I thought it must be coming from the outside door to the den, so I looked through the window expecting to find someone in the yard. Dark as it was, the glow of the street lamp threw enough light to show the yard was empty. Curious but not brave enough to traipse through the shadows to find the sobbing girl, I merely poked my head out the door of the den into the darkened hall. I must have looked like a frightened turtle. I could still hear the soft cries but this time accompanied by an echo. I pulled my head back inside and debated whether to go looking for the noise, the house was still creepy to me sometimes.

On my toes, careful not to make any noise, I walked into the first-floor corridor and paused. The intoxicating rose-scent was only slightly stronger than the sobbing echo. Soundlessly, I tiptoed down the corridor and into the parlor. The rose perfume faded but the weeping continued. Careful not to step on a squeaky floorboard I crept across the parlor toward the open stairway, listening for the source of the crying. Once I crossed the threshold to the foyer - dead silence, the sobbing was gone. I paused there momentarily before remembering to breathe. There was no way I was going back to the den, I sprinted straight up the stairway to the second floor living room turning on all the lights as I went. "When Aidan comes home we'll go together and turn off the computer and all the lights," I thought. I didn't know why I felt afraid but I did, even though there was never a sense of danger.

Chapter 14

Chicago, Illinois – 1891

The heavily lacquered casket was nestled in the elegant but simple apse at the front of the church and remained open during the service. Aaron sat piously in the front pew listening to Reverend Hereford's voice reverberate from the vaulted ceilings along the bas-relief walls and back through the aisles. The echo of his voice was made even more pronounced by the fact that the service was attended by no more than fifteen people, most of them employees of the Palmer House Hotel where Fannie lived the last months of her life. They were joined by three older church regulars who never missed a service of any kind. If Reverend Hereford was in the pulpit, they were in the pews.

Aaron peered anxiously around the expanse of the church; there was no one in the vestibule or at the doors. Did they get the time wrong? Or the place? No, he read the obituary himself this morning. He wondered whether he should give his prepared speech or not. He was inclined not to, not to an empty house.

"I don't understand. What happened? Where are her friends?" Aaron's inner voice queried. This was a dilemma for Aaron. Should he climb those long stone stairs to the platform that held Fannie's lonely little body to deliver his heartfelt thoughts to all of fifteen people? He started to perspire and his breathing became yet more uneven and shallow. This wasn't at all what he had planned.

A quiet voice calmed him as it whispered "This is for you and Fannie, no one else. Say your words to Fannie." Of course she was right. Aaron settled down a bit, the sweat on his neck cooled to a chill causing the hair there to stand on end. A cold shiver shook him and he wondered if he really *did* hear Mother or if his mind was playing tricks. The whole day, *Hell*, the whole trip had been surreal.

Aaron ascended to the front of the church taking the dais just vacated by Reverend Hereford. Nervously stumbling over the last step Aaron took his place behind the pulpit; his was an eloquent eulogy deserving of more ears to appreciate it. Removing the notes from his pocket and taking care to modify it for his new situation, the devoted older brother of Fannie Cavanaugh MacKenzie spoke to a nearly empty church. Following a short pause to collect himself, he nervously offered his heartfelt testimonial.

From the depths of his soul he talked *to* his little sister. It was the hardest thing Aaron had ever done. He felt as though he had been punched in the stomach as he fought back the tears that slowly collected but never quite spilled. Choking on his words, Aaron delivered his speech, pausing occasionally to gain control. In a daze he returned to the front pew, unsteady.

In an altered state of reality Aaron stood dutifully next to Fannie's casket as mourners filed past offering their condolences. The process didn't take all that long with so few in attendance. A young woman placed a white rose on her bodice, it had just the slightest blush of pink tipping the petals. Aaron remembered how Fannie loved roses, the scent of rosewater gently permeating her skin and gowns. He noticed that the woman had a common look about her, wearing a house-dress with tiny flowers. Her hat was far too elegant for her attire and Aaron mulled over her incongruous look as she spoke to him.

"My name's Maggie, sir. I'm a chambermaid at the Palmer House where your sister lived these last several months. I've got her letters here." Maggie slipped a few sheets of hotel stationery into Aaron's right hand. "Her things are boxed up for you. I stored them behind the front desk. I got to know your sister pretty good. She just really needed somebody to talk to, to listen."

"Thanks, Maggie. Let me give you my card, perhaps you wouldn't mind shipping her things COD to Hamilton for me. I'm taking the train tonight and have to manage the casket along with my own belongings."

"Sure, I'll take care of anything you need in Chicago Mr. Cavanaugh. You can always reach me at the Palmer House."

"Thank you for your kindness, Maggie." Aaron just this minute decided not to stay an extra night in Chicago, he was ready to go home. He had plenty of time to change his ticket and get a wire off to Stuart. He had about all the "polite" society of Chicago that he could stomach. Maggie seemed like a trustworthy soul and if not, well there couldn't be much of value in those boxes anyway.

Running through Maggie's mind was the Last Will and Testament she just handed to Mr. Cavanaugh along with Mrs. MacKenzie's letters. Could she trust Mr. Cavanaugh? She hoped so.

Before closing the casket in preparation for the trip to the train station Aaron stood for a few minutes absorbing the sight before him. There lay his fair-haired little sister, looking so peaceful. Finally her wildly erratic mind was set free. An unruly wisp of spun gold insisted on springing across her forehead. Aaron tried unsuccessfully to secure it with the tiny blue ribbon that held her hair back. His

111

fingers lightly brushed her face and he was surprised by the cold stiffness of her skin. It felt like a marble statue, not like the soft and scented baby-skin that was always hers. On her right hand he noticed the diamond encrusted rings that looked grotesquely large for her dainty hands. He clumsily slipped Fannie's rings off her fingers and dropped them in the pocket that held her letters. He blamed himself for not taking better care of her. He promised Mother he would. Then he blamed Lelia for luring Fannie into the world, a world she wasn't ready for.

He closed the massive lid and the casket was secured for travel. Aaron couldn't wait to get home.

Chapter 15

Baltimore & Ohio – 1891

It was nightfall when the train eased out of Grand Central. The station experienced heavy traffic that time of day, so Aaron had to sit near the tracks for a while waiting for the B&O passenger train's turn to move up in the queue. It was a relief to feel the movement of the car, slow at first, then picking up speed. While the train inched gradually through the yard, it seemed to Aaron as though his compartment was stationary and the cars outside were the ones moving. In a matter of minutes the overnight coach was swiftly careening out of the city and into the countryside.

The dark of night loomed outside the window and all Aaron could see was the reflection of the kerosene lamps in the club car and a very weary stranger in a fine silk suit staring back at him. The last several weeks had taken its toll and the last two days were disappointing at best. Where were all of Fannie's friends? Why in the world did no one show up at the memorial? It didn't make sense, not at all. Fannie was a patron of the arts and a

regular at all the society gatherings in this town; she
attended all the balls, all the charity functions. Father made
sure she had enough money to dress in the latest fashions,
to make her place in Chicago's most prestigious circles.
Today Aaron did his part to give them a social event to be
remembered. Where were they? How dare they snub us!
The Cavanaugh family served presidents and dined with
royalty. How dare they!

"Drink, sir?"

"Yes, please." It was a different bartender on the
return trip, "Make it a double Royal Strathythan whiskey
on ice, and I'll settle the tab at the end of the trip if you
don't mind."

Merciful Heaven, Aaron would burst a blood vessel
if he didn't settle down. He just couldn't get this whole
thing out of his mind, couldn't let it go. He would have
ordered the whiskey straight up but thought better of it and
decided to start slow. After his first double-shot the blood
still hadn't drained from his face, he could feel the heat in
his cheeks. The next drink he downed without ice in just a
couple quick gulps. The Cavanaugh fury was beginning to
ebb, Aaron's bulging eyes and the veins on his temples
shrank to their normal size and the warm familiar buzz of a
good Scotch malt whiskey was settling in. Aaron loosened
his new silk tie and began to relax. He looked around the

club car noticing that it was a bit more crowded than the trip up, but still the car was only half-full. There were several groups engaged in conversation, no singles with the exception of Aaron.

The new bartender was good; he kept Aaron's drink replenished without waiting. He was an older gent, white-haired and clean-shaven; very polite, obviously he had mastered his craft. Starting with a full glass Aaron, who was slowing down rather quickly, took a sip then pulled the papers from his pocket. He had been tempted all day to take a peek but wanted to read, no pour over, his sister's letters at his leisure.

The first document was written on hotel stationery from the Palmer House, dated 18 April, 1891. Aaron lost himself at first in her simple beautiful script. Drawing the paper to his nose, he longed for her scent.

Chapter 16

Hamilton, Ohio – 2002

The music was so loud it caused my body to tremor in synch with the beat as vibrations pulsed through the room. The melody simply melded with the boisterous banter that grew ever louder as each tried to be heard over the contemporary mix blasting from the speakers. Escaping the ruckus of the pub I made my way to the parlor where I could silence the ringing in my ears. I heard the scrape of the heavy door as it dragged over the threshold. Someone evidently didn't know you have to lift the heavy door, a trick most of the neighbors were aware of; must be someone new.

In this old neighborhood, known as Millionaire's Row in its glory days, our house represents that bygone affluence the *least*. In the mid-1960's it was gutted of all original woodwork and stained glass. Those vintage treasures were then auctioned off to cover the mortgage by the owner at the time. Very little remained, but slowly one room at a time, we tried to replace those precious but lost artifacts. A startled expletive emanated from the foyer; based on the exclamation this new partygoer must have noticed the parlor – usually a hit - with its pastoral murals trimmed in gold leaf accenting the deep burgundy walls. My grandmother's sterling candelabras were freshly polished and the soft glow of burning candles delicately lit the less than perfect room giving it a romantic glow. I've always been a little embarrassed when the neighbors come to our soirées. Our home is far removed from the Victorian mansion it was at the turn of the century. When our guests see the house by candlelight I feel comforted by the knowledge that the imperfections are hidden in shadow. And after a few drinks, the party is about friends and the special sense of community that we share, not about the half-stripped windows with a hundred years of chipped paint skillfully hidden by satin drapes.

That night our private Pub was packed with rowdies, and it didn't take long for the karaoke to roll things into high gear. We have quite the setup; a stage with double microphones on stands, a large TV scrolling the words and more musical selections than most karaoke bars. It probably doesn't hurt that the liquor flows freely here.

Most mansions in "The Row" have been converted to apartments, but ours had been reconfigured in 1947 as a church with a second and third floor rectory for the pastor's family. What do you do with a huge, and I mean gargantuan, church nave? Well, if you're Irish, as my

117

husband is, you turn it into a Pub and the favorite party place for an eclectic collection of friends and neighbors. The overriding rule at our regular Sashay is that no one drives. That's why it's usually limited to the locals, so they can walk home - or someone can help them walk home.

So, who was this stranger at the door? I would soon find out.

It's no easy task to get the party to *leave* the Pub at a decent hour for the next house for a couple reasons. First, and probably foremost, everyone wants their chance to perform at the microphones, and most are pretty uninhibited by the time we need to move on because this Irish Pub stays well stocked. If someone is too shy to sing when he comes in, it's definitely not the case by the time he leaves. With a party-monger like my husband tending bar, no one ever has an empty glass. And he makes sure everyone leaves with "one for the road" - to tide them over while making their way to the next home. It's not always - okay never - a dignified parade.

"Hi, my name is Susan. I rent the third floor from Jack Lawrence and this is my friend Meghan. She's visiting me today from Oxford, we're both students there."

"Well, I wondered who our new guest was. I heard you come in the front door - *and* what you said, was there a problem? That's usually not the reaction we get to our parlor."

"I love your parlor! But that's not the reason for my... um, comment," Susan said sheepishly, embarrassed that someone heard her crude remark. "Don't get me wrong, your murals are beautiful, really. And I don't think I've ever seen those colors in a house before. You definitely need large rooms like yours to pull that off."

"Thanks, Susan, I think. But wait until you see the other houses on the Sashay tonight. They haven't changed in over a hundred years, I'm so jealous it makes me hate to come back home. What can I get you to drink?"

"A light beer is fine."

"How about you Meghan?" I asked, trying to draw Meghan into the conversation.

"I think I'll just have a soda for now. I can't stay long." Meghan mumbled. I could barely hear her since Karaoke was in full swing. It was loud and definitely animated.

After Meghan took her soft-drink she seemed to blend into the background, finding a vacant bench in the corner of the pub where the ambient light doesn't find its way. I intentionally lowered the lighting to soften the mood, and she intentionally found the darkest spot in the room.

"Is she OK? I hate to see her over there by herself."

"She'll be fine; I'll take her home in a few minutes. I should be back before everyone leaves for the next house. I'm so glad I moved into this neighborhood, what a great bunch of fun-loving people!"

With that my new acquaintance started making her rounds, talking to those she knew and introducing herself to those she didn't. What a grand addition to the group. She would fit right in. It was only fifteen minutes later when Susan and Meghan approached me to say their goodbyes.

"Before we leave, we wanted to ask you a question. I hope you don't think we're nuts." Susan said.

"Of course I won't think you're nuts! Besides, anything goes at these parties. Everyone's already a little tipsy and we're just getting started. What's your question?" I asked.

"Has anyone ever mentioned seeing spirits in this house? This may sound crazy, but when Meghan and I walked in after fighting that front door, we looked up your open stairway - very elegant by the way. Well, anyway, like, uh," Susan hesitated as she struggled with the words, "well, like, Meghan and I *both* saw something on the stairs, something moving," she blurted out. "It was like a mist floating slowly up the steps."

"Oh goodness, don't be afraid," I tried to reassure her, "I *always* feel safe in this house and there's nothing to be afraid of. Is that why you want to leave Meghan?" I asked, once again trying to draw her into the conversation. I hoped she wasn't subdued because she was spooked.

"No, honestly; I have a lot of work to do over the weekend. I'm just not much of a partier I guess. I shouldn't have come; it's just not my *thing*, if you know what I mean."

"Well guys, promise that if I tell you the truth you won't be afraid to come back. Susan, you will come back, won't you?" I said this but at the same time wondered if I should open my big mouth at all about all the things that happen here. Who would believe it anyway? But I was loose-lipped from the wine and already said too much.

"Of course I will," she said. "I just have to make sure Meghan gets home to the dorm before they lock the doors. But, tell me, has anyone else seen someone on the stairs, or is my imagination working overtime in this huge old place? But then Meghan saw it too, right Meghan?"

Meghan nodded a yes, not much of a talker this one. I could relate, though, I understood how uncomfortable she must feel trying to fit in with this outrageous bunch.

"Well, as a matter of fact," I started, "several people have seen a woman in white on the stairs. Mostly, though, our guests only get a sense of movement in the parlor when no one's there, or feel a cold draft that makes them uncomfortable. Occasionally there is an overpowering rose or floral scent. But, personally? I have *never* seen anything."

"So I'm not crazy then. Has anyone here seen *her*?" asked Meghan.

"Only a few who came through our open house at the May Promenade. Every year the houses are open to the public; we learn a lot of history about the neighborhood that way. Several have told me about coming to church here and seeing the 'lady'. And then there's my husband, Aidan. You know, that crazy Irishman over there?"

"Your husband has seen her?" Now Susan was being completely drawn into the whole haunted house thing. She had this amazed, incredulous look on her face. At this point I was thinking she would believe anything I said, but I felt the less said the better. I needed to gracefully end this conversation.

"He has seen a few things I think, that he'll admit to anyway, but he's a skeptic and a storyteller, so who knows? I, on the other hand, am a believer but have seen absolutely nothing; nothing provable – no concrete evidence, nothing indisputable – only perceptions."

If I had been honest, I would have told her about the Civil War soldier in the tri-cornered hat that materialized in the second-story kitchen. Or, the bloody scratches on my

122

stomach, and another night several months later when the scratches appeared on Aidan's arm. They were really more than scratches. They looked like the smooth swipe of a wildcat's claw. Deep and cleanly delivered. Mine mysteriously appeared during the night, three evenly spaced cuts secreting enough blood to soak through my pajama bottoms. I sported a smooth white belly when I went to bed and woke up with a painful four-inch wound. Aidan was wide-awake when he had a similar experience. He was home only a short time after returning from a board meeting; took off his suit coat and noticed a little spot on his white silk shirt, just over his bicep. When he slipped the shirt off we noticed the familiar claw marks oozing blood on his arm. What we found most puzzling was that there was no mark on the jacket or white silk shirt to indicate a wound that severe. Definitely there was something happening in the house that couldn't be explained. I didn't know how much of this I wanted to share, though, especially with someone I had just met.

"I'd really like to talk to you guys about this sometime. Maybe when I get back from taking Meghan home? Maybe you should have a séance here; wouldn't that make a great theme for your Sashay?" Susan was getting too caught up with the whole topic; she didn't know how serious it was. It's not something you play around with. I was going to have to dodge her when she came back, before I ended up telling her something I shouldn't.

"We'll see how that sounds after a few glasses of wine. Not everyone in this room believes in this stuff, you know. I don't really talk about it with anyone unless I know their convictions." I remarked, backpedaling now as I tried to ease myself out of continuing this discussion when she returned.

"Thank you so much, Erin, for inviting us. I'll meet you at the next house and we can talk about this some more. It's creepy, but very intriguing."

"Yes, thank you. And thanks for the soda. Sorry I'm not in the party mood." Having said her goodbye, Meghan quickly gathered up her things and started edging towards the door. She actually was pretty nice, I shouldn't have jumped to judgment; I react pretty much the same way when dragged to a party where I don't know anyone.

I was tempted to go directly over to Aidan and tell him about the "lady" making an appearance, but he was surrounded by seven or eight half-lit men hanging on his every word as he acted out one of his horrible Irish jokes. And they laughed harder and louder than the joke deserved because Aidan had such a way about him. This could wait; I'd tell him after everyone left for the night, in private.

Chapter 17

Hamilton, Ohio – 2002

"Honey, take a look at this," I said. "I finally found an obituary for Fannie."

Aidan followed my voice to the den to better hear what I was ranting about. "What did you say? I couldn't hear you from the pub. What have you got there?"

"An obituary for Fannie MacKenzie and an end to the mystery I think. I mean the trial articles *allude* to something tawdry or unusual with her death but now I have the details."

"Where did you get this," he said looking at the obituary.

"I've been emailing someone I met in a genealogy forum and she had this in her collection. No other information, just this clipping."

"You're getting way too wrapped up in this thing Erin. A forum?" When he saw the hurt look on my face he softened his tone and said "Let me read it." He took over my chair and computer while I read it again over his shoulder.

"Interesting," Aidan said, trying to make up for his earlier brusqueness. "Suicide huh? Why do you think she committed suicide? There has to be more to the story, don't you think? It's starting to sound like a soap opera."

"At least I have a new direction to follow. Maybe I can find out more about Fred MacKenzie now that I know he was manager for Fay Templeton. I never heard of her, have you?"

"She was a character in *Damn Yankees* or something like that," Aidan offered, "some George M. Cohan production. That's all I know and I'm not sure I even got that right"

"And since this article tells me that she died in Chicago, maybe I can find more in the archives of the Chicago papers. Just a little piece of information like this can open so many doors."

"Are you almost through messin' around with this?" he droned.

"What do you mean?"

"Sorry, I meant are you through working on this for tonight?"

"Well, I wanted to look a bit more to see if I can find anything else on Fannie," I said.

"Why don't you do that tomorrow so we can go

upstairs? I'm starving, let's have some dinner and you can work with Fannie in the morning."

It was so hard to stop now that I had these leads. I couldn't get enough information to satisfy me. Why did she commit suicide? What happened at the Colonnade to cause her to be committed to a mental institution? I had so many unanswered questions; it was too compelling to stop. But I did.

"OK then, I guess. I'm right behind you." I followed Aidan up to the second floor and put my research aside for the night. Well, for the evening anyway, because I dreamed about Fannie all night long. In the dream I was the spirit. My dreams lately were too strange for words.

In the dream I'm afraid. For the longest time I've wanted proof that the ghosts are real, since I first heard about the hauntings. But not tonight, not tonight. I'm lying in bed next to Aidan, and I'm having trouble breathing. My heart palpitates like the wings of a hummingbird - that fast. I'm tired and wishing I could get a good night's sleep. My fear and apprehension are building by the minute; because I don't feel like I'm dreaming, I feel awake again. I'm

127

not one prone to anxiety attacks but if I had
one I think it would be like this.

One minute I'm lying in the bed next
to Aidan and the next minute I'm out of the
bed **looking at me in the bed***! Am I a ghost,*
this MUST be a dream. But I can't wake
myself up, even though I know how to do
that if I'm having a nightmare. I decide to
just "go with it".

I glide out of the bedroom and into
the hall.

"Lelia, what's wrong with
you?" A soft female voice fills my head.

I'm not ready for this. In the
hallway is a frail little girl. Older, really
than a little girl, a young woman, but very
tiny and very young looking. It seems very
real but intellectually I know I'm dreaming.

"Fannie, what are you doing here?"
I hear the words spoken from my lips, but
the voice is not my own.

"I'm lost Lelia," the faint little voice
replies.

"I'm sorry Fannie. I'm sorry for
what I did, and I wanted to tell you that all

along, but you wouldn't talk to me."

Fannie disappears, just vaporizes like steam from a hot cup of tea.

"I'm sorry," I say watching her melt into the dark hallway.

The next thing I'm aware of is lying next to Aidan in the bed. I'm half awake- half asleep.

"What are you mumbling," Aidan said sleepily, "are you having a nightmare?"

"I'm sorry," I whispered.

"Sorry for what, Honey? Try to go back to sleep, you're just dreaming. Forget about it and go back to sleep." Aidan turned his back to me and was snoring before I had a chance to even talk to him.

I tried to drift off again, thinking of something different so I wouldn't have the same dream. Heavy intoxicating sleep slowly took control of my senses leaving me incapable of stirring, like the overpowering effects of a strong drug.

"Lelia, I'm lost. Help me..." I hear the faint frail little voice drifting down the dark hallway as I glide out of the bedroom

*door. I didn't open it; I just **floated** through it, following the siren's call.*

Chapter 18

Baltimore & Ohio Passenger Train – 1891

Aaron opened the first document, written on hotel
stationery from the Palmer House and dated 18 April 1891.
He recognized the simple beautiful script as Fannie's.
Drawing the paper close he searched for Fannie's scent
before reading her final wishes.

Last Will and Testament

Being of sound mind and in full possession of my
senses, I Fannie Cavanaugh MacKenzie, bequeath all my
earthly possessions, to include my assets in Hamilton,
Ohio, all my clothes and millinery, jewelry and personal
items to Maggie McPhee, my devoted chambermaid and
the only person who cares about me on this earth.

It is my utmost desire that my body be interred in
Rosehill Cemetery of Chicago, the plot and all funeral
arrangements having been fully paid, and that no notice of
my death shall be sent to any member of my family in
Ohio.

Duly signed and dated by:

Fannie Cavanaugh MacKenzie this 18th day of April 1891, Chicago, Illinois.

"Well," Aaron thought, "if that's what she wanted I guess she'll never know she didn't get it. I might have let Maggie have some of her dresses, but judging from that hat today I'd say she's already gotten her share of Fannie's clothes. Poor little Fannie, didn't she know that we were always watching? I had to report her every move back to Father, had to make sure that Fred didn't get even a penny of the Cavanaugh fortune or hurt our precious Fannie ever again." Aaron decided to withhold his detective's final commission, considering the man's incompetence, and certainly he would never use *his* services again. Fannie was more cunning than anyone imagined if she could commit suicide right under his nose.

Gently refolding the paper that held his sister's final wishes Aaron returned it to his breast pocket with the rings. He opened the second sheet that had also been folded in thirds. Again it was in Fannie's stylish handwriting and on Palmer House stationary. A line drawing of the hotel was centered at the top of the page. The letter was addressed to Maggie McPhee and dated the day before Fannie was found.

20 April 1891

Dearest Maggie,

You more than anyone know of the terrible anguish I am feeling because of the hurtful actions of my Frederic. This Sunday last he divorced me after a long battle – I have no fight left in me. I haven't been able to hold my head high since returning to Chicago, now this disgrace will prevent me from ever showing my face again. In spite of all the kindness you've shown, and I appreciate your patient attention to my worries, with the loss of Frederic I have no one. I am totally alone. Even though he treated me poorly, so did I him. He was all I had.

Grant me one last favor, dear Maggie. Keep my passing from my father and brothers, and especially from Lelia. Since learning in Philadelphia that she slept with Frederic, she is no longer my sister. It's best that none of my relatives know until I'm safely put to rest in Rosehill. Arrangements have already been handled and bills of sale are attached to this letter.

Take care, Maggie, forgive me. For all your troubles on my behalf please take what you want of my belongings.

Eternally grateful,
Fannie Cavanaugh MacKenzie

Behind the letter Aaron found a bill of sale for a cemetery plot, a cherry casket with brass fittings, embalming and burial. Oddly enough there were no flowers and no service included in the itemization.

Putting the suicide note aside Aaron opened the only other paper in the packet, a note from Maggie McPhee to Mr. Cavanaugh. It wasn't written on stationery, but rather a rough white notepaper. The handwriting was childish and the spelling and grammar made Aaron think that she must not have made it past the elementary grades in school. In it the young woman gave her regrets to the family and repeated the offer of her services, if ever they were needed. Maggie shared the story of Mrs. MacKenzie who lived a sad ghost of an existence since moving into the Palmer House Hotel. She explained in detail how she found Madam's body Sunday morning when she went in to make up the room. At first the dutiful chambermaid thought her mistress was still sleeping but when it came time to make the bed she couldn't rouse the listless slip of a woman. An empty morphine vile lay on her nightstand where a half-full one lay the night before. Maggie ran to fetch the doctor, but Mrs. MacKenzie was dead by the time they got back to the room. Again Maggie expressed her sorrow for their loss and included her address in Chicago in case they had to reach her.

Aaron tucked all the documents neatly into his breast pocket and eased back into the plush divan as he contemplated the words he just read. He was overcome with grief and remorse for his last conversation with Frederic. His head hung low as his breathing became labored. Just the thought that his arrogance may have had anything to do with this brought on a familiar anxiety attack. Control, control. He tried to take deep breaths, to change the thoughts racing through his mind with something less disturbing.

Having put the disaster of the memorial this morning behind him, he signaled the bartender for another blended scotch whiskey. Along with a slightly watered-down drink the thoughtful attendant brought a sizeable bowl of mixed nuts and placed them on the table at Aaron's side. After so many years working the club car, the bartender knew only too well that too much whiskey on an empty stomach wouldn't be good for his patron, nor the person cleaning up after. Aaron slowly sipped his refreshed drink and played with a Brazil nut, his breathing becoming more even as he succumbed to thoughts of happier times.

He remembered the summer that Lelia was gone from the house, living in relative isolation in Dayton until after her pregnancy. Fannie turned sixteen and she and Mother were planning her cotillion. It was a time when Aaron was happy to the point of giddy as he helped prepare Evergreen for Fannie's "coming out".

Chapter 19

Evergreen – 1869

The day was absolutely perfect for a garden party. Fannie turned sixteen in May and on this beautiful June day she would be presented to her friends and their families at one of the most sensational coming-out parties the county had ever seen. It was, to Fannie's young mind, much like preparing for a wedding. She spent months on the guest list; Fannie's list consisted of her best friends and just about every person she knew from school. In addition, Mother's list included most of the founding families of the area. Then of course Aaron and Father had their list of business associates. Easily the guests could number in the hundreds, at least that's how many Cook was preparing food for.

Evergreen was buzzing with activity, but Fannie's only concern was looking beautiful. The plans were in place, and it was up to everyone else to carry them out. This was to be Fannie's day, it was all about her. Her only job was to look radiant and soak up all the attention. At least, that was *Fannie's* plan.

"Mother, it's in the paper, did you see it! It had a

big headline on the society page of the Democrat. They called it the social event of the year, did you read it!" Fannie was breathlessly whirling about the kitchen, trying desperately to get her mother's attention.

"I saw it. Now settle down Pet, you'll be done-in before the party even starts. I don't want you sweatin' out those beautiful curls, besides you're a proper young lady now and should act like one. Ladies don't bounce around the house in circles, jumping up and down. I know you're excited, but you're all grown up now and mustn't be all giggly and wiggly!" she teased. Mother turned her attention to the apple compote, one of the many desserts in various stages of preparation. It was Mother's specialty, and the apples were from their own orchard, put up and stored in the root cellar by Cook last fall. "Now go out and see what your brothers are up to, and try not to make a mess of yourself. I still have a lot to do in the kitchen – I can't be mindin' you."

Fannie let the screen door bang behind her, "Aaron! Aaron!" Fannie called out trying to get her brother's attention. Nothing ladylike at all in that yell. "Aaron, did you see the Democrat! It's in the paper today! It's all about me!"

"I saw it Sweetie-pie, it's a great article. It makes you look like you're very important, and you are! You'll be the talk of the county after today. It's your day Fannie, enjoy it. Now I have a lot to do before the party, so you go in the house and just make yourself pretty. We only have four more hours until people start arriving. If you keep bothering us, Willie and I won't get the dance floor made."

Being especially careful not to mess her hair, Fannie paraded back to the house the way she had been practicing all week. Ladies don't run with their hair and skirts flying in the wind. That's going to be a hard one for her to remember. Tied up in front of the house was a buggy she didn't recognize, so when she pushed through the front door, remembering not to bang the screen this time, she was surprised by the sight coming her way.

"Fannie, my dear, I just *adore* your curls!" Walking across the parlor with her bulbous belly swaying from one side to the other was Lelia in a party dress.

Fannie got a sinking sick feeling deep in her stomach. "Lelia, this is my day. You'll mess it up! You aren't supposed to be here."

"Why Fannie, aren't you happy to see me? I've been gone so long. I just couldn't miss your party, it only happens once. Don't you think everyone would think it strange if I wasn't here?" Lelia cooed, smiling as she shifted her impressive bulk from one foot to the other.

"Fannie's right, Lelia dear," said Mother. It's not

time for you to come back; the town doesn't know you're in a delicate way. You're supposed to birth that child and come back with Harry after the baby is a couple months old; say that you married last winter; you remember the plan Dear. We have it all worked out. Please," Mother pleaded, "Let one of the hands take you home before the guests arrive. We have such a busy day."

"Well, I read about the party in the paper and couldn't understand *why* I wasn't invited," Lelia exclaimed. "Fannie, I'm your closest sister, we share so many secrets," She gave Fannie a knowing look as she stressed that last phrase. "I can't believe you want me to leave."

"Mother, help me!" Fannie begged "Today's my day, and you know how Aaron feels about Lelia and the baby, then for her to show up, he's worked so hard on this party. I'd rather he didn't even know."

"Know what?" Aaron asked, wiping his boots before coming in. One look at Lelia and Aaron turned red and silent. He wasn't going to let Lelia spoil this day for the family and he *wasn't* going to lose his temper.

"Lelia, we weren't expecting you. I thought we all agreed you wouldn't come back until the baby was old enough to appear legitimate." Aaron surprised even himself at how well he contained his anger. "Step outside with me for a minute, will you?"

140

"Mother?" Lelia beseeched with the eyes of a sad puppy begging for clemency. She was afraid to face Aaron without the temperance of her mother to keep him in check. Aaron would never do anything to hurt her in front of Mother.

"Just for a minute Lelia, that's all." Aaron said, taking her arm gingerly and leading her out the screen door. He guided her around to the side porch where they could speak privately.

Fannie didn't know what they talked about, and Aaron offered little information when he returned to the parlor still in a good mood. He said nothing about the conversation – only that one of the farmhands was driving Lelia back to Dayton.

That day really did belong to Fannie. For years after, Fannie would talk about this singular day as the very best time of her entire life. The west lawn was filled with the buggies of every important family in the county. There were tables and tables of food, along with enough seating for three hundred people and every chair was filled.

Fannie was presented by a very proud Father, who, in spite of his best efforts, couldn't control his smile; a smile so broad it took over his face. He walked Fannie through an arbor laden with roses, thousands of roses blocking the ample entry so that the two of them barely fit through. Of course Fannie's dress didn't help. Mother made it herself and labored over every stitch. Aaron had never imagined that so many flounces could fit on such a little dress, and Fannie knew how to walk so they all bounced to her advantage. She had been practicing that entrance for weeks. Her hair was pulled back with a dozen finger curls spilling down her back and a few uncontrollable curls springing loose over her alabaster cheeks. She was magnificent.

Taking care to remember she was a lady now, Fannie demurely danced with beaus long after the fireflies dimmed. The night was lucrative for Aaron and his father as they conducted business while others engaged in frivolous banter. Willie, as the youngest, watched from the balcony of his parents' bedroom as the night turned to dancing and revelry. The Daily Democrat reported it as, "the social highlight of the year," and it was.

Chapter 20

Hamilton, Ohio – 2002

I found a wealth of information on Ancestry.com, as Aidan suggested I might. But with all the material I accumulated I found very little about Lelia. Other than the year she was born and the city directory information from Dayton I found nothing.

Taking out a fresh pad and pencil I made notes about what I knew of Lelia, most of it from the trial articles. I knew she had an illegitimate daughter when she left home, but there was nothing more about the child; not a name or birth certificate – nothing. It was mentioned in trial testimony that she had a daughter after she permanently moved from the homestead. I knew she was arrested for misconduct on the Court House lawn and that Aaron literally kicked her drunken boyfriend off the family farm. She was financially supported by her father, who bought her a house in Dayton and gave Lelia a regular allowance until his death. She claimed to be married but there were no public records indicating that she ever married.

Searching through the newspaper articles, I began

highlighting every reference to Lelia. What an enigma! There was no proof she even existed after she was born, with the exception of these few newspaper clippings.

I wondered if Lelia could be the lady on the stairs, but why would she be in Aaron's house? It was possible, I suppose, but according to the trial transcript he hated her. When she spoke to him he ignored her, didn't even respond. It didn't seem likely Lelia would haunt this house. It was puzzling; there just wasn't enough information about the prodigal sister.

I listed my possibilities for the lady on the stairs, assuming it was someone from Aaron's life, knowing it was quite possible it wasn't. Three names were written on my notepad: Lelia, Fannie, and Mother. Aaron worshipped his mother, maybe it *was* Mother; taking care of him still, even in death.

Gradually shifting into a subconscious fog, I worked through my thoughts for hours until I got the creepy feeling that someone was watching me. My head was down as I wrote on an intuitive level, ideas drifting in and out of my mind. I broke out of my reverie and cautiously looked up.

"How long have you been standing there? You scared me to death! Why didn't you say something?" I scolded.

"I don't know; I had fun watching you. I haven't been here long. What did you find - anything interesting?"

"I did find something today in the transcript, let me read it to you. 'On the stand when Lelia Cavanaugh's illegitimate child was brought up in testimony, her sister Ella testified that Lelia had been a mother to her child, a daughter to her father, a sister to her sisters, a friend to her nephew. Lawyer for the plaintiff argued that because of the introduction of Lelia's daughter into testimony, he had a right therefore to ask Aaron Cavanaugh how he stood on his own three illegitimate children.' Pretty scandalous, huh? Of course there's nothing to be found on Aaron's children, and except for the trial there's nothing to be found on Lelia's," I remarked. "Other than that, I'm drawing a blank. I'm just listing what I've found, organizing my notes. I wish I could find more on Lelia; I have pretty much nothing on her. I think I'm ready to give up for the day."

"Sounds like you have pretty much to me, Erin. Don't be so hard on yourself. Remember, these people lived over a hundred years ago. After the courthouse fire and the Great Flood of 1913, you're lucky to find anything."

Lelia

Chapter 21

Evergreen - 1869

Poor Lelia. The farmhand pulled the carriage up to
the modest two-story frame house. It was near the market,
just a few blocks from the city center. The handsome
young hand took care of the carriage and tack, then fed the
horse before walking over to the train station to catch the
southbound back to Hamilton before the party started.
Lelia was looking for an opportunity to use her charms on
the young man but he left without a word. She waddled up
the front steps and into the kitchen to pour a glass of iced
lemonade before returning to the porch swing to escape the
heat of the house.

Only June but already hot as blazes and humid, she
thought. Lelia tried to relax in the swing, but her back was
aching from the weight of her perpetual burden. She found
no delight carrying this bothersome baby. She felt fat and
ugly and all alone while Fannie was dancing the night away
in a new party dress thinking she was everyone's princess. I
just don't know *why* I wasn't invited! She always gets

everything she wants while all I ever get is a hard time.

Lelia moved to Dayton around Christmas and was all alone over the holidays in this horrible house. She was so lonely. She missed going out, she wanted to party. She missed Harry Reynolds, why didn't he want her? He wanted her plenty until he found out about her delicate condition. Now he's nowhere to be found, and believe me, if he was around Aaron would find him. And if Aaron found him she would be married now, and they would have spent the holidays together in this house. They would have been invited to Fannie's coming out party. Lelia wouldn't be the pariah, or at least maybe not.

Lelia read the article about Fannie's sweet-sixteen party on the Society page. There was a huge headline with a guest list reading like the national census. Everyone except for Lelia was on that list. The only mention ever of Lelia on the Society page that she could remember was: *Miss Lelia Cavanaugh will be going to Dayton to stay with friends for an indefinite period of time.* Although, she made the Police Blotters a few times and she chuckled at the thought of some of the news items about her that *did* make the paper.

Lelia took up her stitching and sat on the porch until the lightning bugs became a twinkling nuisance. Soon moving from the swing to the upholstered chair to ease her

147

aching back, she lit the lamp on the porch while working on her cross-stitch. It wasn't something she enjoyed really, she wasn't much of a homemaker, but it didn't require a great deal of effort and it allowed her mind to roam. Everyone in this small neighborhood thought Lelia was Harry's widow; because that's the story she told, thinking it would give her the fewest problems from the local gossips. They were just a bunch of busybodies in Lelia's opinion, and she didn't want them in her business. After all, it *was* Harry's baby, probably. She would go crazy if she had to live in this house by herself. She needed to find a servant before the baby came.

"There's no way I'm going to be able to take care of this thing." Lelia mumbled.

The darkness of night had crept up fully while Lelia's thoughts worked through her situation and options. The sound of moths popping in the lamplight caught her attention as she gathered her things and carefully made her way back into the house.

Chapter 22

It was the same dream, the one I've had so many times before, about the man who sneaks up and holds me from behind. I think I'm awake lying on the scratchy parlor sofa; it always starts the same way. In fact it always ends the same way and plays out each time with just slight variations.

This time I cautiously rolled off the edge of the couch, hesitating only for a moment to glance around the room for the stranger. I had a gut feeling that he was there, but there was no sign of him. I had no idea what I would have done if I encountered him anyway. My breathing was shallow; I could feel my heart like a little fish out of water flopping around in my chest; my head was buzzing. I sat on the edge of the sofa wondering if I was awake, because it sure seemed like it, yet I wasn't certain.

I looked around to get my bearings before making a dash for the stairway and sanctuary on the second floor. I checked the foyer for the antique wallpaper and massive drapes that were usually the setting for this dream. Just outside the parlor the foyer confirmed that, in fact, all was well as I became aware of the rugged textured plaster painted dark navy that I labored over last winter. "This is good," I thought.

To make sure this was not my recurring dream, I touched the rough walls as I crept up the open stairway. After all, seeing isn't necessarily believing under these circumstances. So I ran my fingers along the walls on the way up. Oh yes, solid and textured for sure, I was awake this time; everything was as it should be.

Or so I thought. By the time I reached the first landing my chest felt heavy and sore. Now, earlier in the dream I pounded my chest in an attempt to wake myself up; maybe I really injured myself. Sometimes I try to talk or feel something and that will bring me out of a nightmare. But that wasn't it. No, I recognized this feeling from my pregnancy twenty-five years earlier; a sensation no mother can ever forget, the swollen soreness and heavy weight of a mother's breasts when her baby's hunger cry brings her milk in.

Once again my heart beat to an unnatural rhythm and butterflies wreaked havoc in my stomach as panic escalated to the next level.

I couldn't work it out in my mind: nothing made sense. Logic told me I was still in the dream because there was no way in hell I could be pregnant. Yet, there I stood on the first floor landing; no doubt about it, I felt the walls, I was awake.

I was just steps away from my escape. I stood on the top landing, opened the door separating the floors and walked through, aware enough to close it behind me so the cat wouldn't slip out. The cat could see them – the spirits; you could always tell when they were around by the way she acted.

Why did I constantly end up on the steps in this dream? Am I the lady? That's absurd.

I crept into the bedroom convinced I was fully awake this time because never before in the dream did I get this far. It always ended the same way with the man (Aaron?) pinning me down. Still I wondered about the pregnant feeling. The throbbing pain in my chest wasn't easing off, the soreness felt too real. It didn't make sense that I would continue to imagine it if I was awake. I stepped on a squeaky board and Aidan lifted his head.

"Am I awake?" I asked.

"Of course you are," he responded sleepily, and a little cranky if you ask me.

"Really, is this a dream or am I actually awake? I feel like I'm wide-awake."

The ache in my bosom was fading and I could feel the pain slowly subside as I walked over to the bed. Now they weren't swollen, not heavy, not hurting. They were just fine, like nothing ever happened, as though when I entered our bedroom I walked into one world and left the other behind.

"I would say you're wide-awake. You must have been sleep-walking again. I thought you went to the bathroom but you've been gone a long time." Softening a little, trying to make up for being short with me, he said, "I'm glad you came back to bed; I miss you when you're not here, it's hard to sleep without you next to me." He put his arm around my pillow to cradle my head, I slipped under the covers and snuggled as close to him as I could get. Then I gave him an abbreviated version of my dream or whatever it was.

"I believe you Honey. You should write this all down before you forget it. Right now - try to sleep."

"This house makes me crazy! Do you believe me

when I say this wasn't a dream?"

"You're squirrelly, you are," he said, "but I married you anyway. I love that there's never a dull moment. And if you say this wasn't a dream – by God it wasn't a dream."

"Don't patronize me, please."

"I'm not. Come here, let's both get some sleep while we still can," he said, pulling me into bed. "Tomorrow morning you can write down everything you remember, but not now.

"So many things happen that don't make sense to me. I need more clues – I need to put this puzzle together."

"Fine," Aidan moaned, "but do it tomorrow, that's just a couple hours from now."

"Sorry, I'll leave you alone." I snuggled up in the curl of his arm for only a few seconds before turning my back to him so I could face the window.

"I love you, Angel." Aidan whispered, before I heard his raspy little snore.

Chapter 23

Dayton, Ohio – 1869

The birth of the newest little Cavanaugh was
attended only by Mother, Fannie (who Lelia considered of
no value whatsoever) and a midwife. The same cute
farmhand that brought Lelia home early summer was the
same one that brought Mother and Fannie this time, but he
had no intentions of staying around while the womenfolk
took care of "women's things", to give an exact quote.
Lelia was hoping he would get a chance to see the REAL
her, not fat ugly Lelia. As soon as this messy deed was
done she would pretty herself up and show him her best
face. Men usually loved Lelia. She may not have been the
prettiest girl but she was attractive, and she was not afraid
to do the things other girls wouldn't. She was her own
woman in every way. She always loved life, and she had
every intention of getting back to it.

It was nightfall by the time Lelia's labor pains
began and Mother sent Fannie for Dr. Hitchcock. Lelia was
not accepting the pain of childbirth with grace.

"DO SOMETHING!!!" Lelia screamed. Never one

with a high tolerance for pain, it was enough that she got through the nine months of carrying her child. She just knew this experience would be the end of her. "Mother! For God's sake DO SOMETHING! I can't bear this dreadful…" and before she even completed the sentence the contraction subsided.

"Lelia, dear, your pains aren't coming close enough yet. You have a while to go before this angel slips out. All women bear this special responsibility in life, why, I've had seven babies of my own."

"And Mary died from the fever having her first one!" cried Lelia. "I don't want to die Mother, and I can't stand the torture this babe is putting me through. Isn't there something you can DO?!!" Lelia screamed as another pain started squeezing her belly like the worst cramp imaginable.

"Hold my hand Dear-heart and squeeze it if you need to. When Fannie gets back with Dr. Hitchcock he'll have some chloroform to help get you through this. Why, when I had my first, I remember we were just beginning the farm, I worked the field until Mary was just ready to pop, and Father helped me into the barn and …"

"I really don't care and I REALLY don't want to hear about it right now." Lelia bit her lip waiting for the "Cramp from Hell" to pass, squirming in her sweat-soaked featherbed.

The midwife came into the room with some warm mulled wine to help ease Lelia's cramps. Clean white linen rags were arranged by the bed in preparation for the doctor. Now it was just a matter of waiting for Lelia's time. All that remained was to make the ladies as comfortable as possible. She explained to Lelia what to expect, but the distorted writhing she-witch in the bed squeezed her mother's hand like there was no tomorrow and didn't hear a word that was said. Patiently the midwife readied the room realizing there could be many more hours of waiting before the blessed event.

It was nearly an hour before Fannie returned with the doctor and Lelia was hell-bent on making everyone's life as miserable as hers that night.

"Oh, come now Missy, don't be a baby. Women go through just what you are every day in this country. Let's take a look at you." Doc Hitchcock didn't have a lot of patience for weak fragile women, especially this young gal who was coming off as a tad spoiled and one used to getting her way.

"Where's the chloroform? Put me out." Lelia insisted.

"I can't do that until the baby starts to come out. That could still be a while yet. Let's get her another glass of that wine elixir you have there ladies, something to calm her down," the doctor advised.

"She's just frightened doctor, you must excuse her beha…"

"Don't speak for me Mother!" she screamed, slipping into a ferocious tantrum as another cramp took over her body. They were coming faster and Mother was hoping it was a sign that this would soon be over.

"Well, I can feel the top of the baby's head little missy. Things should start popping any time now," Doc chuckled, disappointed that his humor was either unappreciated or unnoticed.

"If he calls me missy one more time I'm going to pinch his peanut-head off with my bare hands," Lelia damned him under her breath.

Fannie went about helping the midwife while Mother stayed by Lelia's side offering comfort and support in the way that only Mother could.

Doc Hitchcock opened his black bag extracting a brown bottle and a bit of gauze, a forceps that looked like something out of Cook's kitchen, some white cotton gloves and alcohol.

"Strip her completely down and cover her with the sheet while I go wash up. It won't be long now young lady." And with that the doctor went with Fannie to the kitchen.

Lelia started crying, "Mother, it hurts so bad. I'm ready for this to be over. Oomph!" She winced at the pain as Mother rubbed her back and put a cool cloth on her head. The midwife worked at trying to relax Lelia and helping her to breathe and push.

When the doctor returned he put a few drops of the liquid from the brown bottle onto the gauze and placed it over Lelia's nose. "Just a little bit Dearie, enough to help with the pain without putting you out. I need you to push as hard as you can, OK?"

Oh yes, Lelia thought, I'm going to push this tumor right out of me just as fast as I can. Her screams slowly faded, along with the room and the people in it as the whole scene played out around her with a dream-like quality. Lelia felt like a bystander looking on, and that was fine with her. The pain was still there as she tried to expel the burden she'd been carrying around for what seemed forever. It was definitely there but she just didn't care – thank God for chloroform. How did women ever do this without it, she mused.

"It's a beautiful girl! Well, look at this Lelia, a perfect little girl." Doc said as he removed the tiny package from between her legs, tied twine around the umbilical cord and snipped it just above the knot. After giving a whack to baby's tiny bottom he handed the infant to Lelia, who was still looking on as though she were detached from the process, thanks to a wonderful dose of anesthetic.

As Lelia reluctantly held her new daughter she thought, "How could he say she was beautiful? The thing is bluish, covered with blood and cream-cheesy glop, and looks like she has just been in a fistfight." In her disconnected state, Lelia saw a puffy blue eggplant covered with cottage cheese. Her head was pointed; it was the ugliest baby she had ever seen.

"It's over Doc, let me have some sleeping powders." Lelia said as she handed the infant back to the doctor.

"What about nursing, Lelia? Do you think you should do that if you're going to nurse?" Mother asked in a soft nurturing voice.

"I'm not nursing. Father will just have to pay for a wet-nurse. I can't do this all by myself. He and Aaron wanted me to leave; he'll have to help me pay for things if I'm going to live so far from home. Give me the powder! NOW!"

"I think some sleeping powders wouldn't be a bad idea." Doc said as he passed Lelia a small folded paper containing a white chalky substance and Fannie timidly handed her sister a cool glass of water. Within minutes an exhausted Lelia slept soundly and the ladies began cleaning the mess in the bedroom and disposing of the afterbirth while Fannie tended to the newest young Cavanaugh.

For the short-term Mother left Fannie in Dayton to help Lelia until things got settled. Mother would arrange for a wet nurse when she got back to Evergreen and the whole family would eventually make the best of the situation. After all, the sweet little girl is a Cavanaugh and Cavanaugh's take care of their own. No one can blame the child.

Fannie loved taking care of the newborn, and Lelia loved having Fannie at her beck and call. But, she soon returned to her domineering ways with her little sister. Father not only paid for a nurse for the first two months, he paid off the mortgage on Lelia's house, putting it in her name. Regular stipends came by post to help the new mother and her little girl. If a visitor should come to call, which they rarely did, they would think that Fannie was the mother, for it was Fannie who always had the precious little doll in her arms.

"Hello little LeeLee", which is what Fannie called her, because her sister hadn't bothered to name her OR christen her. Normally Fannie would have found this scandalous, but Lelia was in such a depression after the baby was born. "I love you, Precious. You're Fannie's sweet little girl, aren't you?" a child herself bonding with the small cherub in her arms. Fannie would put her little pinkie in the infant's mouth and it would suck on her finger with ferocity like it was a teat. Fannie loved the way little LeeLee would hold her finger tightly and never wanted to let go. It was Fannie that bathed the little girl, careful to get the cloth under the folds of her chubby little cheeks to get the sweet-smelling cheese that congealed there. Fannie was very attentive while Lelia, poor Lelia, lay in bed all day. Depressed, she felt grotesque because for the life of her she couldn't seem to shed the fat from the baby, gaining fifty pounds during her pregnancy and losing only ten in childbirth. She wanted her life back and in her current state she couldn't see any options, so Lelia lay in bed with curtains drawn, feeling sorry for herself while Fannie played the role of mother to Lelia's little girl, a bond quickly forming.

For two months Fannie attended Lelia faithfully while providing the love and nurturing to her daughter that Lelia couldn't find in her heart to give. Fannie would have stayed longer, but Aaron himself came to fetch her home. It was hard for Fannie to leave the little girl and Aaron could see that she was getting too attached. No, the time was right, in fact past right. Fannie, in Aaron's estimation, had stayed long enough. It wasn't good for any of the girls,

Lelia nor the baby but especially not for Fannie.

Aaron took the child from Fannie's arms and carried it like a sack of flour tucked loosely under the crook of his right elbow.

"Be careful of her neck, Aaron. She's just an infant" Fannie cried.

"Fannie, I've handled all you kids when you were little, I think I know what I'm doing." Aaron was stern and impatient in his response.

Aaron lumbered across the parlor and into the darkened bedroom to Lelia, still bed-ridden. The jostled baby screamed from insecurity, arms and legs flailing. Fannie believed her precious little Pet screamed for her Aunt Fannie.

Aaron deposited the bundle in Lelia's arms but the infant continued to scream, after all, she didn't spend much time with her mother.

"Lelia, take care of your screaming waif. We have to leave and you're just going to have to get out of bed and accept responsibility for this baby you made."

"Why are you so mean to me Aaron? I'm faint when I stand up, and that child is so damn needy! Goodness, I just don't have it in me to jump every time that thing cries! Don't leave me here alone, she doesn't like me, she cries when I hold her."

"Lelia, this is your problem. Handle it! I'm taking Fannie back home today and you will just have to get hold of yourself. Get out of bed, and take care of your baby. The baby's yours, not Fannie's."

Aaron left the child screaming as it lay on top of Lelia's bedcovers, the poor baby gasping for breath as a panicked Lelia tried to offer comfort with no effect. Taking Fannie firmly by her hand Aaron coaxed her out of the small frame house on Samuel Street, into the carriage and back to Evergreen.

Truth be told, Aaron waited as long as he could to retrieve Fannie. Mother was not well and spent much of her day in bed with a serious case of influenza. Of course she insisted she just needed to rest a spell and could get by with the help of Katie who occasionally stopped by with chicken soup and a fresh camphor poultice. Fannie was the only daughter left at home and she needed to be by Mother's bed, not Lelia's.

In the weeks that followed a pall settled over the Cavanaugh home as Mother's condition worsened. Doctors and family were in and out of her bedroom at all hours, but Fannie never left her mother's side.

The screen door was thrown open with a bang and Lelia flew in like a winter storm and twice as frosty.

"Why didn't you tell me about Mother? Why the

163

hell didn't you send for me Aaron?" Lelia ranted while her squealing little girl flailed loosely in her arms.

"Lelia, you're just making matters worse. Take care of that screaming brat of yours." Aaron insisted. He wasn't in the mood for Lelia's self-indulgent tantrums, his thoughts were on his sainted mother lying, possibly dying, in the bed upstairs.

"Why am I always left out? I'm a part of this family. I love Mother as much as anyone, she would want me here. Did she ask for me? I know she must have, and for her granddaughter." Lelia's older sister Ella crossed the parlor and took the child from Lelia's arms. In a matter of seconds the little girl stopped her crying and made just little sniffling noises, then cooing in the experienced arms of Ella.

"See Lelia, it just takes a firm nurturing hold to make her stop crying, so she feels secure. If you're nervous and upset it makes the baby upset. That's why she cries." Ella offered in a friendly tone.

"Thanks, Ella, but I don't need your interference. Aaron, I want to see Mother."

"Not right now, Lelia. You'll just upset her and she needs to stay calm and rested." Aaron returned impatiently.

"God, Aaron, why am I always shut out? I'm not going to make trouble; I don't know why you think I will."

Lelia was furious at her brother. Ella, Willie and Kate just faded into the background before the fight became physical between brother and sister, as it too often did. No one wanted to get in the middle of Aaron and Lelia. One's temper was just as volatile as the other's. No, they just took the now sleeping baby into the second parlor and waited for word from Father and Fannie who were upstairs with Mother.

Aaron would have no part of Lelia; he wasn't going to feed her paranoia. He took her roughly by the elbow, depositing her in the second parlor with the rest of the waiting family, and crept up the creaky stairs as silently as possible. Father came out of the bedroom looking like a helpless child; Aaron took the door from him and quietly peeked into the darkened room.

Fannie was kneeling next to Mother's bed. A shaft of light broke through a small opening in the draperies, little specks of dust riding the sunlight as it made its way across the gloomy bedchamber. Fannie's head was bent over Mother's shrunken form, gently kissing her pale hand, praying to a God who couldn't hear her petitions. Her wild hair caught the sunbeam and threw off a glow like a halo.

Later after the supper hour, the doctor came in one last time. There was nothing he could do, unfortunately, but comfort the loved ones. Influenza was touching nearly

165

every family in the county and Mother's case was the worst he had seen thus far. He suggested they make her as comfortable as possible and call him if she's still holding on in the morning.

In the middle of the night, Ellen Cavanaugh silently slipped away. Fannie stayed by her mother's side until the end. Pa was devastated; Aaron lost his rock, Mother was the only person who really understood him. Aaron grieved more than anyone realized over the loss, but of course he would never show it. He was the strong one, everyone depended on him.

The day of the funeral a cold drizzle fell steadily, soaking the landscape and coating everything with a patina of ice. Earlier in the day a grieving Fannie helped Lelia find a suitable dress, one that would fit her expanded figure; she didn't exactly have the small waistline she once had. With the help of a corset and a determined Fannie, Lelia was able to get into one of Ella's old mourning dresses.

Lelia followed the procession to the family cemetery plot riding three carriages back with her sisters Fannie and Ella, having left the baby at Evergreen with the servants. Aaron rode in the front carriage with Father, the carriage behind them held Willie and Grandpa Schlager who never expected to bury his daughter now that she was beyond child-bearing years. It was a quiet and dignified service with Mother's friends from church, a few of the extended family and the immediate family. After the service, most came back to Evergreen for a generous meal of turkey, ham, vegetables of every kind put up from the garden and a variety of desserts. Fannie tried to make Mother's apple compote, it wasn't as good as Mother's by any means. Now that she was gone, though, she really had to practice that recipe; today she would make it as a tribute to the beloved matriarch.

It was a long day for Lelia, for everyone really. Lelia spent the night at Evergreen, as did the rest of the family; sister Ella, who was experienced from several children of her own, took care of the baby. It was a relief for Lelia to be around family, her only company the last couple of months being that bothersome babe. She missed adult conversation. Even though the circumstances were devastating it was a much-needed respite for Lelia. She felt special that her mother was there for her when the baby came. At least Mother loved me, she thought.

A reluctant Lelia left early for Dayton the next morning, she just didn't feel welcome at Evergreen. Ella and her family returned to their home in Hamilton, while most guests left the evening before. Lelia felt Aaron was overly-protective of Pa and Willie, who was Aaron's shadow, not that she had much to do with any of them anyway. In her opinion young Willie needed to get away from the farm so he wouldn't be corrupted by Aaron, but her words held no value here. Fannie was the only woman left on the farm now that Mother was gone. Poor Fannie, thought Lelia, to be stuck at home with the bossy Cavanaugh men. No, it was best she leave; Lelia felt unwanted, like an outsider. It was probably best that she go back to her lonely existence on Samuel Street.

Fannie was the one person sorry to see Lelia go, and more than Lelia, her precious little girl. She was so grief-stricken over the loss of Mother; the baby had been a comfort. Just five short months ago it was the happiest time of Fannie's life as she danced the night away at her sweet-sixteen party, and now she was spiraling down into a dark abyss. From her bedroom window she watched Lelia's carriage wind slowly down to the end of the lane until it was no longer in sight.

"She promised she would take me with her," Fannie sobbed, overcome with emotion.

Chapter 24

Dayton, Ohio – 1870

Lelia tried with the baby, she really did. She felt housebound. Once the nurse left and it was just mother and daughter Lelia found herself crying most of the time.

"I don't know why this thing is fussing so!" wailed an over-wrought and still quite overweight Lelia to an empty house. Lelia spent her days and nights eating, crying, many days not getting out of her bedclothes and trying to tend to a baby that Lelia had no motherly affections for. That maternal bond never formed between the two. For Lelia, who was used to being the needy, self-centered one it was difficult to constantly answer to someone more demanding than she.

Lelia rose early that morning; bathed, scented herself and slipped into one of the few housedresses that actually fit her. She also took the time to bath and dress the infant, struggling to get a wiggly baby into the lace gown given her by Ella when she was home for the funeral. The baby still hadn't been christened but everyone called her Little LeeLee so that's the name Lelia used for her. The baby had been completely unmanageable from colic and Lelia couldn't console her. She tried the remedy from the apothecary down the street; it seemed to help a little bit. "With any luck," she thought, "the child won't start screaming when Ms. Haines arrives." Lelia's meddling neighbor said she had been using the belladonna way too much making the baby sleep more than it should. A sleeping baby worked for Lelia, but perhaps the neighbor was right, after all she didn't want to poison the thing. Lelia tried Ella's suggestion, soaking a rag in fennel water, which didn't work nearly as well. The baby was sucking on the rag now and was only whimpering instead of screaming as before. It wouldn't do to have Little LeeLee knocked out when the ladies from the Montgomery County Children's Home came later in the morning. She had convinced herself that putting the child up for adoption was the best decision for everyone. The baby would get a real family that wanted her, loved her and could take care of her properly; then Lelia would get her life back. Lelia was too young to give up all her hopes for the future, to center her every action on this baby. Yes, she was convinced she was right; it was the baby's only hope for a decent future; and hers. Some people are just never meant to be parents. What else could she do? After careful consideration, this seemed her only option. She didn't expect Father or Aaron to understand, no need to tell them. A man has no idea what women go through; and besides, that baby needed a mother AND a father.

For the second year in a row Lelia spent the holidays alone in her modest little home. Christmas found her crying constantly, for Mother, for little LeeLee. Did she let Mother down? Was she watching from above as Lelia gave away the only thing truly hers? The more time that passed the more Lelia glamorized her lost motherhood, she forgot about the sleepless nights, the screaming inconsolable infant, and the bouts of depression. At night, when she closed her eyes trying to sleep, she would see the face of her little girl and quietly sob into her pillow. She should have given it more time; LeeLee was her flesh and blood; a piece of Lelia and the only part of Harry that she could ever possess. The devastating thoughts of what she had done gave her the feeling of having been punched in the stomach and nauseated her; Lelia would turn over her dampened pillow and try to sleep. This was her routine for several months. Her dreams were colored by her longing for Mother and her sweet LeeLee. Lelia's depression permeated her life.

Chapter 25

Dayton Spring – 1871

Fannie felt quite grown-up stepping off the train and flagging her own carriage. This was her first train ride unescorted. The hansom cab, carrying an excited Fannie up for an adventure, pulled out of the station and onto the toll road, making its way to the little house on Samuel Street. Finally Aaron relented and allowed Fannie to visit Lelia and the baby after the winter thaw. Following Mother's funeral Pa came down with the influenza himself and Fannie dutifully nursed him back to health. The thought of losing both Mother and Father would have been unbearable. Aaron simply wouldn't allow her to leave until the household was back to normal.

Fannie was over-the-moon with excitement; she was very much looking forward to this trip. She needed little LeeLee to help her out of her despair after losing Mother. And certainly Lelia could use an extra pair of hands around the house; it would give her a needed break, a chance to get out a little bit.

The door was unlocked. Slowly Fannie walked through the front parlor, at first it looked as though Lelia wasn't home. The house was dimly-lit, silent; there was no sign of activity. Curious, Fannie called as she walked through the small house. Finding no one in the parlor or kitchen she climbed the stairs to the second floor checking first the baby's room, which was oddly empty, then Lelia's bedroom. Lying on the bed in the darkness, shades drawn, was Lelia. Fannie thought she must be dead, there was no acknowledgment of her as she walked into the room calling Lelia's name. Nervous with what she'd find she silently prayed, walked over to the bed and jostled the lifeless frame.

"Lelia, are you OK? Are you sleeping?" Fannie whispered. "Where's the baby?"

Lelia began sobbing, and when she managed to speak she whimpered. "She's gone. I'm a terrible person Fannie, I gave her away."

Fannie didn't know what to say; she was in shock. "Lelia, tell me it isn't true. How could you do that? Why didn't you send for me? I would have come to help, or taken LeeLee back to Evergreen to give you some time. I would have taken her gladly."

"Putting her in Aaron's control was *never* an option," Lelia replied angrily. Then, in a defeated voice she added, "I thought I was doing the best thing, I really did. Now I'm so sick I can't even get out of bed, I don't want to wake up in the morning. I have no one now Fannie, I'm so lonely. I just don't want to live." Lelia's shoulders began heaving as her sobs broke into uncontrollable weeping.

Fannie put her arms around her big sister and whispered tenderly, "You have me. I'll get you through this Lelia. I can stay awhile, until you feel better, until you are yourself again." Fannie held her sister, lovingly rocking her gently in her arms. "I'll take care of you Lelia."

Within a few short weeks, in the company of Fannie, Lelia started to recover. The nightmares didn't go away, but they weren't as frequent. She still cried herself to sleep, but woke up to Fannie's nurturing words. Her little sister was like Mother in so many ways.

"Lelia, let's go to the theater this week, won't that be fun?" Fannie called from the kitchen as she tried her hand at a home-cooked meal.

"Not on your life. I'm still fat; I've lost hardly anything after the baby. Besides, I wouldn't have anything to wear. Nothing fits anymore, and I certainly couldn't wear anything of yours, you don't have anything larger than a hankie."

"You could wear the party dress you wore to my sweet-sixteen last summer; I'll take it in for you." Fannie offered.

"That's the problem; you probably wouldn't have to take it in." Lelia pouted. She really didn't want to go out on the town looking like a whale. She wanted to be her old self, and she wasn't yet.

"Come on, it will be fun. We'll dress up, and I know once you dress up and fix your hair you'll feel just how pretty you really are! Come on, let's go," Fannie persisted. Fay Templeton is in town with Lillian Russell in *Evangeline*, I heard Fay Templeton is the hottest thing in burlesque right now. It's our chance to see it before the company takes it to New York. Just look at her picture in the Daily News, she's no skinny bird and she's the darling of the theater. You're much better looking than she is; besides, it's all in how you carry yourself. Mother always told us that. A night out will do you so much good."

After much pleading and skillfully plying Lelia with compliments, not too bold, Fannie convinced her sister to go. The two of them were like a couple of twittering birds getting ready for their night on the town. Fannie would pay for a carriage and driver for the night. They would dine at the Algonquin, one of the finest restaurants in Dayton, then

175

on to the Victoria Theater where they would try to slip through the crowds to meet Ms. Templeton backstage. Lelia insisted that would not be a problem. Now they were talking about what *she* could bring to the table, Lelia was a master at sneaking into places. Planning the event was as much fun as actually going to the opera for the sisters.

Lelia strutted with her old familiar air of confidence as she and Fannie entered the Victoria. They had seats in the orchestra section thanks to Fannie's generosity. Fannie wanted this to be a night to remember for Lelia, who desperately needed to snap out of her depression. It actually helped Fannie, putting her energies into making Lelia feel better. Otherwise she would be wallowing in that morose state of depression herself. Lelia really didn't look as bad as she imagined. Her hair was washed to a lustrous sheen and Fannie pulled it up into a fashionable pile of twists and curls entwined with feathers and costume jewels. A nip here and tuck a there on the dress by her skillful sister made Lelia's gown slimming and one would never know its original use as a maternity frock.

Fannie wore a stunning evening dress of ecru embroidered lace adorned with miniscule golden beads worked through the delicate fabric that fell to the floor in soft folds. Her long flaxen hair, piled high on her head, was secured by a modest rhinestone comb and a simple white baby ostrich feather. Unlike Lelia, she didn't need rouge to color her cheeks, which had a natural pinkish glow. Tiny blue veins showed through her pale delicate skin, making her look so fragile she could break at the slightest roughness.

Together they watched as Fay and cast cavorted and presented Longfellow's popular poem, *Evangeline* in a way that hardly resembled the original work. There were plenty of young ladies in tights and an incoherent plot that whisked the girls from Africa to Arizona. Although close to incomprehensible, the material was clean, and the Midwest family audience loved the spouting whale, the dancing cow, and the performance of the inscrutable Lone Fisherman. Lelia couldn't remember when she laughed so hard nor had so much fun, it was cleansing. Not once all night did she even think about her recent trials, her lonely existence, or what her future held.

A grateful Lelia took Fannie by the hand up the stairs left of the stage and into the narrow hallway that led to dressing rooms. The passage was crowded and at first they had no difficulty maneuvering their way. No one stopped them until they sidled past the throng to the other side near the costume racks and dressing rooms. Waiting for them with a stogie in his mouth and the end of a velvet rope clutched firmly in his hand was the "guardian of the gate". They were stopped by a gruff security guard outside Ms. Templeton's door.

The older man with a balding pate blocked their way saying "Sorry girls, you ain't allowed back here 'less you belong with the company." He was polite but firm, and wouldn't allow them to pass.

Standing only three feet away, outside Ms. Templeton's dressing room, Lelia spied an uncommonly handsome young man and then heard the popular star call through the door "Freddie, Freddie! I need your help in here please dahlin'."

Lelia, feeling a bit of her old self, turned back to the podgy guard and slathered on her charm. "But Sir, we are here at Freddie's invitation. Aren't we dear?" Lelia turned to Freddie and conjured up her most demure smile and gave the handsome young man a wink.

Freddie MacKenzie, never one to turn down an opportunity with such a willing and fine young filly extended his right arm towards the girls and called out "Yeah, you can let 'em in. They're with me." He returned their smiles tenfold, winking at Lelia with a twinkle of expectation. Lelia and Fannie slid past the fleshy stagehand towards Ms. Templeton's door as Freddie greeted them with outstretched arms, "Ladies I'm Freddie MacKenzie, Ms. Templeton's manager. I'm so glad you could make it tonight." Fred increased his volume on the last several words for the benefit of the nonplussed guard who was in the process of returning the red velvet rope to its position across the entrance.

Lelia was feeling fantastic. Being noticed by such a good-looking man of the theater, someone who must know all the famous people from burlesque and vaudeville, made her feel back in stride.

"Mr. MacKenzie, sir, my name is Lelia Cavanaugh and I was hoping to introduce my little sister to Ms. Templeton. She's such a fan, my sister that is." Lelia said in a soft lilting voice. She was definitely smitten with this man and if she had the chance she would bed him for sure. "Mr. MacKenzie..."

"Call me Freddie; it's a bit less formal."

"Why, thank you, Freddie; you may call me Lelia. This is my little sister Fannie Cavanaugh," cooed Lelia in her most alluring voice. Hearing her introduction Fannie stepped out of the shadows.

Young Fannie took Freddie's breath away. Someday, somehow he was going to have that little doll. Collecting himself he bowed from the waist with a flourish and invited them in with his most charismatic smile.

"Come on in ladies, this is Ms. Templeton's dressing room." Freddie opened the door escorting them in. "Fay, I have a couple admirers that are dying to meet you."

"Hello girls, so nice to meet cha. Did ya enjoy the show tonight?"

Sitting at the dressing table singing "Rosie, you are my Posie" before a lighted mirror, quite obviously to herself, was the short, feisty, throaty-voiced brunette that returned for three standing ovations just minutes before. She was the most glamorous woman Fannie had ever laid eyes on. Still wearing her costume, scandalous by Midwestern standards, Fay pointed to the divan and graciously entertained the girls while she removed her heavy makeup. The small room looked like it had belched sequins, feathers, fancy hats and gowns, so finding a place to sit without spoiling the costumes was a challenge. Fannie felt so grown-up and was enamored with the exciting lifestyle of burlesque and the theater that she was a part of tonight; she floated through it like a dream. Lelia was captivated as well, not by Ms. Templeton with her fancy wardrobe but by the charming Mr. MacKenzie. Lelia trained her eyes on what could well be her way out of a lonely existence: Freddie.

After an acceptable amount of time passed Ms. Templeton politely sent the ladies on their way. When the door shut soundly behind them she turned to her manager with a scowl and said, "Freddie, ma deah, don't you evah do that to me again." Freddie lightly positioned his bowler on his head and with a rakish grin, turned on his heels and walked out.

"Scalawag," Fay murmured, and went back to her song.

Fannie felt in awe of Lelia's talents, her bravery and cunning in getting them backstage. The carriage ride home was such a gay time for the two sisters, talking about the production, Fannie comparing it to Longfellow's poem *Evangeline,* which was nothing like the play. They sang snippets from the songs they remembered, Fannie going on and on over Ms. Templeton and Lelia going on and on over Mr. MacKenzie.

At that moment in time, in the dimly lit bowels of the Victoria Theater where the youngest Cavanaugh sister stepped out of the shadows, that singular moment was a turning point in Fannie's life. That was the night that set in motion events that would change the Cavanaugh family forever and not for the better.

Fannie departed Lelia's company just a few short weeks after the opera. Lelia was feeling much better about herself and Aaron needed Fannie back at Evergreen. After mother died Cook and the maid left within months. The Cavanaugh men weren't the easiest to work for; they could be quite demanding and intimidating, so now Aaron faced the task of replacing the household staff. If Fannie agreed to help Willie out with housekeeping until Aaron could arrange new servants, he would send her to university for two years at the Western Female Seminary in Oxford, a school that offered women the same education men expected but women were denied because of the mere accident of their gender.

Now that Fannie was back at Evergreen Lelia, who had shaken her melancholy, set about putting her life in order. She worked on her weight, determined to situate her sagging bosom and pudgy stomach back where they belonged. As she began slimming down she ordered new dresses made, sending the bill to Father naturally. Every time Freddie's theatrical troupe came to town Lelia attended the theater. It didn't take much for Freddie to be coaxed into her bed. Not every night he was in town, for he did entertain other female friends who demanded his attention, but enough to satisfy Lelia.

While Fannie toiled away at school, Lelia was developing a regular affair with Freddie. Much to Lelia's dismay Freddie's mind was on Fannie, that elusive vision he caught a glimpse of only once; he had memorized every detail of her being - the memory of it growing more glamorous with each passing day.

Arms and legs tangled among flounces of eyelet and lace bedcovers, Lelia arched her back and stretched the full extent of the bed, then turned over and provocatively blew what breath remained over her lover's sweating body.

"Lelia, baby, don't make me beg. I love the way you do what you do. You know what I like, that's why I keep coming back. I can't resist you."

"Just trying to please my man," Lelia coyly cooed. If lovemaking was Lelia's special talent, the afterglow repartee was her gift.

"I'm talking about your sister and you know it. For a year now you've been promising me. I want to see her again Lelia; arrange it. Don't make me beg"

Freddie willingly lay with Lelia, but after every encounter he would ask about her sister.

"Next time my love. The next time Fannie's home from school and you're in town, the three of us will get together. I promise."

"You promise every time," Freddie pouted. It angered him that Lelia had this control over him, but he didn't want to spoil his chances with the woman of his dreams by turning Lelia against him. He hated that she called him "her man" and "her love". She was only one of many who took care of his needs, like the grocer took care of his hunger. It was nothing more. Until he possessed

Fannie, he'd let her get away with it, but only until then.

The Christmas season was a bittersweet time for Fannie. It had already been a year since Mother died. She had so many wonderful memories of the holidays with Mother in the kitchen: beautiful gifts, wonderful food, family all around and weeks of holiday parties. Christmas was indeed a special time of year in the Cavanaugh home. Now her thoughts were filled with Mommy dying in her bed, the horrible cold rain that did nothing to relieve the pain of losing her, the cold grave at Greenwood swallowing Mommy whole while the incessant rain turned her final resting place into a lake of mud.

Fannie didn't want to go home, she thought a trip abroad would do her a world of good, but her sense of duty won out. It wasn't at all what she wanted to do but out of obligation she returned home to Evergreen for Thanksgiving and Christmas. Lelia begged her to stay in Dayton for the holidays but Aaron would never let Fannie hear the end of it if she did. Instead she spent her break from school through Christmas Eve with Father, Aaron, Willie, Ella and Ella's family. Christmas morning, after attending church with Ella, Fannie took the train to Dayton to spend a few days with Lelia before returning to university.

Evangeline and company was again touring the
Midwest, playing to packed houses in Chicago over the
Christmas holidays. Not wanting to pass up an opportunity
to become reacquainted with the beautiful Fannie, Fred
took the train out of Chicago and arrived in Dayton on
Christmas morning. Lelia arranged to take Fannie for a
holiday breakfast at one of the larger hotels downtown.
"Coincidentally" thanks to Lelia, Fred MacKenzie was
checking into that very same hotel AND "coincidentally",
he saw them in the restaurant and walked over to weasel his
way into their conversation with the hope of getting an
invitation to breakfast.

"If it isn't the lovely Cavanaugh sisters, how
fortunate for me to run into you here," the charming and
debonair Freddie sidled up to the table acting genuinely
surprised. He played his role quite convincingly.

"Why Mr. MacKenzie, how wonderful to see you in
town," Lelia cooed, playing along nicely.

"Please, call me Freddie," he said as he lifted
Fannie's tiny pale hand to his lips, bowing from the waist
and kissing it lightly.

"Frederic, how nice to see you again." Fannie spoke
shyly with her eyes cast downward, her silky brown lashes
sweeping her cheeks.

"Freddie," Lelia interrupted the moment, "why

185

don't you join us? Are you just getting into town? Is the opera playing at the Victoria, or are you just conducting business here?"

Freddie eagerly pulled up a chair and signaled the waiter. This was his chance and he wasn't going to waste one minute of it. His plan was to be aggressive and arrange another meeting with Ms. Fannie before leaving. Suave Freddie. He was feeling no doubts about his abilities in that department. He had a way with women; it was his gift in this life. God blessed him with good looks and charm, or so he thought.

Frederic's pursuit of Fannie didn't flow as smoothly as he had hoped, certainly not with the same ease as her sister Lelia. So Fannie returned to school and he communicated with her by post, letters that turned more amorous as time passed. During Fannie's breaks from school Freddie managed to see her, even if the burlesque company was not in town. All the while, foremost in Fannie's mind was to present herself as a lady, someone her mother would be proud of were she still alive. Fannie's consummate need to maintain her status as a lady made Fred's attempts at wooing her that much more difficult, but for Fred, the more challenging the chase, the sweeter the prize.

The summer after Fannie's graduation from

Western Female Seminary she saw Frederic at every opportunity, thanks to Lelia who was secretly conspiring on Freddie's behalf. In Fannie's mind it was a most proper courtship; Freddie secretly hoped for something much less dignified. Even though Freddie was busy pursuing her sister, Lelia had no problem continuing her affair with him. It had never been more than a casual relationship as far as Lelia was concerned and had nothing to do with love. Freddie's pursuit of Fannie was, in his mind, the closest thing to love he had ever experienced. With Lelia's inside information of how he could endear himself to her sister, Freddie made tremendous inroads that first summer. By the Christmas holidays that same year, after courting her all through the fall as best he could and still maintain his job as Fay Templeton's manager, Freddie was ready to propose. Fannie was doing the suitable thing for a lady, saving herself for the marriage bed. The only way Freddie would be able to claim his prize was to make her his wife, and the love-besotted Freddie was prepared to do just that.

Lelia accompanied Freddie to the more exclusive jewelers in town searching for just the right engagement ring, one that Fannie would never be able to refuse. Their plan was to invite Fannie to Dayton for the holidays where Freddie would propose marriage. Fred wasn't accustomed to the insecurity this situation posed. He actually feared she would say no, so Fred and Lelia planned every detail to his advantage.

It was Christmas Eve, the busiest night of the year at the prestigious inn, so Freddie walked into the Golden Lamb half an hour early. Positioned midway between Cincinnati and the National Road the Golden Lamb was the oldest and finest inn and restaurant in the state, hosting many presidents and prominent statesmen. Freddie wanted to make sure that the table and meal were beyond perfection. He approached the proprietor to confirm his arrangements.

"Sir, a minute of your time please," Freddie said, slipping a folded bill into the man's hand, "I have a very important dinner engagement this evening, a reservation for 7 o'clock. If it's possible I'd like to have that private table in the back corner, by the window?"

"Certainly sir, I don't expect that will be a problem. I'll have a reserved sign placed there to ensure you get the table you want," he replied.

"And also, if possible," Freddie asked, "some flowers? As I said, this is a very special occasion."

"I'll send someone down the street straight away to get an arrangement for you. And some fine champagne for the table perhaps?"

"That would be fantastic," Freddie said. Is it possible that I'm nervous, he thought? I've *never* been nervous around women, only Fannie. He couldn't figure out the hold she had over him. Never had he worked so hard to pursue a woman.

When Fannie walked through the restaurant door all eyes turned her way. She was a vision in a baby blue silk gown that draped sensuously from her tiny hips and bosom, her hair tucked as neatly as possible in an upsweep captured by matching blue and pearl combs.

Freddie met her at the maitre de's podium and guided her to the back corner of the restaurant and a table perfectly appointed with fresh flowers, soft candlelight and a silver bucket of chilled champagne.

"Freddie, you've outdone yourself," Fannie purred.

"I want tonight to be special Fannie; after all we've been together for a year now."

"I wouldn't call it together really, friends maybe."

"Well, I definitely would like for us to be more than friends, my Dear." Freddie fumbled in his pocket for a little velvet box. He had no plan to get down on his knee to propose. That would be taking it a bit too far in his estimation. The ring should be enough to close the deal.

"Fannie, you are all I think about, I am consumed

by your beauty and sweetness," Freddie struggled to get his words out, hating that he felt so anxious. He placed the open ring box on the table between them. Six dazzling diamonds set in platinum caught the light from the candle perfectly and sparkled with breathtaking brilliance. The unknowing waiter stopped by the table to pour the champagne and take their order but was summarily dismissed by the wave of Freddie's hand.

"I'm hoping you'll say yes, will you marry me Fannie?" Freddie retrieved the ring and waited in anticipation.

"Frederic, I'm overwhelmed! I've never seen such a stunning ring and quite honestly, I wasn't prepared for this." Young Fannie was star-struck. Here was this handsome man, well-traveled and nearly famous as Ms. Templeton's manager, and he wanted *her*. She felt life couldn't get any better, that she would never find another as charming as Frederic.

"What did Father and Aaron say?" Fannie asked.

"What?"

"When you asked for my hand in marriage."

Damn that Lelia, he thought, she was supposed to pave the way so nothing was left to chance.

"Fannie, my love, you are my obsession. No one could love you; no cherish you, more than I do. I want to

190

take care of you for the rest of our lives." Freddie thought talking to the father was taking the "proper" marriage proposal a bit farther than he cared to go, but he was consumed by his lust for her.

"Well, I haven't asked him yet," he replied, "but I will. I can visit over the holiday before I return to Chicago," he said with some reluctance.

"After you talk to Father we can set a time, I think perhaps a year or maybe two would be a suitable engagement."

No way could Freddie wait that long, but once this was settled he felt he could manipulate the situation. The waiter was patiently waiting at the periphery looking for the right time to once again approach the table.

"Sure Honey, we'll see." Freddie looked up and saw the waiter biding his time and motioned him over. It didn't go exactly as planned, but it could have been worse, Freddie thought, she could have said no.

Frederic arrived at Evergreen on Christmas evening to meet with Mr. Cavanaugh, a bit nervous which was a new sensation for Freddie, one he didn't care for. Fannie met him at the carriage and they walked in together. She meekly made the introductions to Father and then to Aaron.

Not long after meeting the famed Cavanaugh men

Fred strode brusquely out to his borrowed Landaulet carriage, having been tersely dismissed by Aaron. Indignant, Freddie barked "Well THAT was the worst experience of my life. Now what, Fannie, after they said no?"

"I'll leave Evergreen. We'll get married whether they approve or not. They don't own me Frederic. I'm strong, my own woman. We can get married in New York, Lelia will stand by me. It will be fine, trust me dear. Eventually they'll come around."

Chapter 26

New York City, New York – 1872

Fannie's love for Frederic became all-consuming. Oh, she had several boyfriends at home and dated a few while at university, but none of them loved her with the passion of her Frederic. She found it an overpowering emotion, a new experience inflamed all the more by her imaginative musings of what their life would be. By the time their wedding *did* arrive her every waking moment revolved entirely around this man.

Freddie's sordid affairs with a multitude of women, the likes of Lelia and minor players in the theater group, allowed him to maintain his sanity in anticipation of the marriage bed. For certain his expectations were vastly different from Fannie's fairy-tale visions.

After a short engagement, only a few short months instead of the year or two Fannie wanted, they married in lavish New York City style while *Evangeline* was on hiatus. Fay Templeton, recently divorced from her first husband Billy West, a minstrel man, was escorted by her new husband Howell Osborne. The entire company attended the extravagant affair at a Fifth Avenue Hotel.

Lelia and Fannie took the Baltimore & Ohio Passenger train from Sandusky to New York. Frederic met them at Grand Central Station and sent their bags ahead to the hotel. Excitedly he gathered up the sisters, one in each arm, and led them to the elevated train line. Lelia and Fannie were so much in awe as they stepped out of the Pullman Sleeper and into the cavernous noisy station, it was all Frederic could do to get them out of the terminal and into the city.

As the three rode the train above the streets of New York City Frederic played the perfect tour guide, explaining little known facts about all the landmarks that he lived with every day but rarely visited. The women had never seen the likes of a steam engine gliding across the rails high above the city. They approached Manhattan and traveled along Sixth Avenue; a site that Lelia and Fannie couldn't take in fast enough. Among the tall buildings were situated designer shops and storefronts in European style. They looked down on streets crowded with people hurrying in every direction.

"More shoppers arrive daily from all over the city, hell, from all over the country and world!" Frederic enthralled them with clever tales as they stared at ladies in bustles and gentlemen with perfectly waxed mustaches

194

clogging the sidewalks.

"This was once home to well-to-do people like Horace Greeley, the Roosevelt's and Washington Irving. Now it's known as 'Ladies Mile' because of the profusion of fashionable women."

Streets were congested with horse-drawn street cars, broughams and coupes carrying ladies from all over to shop the splendid stores for the latest fashions from Paris. Frederic wondered if the girls were listening to anything he said, they were so busy trying to take in every cast-iron store-front adorned with European window dressing, all the while cattily critiquing the style and dress of every woman on the street.

"Oh, Frederic, I think I'm going to swoon. This is beyond my dreams even; I never knew anything so exquisite existed!" Fannie exclaimed breathlessly. "In Ohio the buildings aren't nearly so tall; no magnificent shops with styles found only in fashion magazines."

Lelia tried to appear nonchalant but wasn't convincing anyone. "I can't wait to go shopping. I *do* need a new dress for the wedding Fannie, let's go out tomorrow. Or maybe tonight! If only those home-spun crones back home could see me now. They'll want me at all their little small-town parties; but I'll play hard to get. They won't be snubbing me anymore when they see me in my New York gowns; they'll be so jealous."

"And hats! Look there, Fannie, in the window of that milliner's shop." Lelia couldn't contain her excitement, as hard as she tried.

Frederic led them off the train at the Sixth Avenue and Twenty-Third Street platform. The three walked carefully down the steps to the street where Frederic hailed a Hansom cab to take them the short distance to the hotel.

"Oh, let's walk Darling. I want to see the store windows up close." Fannie begged in a way he could never refuse.

"I know you two. You'll be going in shops, looking and trying on everything, you know you will. We don't have time for that. It's best that you not see them at all because we can't stop and browse," he insisted. "Everyone is waiting for us at the hotel. Fay has a luncheon planned in our honor."

Lelia jumped in, "No, we won't, I promise Freddie. We just want to get the feel of being here, of being a part of the big city."

"Ple-e-ease?" Fannie dragged out the word to three syllables.

"How can I refuse? But we aren't stopping, so don't ask me."

When Lelia and Fannie turned the corner at

Twenty-Third Street they stared skyward as they strolled along the white marble façade of the old Fifth Avenue Hotel, which for nearly fifty years entertained only the most noted persons who came to New York. Freddie boasted that it was the most exclusive hotel in New York City; that presidents Grant and Arthur and the Prince of Wales actually stayed here. The hotel took up the entire block between Twenty-Third and Twenty-Fourth Streets. Adjoining the hotel at Twenty-Fourth was The Madison Square Theatre advertising "an original Domestic Comedy-Drama." The poster promised an extraordinary cast and novel mechanical and scenic effects. Frederic was moving them so fast that Lelia didn't have time to read the entire billboard.

"Tomorrow," Lelia whispered to Fannie, "you and I can tour the theater before shopping. The way Freddie is rushing us now, we wouldn't enjoy it anyway."

The Fifth Avenue Hotel was the first modern New York City hotel, the meeting place of princes, financiers and anybody who was anybody. The Cavanaugh girls followed Frederic into the expansive white-marble lobby with high ceilings and Austrian crystal chandeliers the size of Lelia's whole house she thought. Gigantic flower arrangements were everywhere, positioned around plush leather chairs and divans. Fannie's jaw dropped in amazement and for once Lelia was speechless; they thought they had seen it all. There couldn't possibly be anything to top the extravagance of this hotel lobby. Fannie, enchanted, tried not to present herself as the small-town girl she was, gliding across the floor in her practiced lady-like walk; just like mother taught her so many years before.

I wish mother could see me here and now; she would be so proud Fannie thought to herself.

Trying to take everything in, the animated sisters followed Frederic through the lobby to a huge and peculiar brass door that looked more like a gate.

"An *elevator* ladies," Frederic announced impressed with himself, "I bet you haven't seen one of these before.

"Why, whatever is it for?" Fannie asked as she curiously studied the shiny brass contraption.

"I read about this," Lelia offered. "It's like a moving room, going up and down from floor to floor."

"It's going to take us to our rooms. You wouldn't want to walk to the eighth floor, would you Fannie dear?" teased Frederic.

Freddie pulled back the gate and with a bend at the waist and a flourish of his arm indicated the ladies step into the brass box, "Ladies first."

Fannie and Lelia took their first elevator ride. Cautiously the girls stepped off, trying, unsuccessfully, to look like this wasn't their first time; like they rode elevators every day and this was nothing out of the ordinary. Frederic grinned as he led them to their separate rooms. Lelia and Fannie in one beautifully appointed suite and Frederic in a separate single across the hall.

The wedding of Frederic MacKenzie and Fannie Cavanaugh took place in the ballroom of the elegant Fifth Avenue Hotel. It was a civil ceremony and the only Cavanaugh family member in attendance was Lelia, although all were invited. Fannie thought at least Ella and the Byron's might attend, after all Samuel Lee was a congressman and they spent most of their time in Washington now; they weren't that far away. It was probably just as well; Ella was so active in church, chairwoman of the Browning Club and all. She was probably too busy; and certainly she would think Fannie's wedding gown scandalous anyway.

"Whatever will I do Lelia," Fannie lamented. "I can't walk down the aisle unescorted."

"Of course you can Honey. You'll be fine. You can do it."

"I CAN'T, I'm too nervous and the bodice on this dress is too tight – I'll faint, I know I will. I need someone to hold me up; I can't believe Father isn't here on my wedding day," Fannie cried, a panic setting in.

"Settle down, you silly ninny, or you WILL faint. Stand tall, be a woman. I'll see if I can find someone to get you down the aisle." Lelia left the room and began her search for someone to walk with her sister, not necessarily someone appropriate, but just anyone.

Fannie stood in her makeshift dressing room, she just couldn't get a good breath; she felt like she was suffocating.

"I need to sit down, but that's impossible in this gown," she said to herself. She was hurt that no one from the family even bothered to contact her, to wish her well.

"If that's the way they want to be, that's fine with me," she said stubbornly. "Frederic's my family now. Who needs them?" Fannie was now talking aloud, even though she was the only one in the room. "Mother would be here," she added. Her words said she didn't care, but there was disappointment in her voice.

Fannie marched into that ballroom like she owned the world, escorted by a suited stagehand, filling in for her father. Fannie had no idea who he was, having never met him, but was so very grateful for his arm to steady her. All eyes were on Fannie in her exquisite courtier-style wedding dress, but her eyes were trained on her beloved, Frederic.

Fannie's designer wedding gown was created by Mme. Marechal of Paris and was constructed from gorgeous silk-satin and taffeta brocade. The background was pale celadon green with tiny pink and green brocaded flowers and pink iridescent taffeta stripes interspersed. The squarish-round neckline was revealingly low cut, showing a bit of décolleté. The French corset-style bodice cinched her waist with front laces winding through hand sewn holes. Appliqués adorned the cap sleeves with silk-satin stitched floral with the backside delicately revealing her slender figure by curving into a V shape.

Lelia stood next to the man she had shared a rollicking bed with so many times herself. But he only had eyes for Fannie now, and stood mesmerized by the beautiful sister who glided elegantly down the aisle that separated nearly a thousand newly-made friends and spectators. Lelia watched Fannie slowly approach the front of the ballroom, desperately clutching the arm of the handsome young man Lelia had "connected with" the night before in a vacant broom closet. Lelia slyly exchanged a knowing glance with her new paramour; she would thank him properly later for standing in for Father.

Fannie took her place between Lelia and Frederic and as Lelia turned with the wedding party to face the minister she watched the young man take his seat in the audience, her mind wandering to something totally foreign to the wedding about to take place.

As vows were exchanged Fannie's eyes filled with tears of joy, an occasional tear escaping those brilliant blues and spilling over the brim to the crease of her nose. Freddie was daydreaming of the night to follow when he could claim the prize he had longed and schemed for, it had been a torturous wait. His body ached for her since the day began.

The actual ceremony was short, no more than ten minutes of readings and vows, leaving the remainder of the night for partying and dancing.

After a lighthearted evening of introductions, dancing, laughter and champagne Frederic led his beautiful bride to the suite which now the two of them would share. Lelia entertained in the smaller single across the hall, it suited her needs just fine.

For two long years Freddie waited for this night, the night they would consummate their marriage. Whirling through Fannie's head was her romantic vision of the marriage bed; thoughts of the children she would share with her adoring husband, maybe a house in the country; the kind of life Mother had.

Frederic quickly undressed, while Fannie was still working on the pins in her hair.

"Here, let me help you. You're so slow, Fannie. I guess you aren't used to the champagne, it's slowing you down. Let me give you a hand," said a very anxious Freddie, who was adept at these things. He swiftly had her down to her corset.

Fannie was nervous, in her dreams it never got this far. She hadn't thought about the prospect of facing him without her clothes. Lelia had always called her a prude, but Fannie insisted that wasn't so. She just wasn't comfortable with nudity, it destroyed the romance. Some things are better left to the imagination.

"Let me take care of it from here. If you'll just loosen the corset," she whispered, "I'll step into the dressing room and put on the lovely silk nightgown I bought to celebrate our first night together."

"What do you need that for? You don't need that Sweetness." Freddie was ready, and he wanted no more delays.

"Please, Frederic. This is a special time; I have a gift for you that I'll never be able to give again. I want it to be special. I love you so much, let me make it special."

Freddie humored Fannie but the tension was so great, he didn't know how long he could contain himself. He would be a gentleman as long as possible, but that intention wasn't compatible with what he had in mind and was fast fading.

Fannie stepped out of the dressing room, her

signature rose-water scent perhaps a bit too bold, and glided across the candle-lit room in a pink silk full-length nightgown with a bodice trimmed in French lace and miniature rose appliqués. The flimsy straps were barely enough to hold even her tiny bosom and the strain caused by the curves of her body on the silk fabric was driving Freddie wild with anticipation.

Freddie was already in the huge four-poster bed when Fannie walked into the room. "Come here by me, Fannie darling. Quite honestly, Sugar, I really can't wait any longer."

To Fannie's surprise under the covers was her completely nude husband, elongated appendage demanding immediate attention. She wasn't ready for this, she was nervous – her breathing labored.

"Lovely gown dear," and Freddie immediately tried to pull it off.

"Wait! I'm not ready. Let's talk for a minute."

"About what? No, let's not." He was still trying to get the silk gown off a squirming Fannie.

"Frederic, please! First blow out the candles." Fannie begged.

"I want to see you, Sweetheart. Let's leave them lit." Frederic tried to be as patient as possible under the circumstances, but he was about to lose it with his heightened excitement and her damned modesty.

Fannie extinguished the candles by the bed. "Frederic, you have to have patience with me. I'm nervous and I'm scared."

In the dark Fannie allowed Frederic to remove her new silk gown, but when his hands started roaming all over her body and touching places that had never been touched she went into a panic. He became more and more aggressive and there was little she could do but resign herself to the inevitable. Freddie was all about pleasing himself and was deaf to her pleas to be gentler.

"You're hurting me," Fannie whimpered. She lay there praying *Oh, please God, let it be over soon.* She endured his callous thrusting and grunting until she thought she could take no more when Frederic slumped on top of her, sweaty and exhausted.

After he had his pleasure, Freddie lifted his head, his eyes closed, and kissed his little bride. He felt the wetness on her face and finally looked at her. "What the hell? Why are you crying?"

Fannie felt so humiliated. She didn't know making love was about a grunting animal on top of you, pounding you - hurting you. No one had told her; why didn't Lelia warn her? It wasn't at all like her daydreams.

"I'm sore, that's all." Fannie told him a half-truth.

"I'm sorry Sweetheart. Let's try it again and I'll be gentler this time."

"No, please Frederic. I'm so sore. I'll be better tomorrow, we'll try again tomorrow. It's been a long day, beautiful beyond imagination, but long." Fannie said trying to control her tears.

"Sure Sweetheart, tomorrow." Freddie turned over and was asleep by the time Fannie washed his traces off her and slipped back into her soft pink gown.

He didn't even really see it, she thought, and I bought it just to please him. She eased into bed next to him and turned her back to his, but she couldn't sleep. She lay there and quietly sobbed, nervous and anxious, wishing her mother was still alive. *She* would have been here for her wedding. Is this what Mother went through? She must have, but how will Fannie ever get used to it? "I guess I'll have to if I want children," she told herself, as her thoughts skipped all over the place, keeping her awake 'til the sun peeked through the drapes. She couldn't relax enough to sleep beside his naked body, so close.

Freddie woke, washed, dressed and went down to breakfast (Fannie said she didn't want to eat). Only then did Fannie fall into a deep sleep and didn't rouse until late afternoon. When she *did* wake she found Freddie sitting quietly by the bed, watching.

"It's about time Sleepy-head; your sister is waiting to go sight-seeing."

"Sorry, give me a half hour and I'll be down," Fannie whispered.

"We'll meet you in the lobby, unless you want me to help you get dressed," Freddie added playfully.

"No, really. You wait with Lelia, I'll be right there."

By the time Freddie located Lelia and they made their way to the lobby Fannie was already stepping off the elevator. The three took the elevated train to the Bowery where they discovered a fantastic eatery. It was great fun and Fannie soon had her mind on the adventure and not the throbbing pain between her legs.

Chapter 27

Hamilton, Ohio – 2003

On October 21 we were fortunate enough to have one of those mild Indian summer evenings that you hope for but rarely see, the kind with a full *Orange Harvest Moon* hanging low in the sky. The night was perfect for a stroll through a haunted Victorian neighborhood. If you ignored the cars parked at the curb and the occasional traffic noise, you could easily imagine you were in the nineteenth century. The lantern-led stroll began at the Wolf Gazebo in Cavanaugh Park. The weather cooperated and gave us a slightly cool cloudless sky, the waning moon just barely less than full. The excitement was electric as guests shuffled through the decaying fallen leaves on their way to the gazebo, stirring up the familiar earthy scent that says summer is gone and winter is not far off. There were very few children as people fully expected to encounter ghosts and they chattered anxiously about the prospect as the host, dressed in cape and top hat, waited for enough patrons to begin the first tour. Skeptical district board members planned on no more than thirty to fifty paying guests, and were pleasantly surprised as they tried to accommodate the gathering of more than three hundred who showed up that night. Mingling among the waiting thrill-seekers were bona fide ghost hunters carrying their portable equipment and cameras, adding to the already elevated vibration generated by the crowd. Excited guests jockeyed for position to make sure they got into a group with one of the investigators.

The previous Saturday a group from a local church, led by a descendant of the Cavanaugh family, sponsored a "Holy Ghost Walk" publicly offering up prayers over the neighborhood and residents after they failed to halt the fundraiser. They felt some things were best left buried; that we shouldn't agitate the spirits but allow them to rest in peace. *What were they trying to hide?* The controversy caused by their demonstration, which could have forced an end to our historical spin on Halloween, in fact ended up generating even more interest in the tour. Everyone was "abuzz" about the *Victorian Ghost Walk*, an event which drew visitors from three neighboring counties. Two more nights were added to accommodate the growing numbers who didn't want to miss out on seeing a real apparition.

Ten homes were on the walking tour, one of which was ours. The costumed host would lead a group of fifty to a hundred through the neighborhood telling tales of specters found in the common areas like the park and alleyways. The fascinated audience would pause for five minutes at each of the houses on the tour while the residents would tell of their personal experiences and explain how documented evidence backed up Kevin's psychic impressions. The ghost hunters unwittingly added to the thrill by allowing others to watch as evidence of ethereal beings appeared in their night scopes. Hauntings were a regular occurrence in these old homes. Material was so abundant, nothing had to be fabricated; scripts were based on actual encounters and historical fact.

After checking to make sure things were running smoothly at the park, now overrun with nervously tittering people anticipating their turn, I headed home where Aidan was waiting to share personal anecdotes of the spirits who shared our house. I love that Irish gift of gab; he does know how to turn a tale.

We purposely turned out all the lights in the house to heighten the effect, using a single lighted candle for illumination which Aidan carried to the porch as he greeted the throng in cape and top hat. I sat in the darkened parlor on the couch where I would be inconspicuous but could hear him talk to our guests.

Aidan told them about the soldier he saw in the second story kitchen, about the balls of light the cat would chase until they quickly flew through the wall, about the remote control for the television that sometimes would change channels all on its own without being touched. He explained the history of the house and the early owners.

Pretty good, I thought, as I sat in the dark straining to hear his words from my place in the parlor. My breathing was purposefully shallow so as not to make any noise, the darkness heightened my sense of hearing. My heart began to quiver from the atmosphere created for the participants crowded outside the door. Mixed in with Aidan's voice and the occasional round of laughter caused by his Irish spin on a somber subject, I heard very faint sobbing. I thought it must be my overactive imagination. I quietly rose and crept across the floor in the dark, following the sound. I stopped at the threshold to the foyer, not wanting to cause panic outside with my movement. Where the parlor meets the foyer the sobbing became a bit more pronounced, and the slight smell of roses wafted into the room. I glanced at the stairs and there she was! I had never seen her before. I stood motionless, not wanting to scare her away; like a rare bird that you want to study before it flies off in fear. At that moment I saw Aidan turn and point to the steps, he must have been talking about "the lady." He turned back to our guests, who were hanging on his every word, and finished his five-minute talk that turned into twenty.

I didn't take my eyes off the apparition, who continued to sob. She didn't really look like a lady, but instead appeared to be a gray mist of indistinct shape. The sensation was that of a lady because the sobbing was high-pitched and sounded female. The mist appeared to move but in reality it merely vaporized, like fog in the early morning sun.

Aidan joined me on the parlor sofa after his first presentation of the night; I couldn't wait to tell him. He must have seen the look on my face and spoke first.

"I know," he said, "I saw her."

"Did you really?"

"Yes, just as I turned to point to the stairway through the door, there she was! How perfect was that? I can't believe I saw her and what timing! It's like she appeared just for me. I'm going to include this in my script for the next groups, one more sighting to add to the list."

We sat in the dark, whispering and waiting for the next contingent, explorers who naively thought they wanted to be scared by something not of this world.

Chapter 28

Chicago, Illinois – 1873

Frederic was traveling extensively with the theater troupe as Fay Templeton's popularity grew. They were on the road from New York to Chicago and back again, so much so that Fannie didn't have to worry too much about his insatiable appetite in the bedroom. Frederic and Fannie, Mr. and Mrs. MacKenzie (Fannie loved the sound of that), bought a house outside of Chicago and whenever the group was in the area Frederic stayed at home, commuting to the theater. Sometimes, when the group played in the Columbus and Dayton areas, Fannie would stay with Lelia so she could spend more time near her husband. Unfortunately for Fannie, this was her life for several years, as Ms. Templeton's reputation on the stage spiraled upward.

Fannie couldn't understand why she wasn't able to conceive considering all the times she lay with her husband. Certainly she should be with child by now. During one of these visits Lelia took her little sister to her own "female doctor". Fannie emerged from the doctor's office red-faced and crying.

"Lelia," a few sobs escaped and Fannie had to wipe her nose with a kerchief before going on, "I *can't* have children. I'll *never* have children; Frederic has given me some kind of disease! Now, I'll never be able to have a child!" Her sobbing stopped and her anger mounted at the impact of her words.

"Settle down, little Sis. What exactly did he say?" Lelia was trying to comfort her sister, but knowing the real Freddie she thought she had a pretty good idea of what the problem was.

"I have the French Pox, syphilis, it's a *sexual* disease." Fannie spit the word "sexual" out like she had a bug in her mouth and had to get rid of it.

"Really, he could be wrong, we should get another opinion." but Lelia knew he wasn't wrong.

"I've never been with anyone but Frederic, so he must have given it to me."

Nothing in the world would make Lelia tell Fannie the truth about her husband, absolutely nothing.

"But Honey, look at the life you live, it's so exciting with Freddie, isn't it? And I'll tell you the truth, when I had my baby it was the worst time of my life. I wouldn't be so upset about not being able to have children. Now you can make love all you want and not have to worry about the consequences." Lelia reasoned with her sister.

"I'm not like you Lelia!" Fannie wouldn't be soothed. She was sick to her stomach thinking about just what this meant. She felt dirty. She understood she wasn't the first for Frederic and always rationalized that it was probably best that one of them knew what to do. But this disease! He must have been visiting the Chicago brothels in the Tenderloin District to get something this filthy. Then to pass it on to his wife; Fannie was beside herself with humiliation, not to mention the sense of betrayal.

"Do you want to stay with me awhile?" Lelia asked Fannie.

"No, I want to go home. I need to figure out what to do, what to say to Frederic. I love him Lelia, how could he do this to me? Just put me on the train, I want to go home."

Lelia did just that. She put Fannie on the train to Chicago that afternoon then immediately contacted Freddie to warn him. She knew very well that Freddie was getting his pleasure on the tour from a number of ladies. He didn't have to visit the red light district to get what he needed. In fact, he continually pressured Lelia to return to his bed, but Lelia made a solemn vow that once Freddie married her sister she was through sleeping with him. Nothing could make her break that vow. She enjoyed men, no doubt about that; but having sex with her sister's husband was just too repulsive, even for Lelia.

After Freddie read Lelia's message he decided to avoid the situation altogether and refused to go home to Fannie. He was on the road most of the time anyway, so when the show was on hiatus he returned to New York or Boston or Philadelphia. He had friends and a warm bed in each of those cities, so it was just a matter of where and who struck his fancy.

Fannie waited for months for her husband to return home, she was nearly out of her mind with despair and worry. She wanted a chance to talk to him, to find out what he was hiding from her. She loved him, or her idealized image of him, and was willing to give him a second chance. Maybe they could adopt, they could still have a family. The silence between them was making her crazy; she was fixated on nothing but getting Frederic back. It was imperative that she speak to him. Why was he ignoring her letters? Why wouldn't he answer? Fannie decided to spend a few days with Lelia, knowing that her sister sometimes heard from Frederic.

Lelia met Fannie at the train platform early evening and took her back to the small Samuel Street house.

"Why don't you unpack your valise while I make us a little supper," Lelia said.

"Why won't he talk to me, Lelia?"

"Fannie, put your things up and we'll talk about this over a glass of sherry, OK? I'm going to warm up some haggis and mushy peas while you unpack. Then we'll relax and talk over a drink."

Fannie walked into the kitchen and asked, "Why won't he talk to me Lelia? Why won't he come home?"

"I don't know, Fan," Lelia lied.

"Do you know where he is? Tell me the truth."

"I think he's in Philadelphia, Honey. They're rehearsing another Edward Rice burlesque and some of the cast are there. I know Fay is staying at the Colonnade, so he might be there. I really am not sure." Uncomfortable with the conversation, Lelia knew trouble was brewing and she wanted to stay as far away from it as possible.

"Come with me Lelia. Come with me to Philadelphia. I, I just don't know what I'm going to do, I mean if I can't straighten this out with him, whatever will I do?" she stammered.

"I can't, I really can't. This is between you and Freddie, I can't be in the middle of this and it's not fair of you to ask me."

"Alright then, I'll go by myself. I thought you were my closest sister, my friend, but I guess not. I'll go alone." Fannie pouted.

Supper was quiet and a couple glasses of good Harvey's Bristol Milk didn't do anything to soften the mood. Fannie took the morning train to Philadelphia, her stomach in knots at the prospect of facing Frederic on her own. Lelia stood silently on the platform watching the train shrink into the distance. She could sense the disaster that waited just down the line; Freddie would never accept this confrontation gracefully. Fannie could only make things worse.

"What a mess." With that understatement, Lelia got back into her buggy and drove herself home. "Maybe I'll make a trip down to Evergreen and see Father and Ella for a few days. I haven't seen them in forever and it will take my mind off this predicament." But Lelia knew she would end up following her sister to Philadelphia, to help ward off the impending storm.

Fannie, on the verge of an anxiety attack, stepped off the eastbound train at the downtown Philadelphia station. It had been such a long time since she talked with Frederic even by post; she wasn't sure what she would say – or how he would react to seeing her. She found a willing porter who arranged a carriage to the hotel and stowed her single bag beside the driver for her. The Colonnade Hotel was an opulent palace-like hotel on Chestnut Street that

sometimes doubled as a stock exchange. On her arrival
Fannie immediately made her way to the reception desk
and asked for Frederic MacKenzie's room number.

"Is he expecting you Madam?" the clerk asked.

"No, it's a surprise. I'm his wife," she replied in a
huff.

"I'm sorry, Madam, but Mr. MacKenzie is out and
I'm afraid I can't give you his room number. You can
write him a message if you like and I'll see that he gets it as
soon as he returns."

Freddie in the meantime was in the smoking room
with a few of his friends from the theater, joking about his
dilemma.

"Why do you stay with her Freddie? You don't
need that kind of aggravation, just divorce her. That's what
you do now-a-days if it don't work out."

"Believe me, gents, I've thought about it. But her
father is some kind of business tycoon in Ohio; they say
he's a millionaire. I can't turn my back on that kind of
money. Things are working for me right now. If I play my
cards right some of that money will be mine someday."

"You're a shrewd one Freddie. I guess that's why I
like you ol' man. That and because you attract the ladies
like a magnet! I'll take your castoffs any day of the week
Friend." Peals of laughter filled the mahogany-paneled

room along with clouds of cigar smoke.

"Now, now gentlemen, I think I could take them all if my energy level was up," Freddie boasted. Hardy laughter once again rose above the din.

No one noticed a slender woman in a lovely garnet reception gown soundlessly slip into the smoky lounge. Fannie was intimidated by the swaggering men; no other woman would dare to invade this private space. But she heard Frederic's voice and it pulled her in. She was determined to straighten out their little misunderstanding.

"Now there's a hot one for you Freddie boy," said one of the chaps. Catcalls and whistles bombarded Fannie who self-consciously walked across the room as each man tried to outdo the other with lewd comments and derisive laughter.

Freddie turned around ready to make his move on a new conquest. Standing demurely behind him was Fannie, thrown a bit off-center by her vulgar reception.

"Frederic," she was noticeably trembling, "I really need to talk to you. Could we leave this place, maybe go to your room for a few minutes?"

"Fannie, I'm busy. We're conducting business here, aren't we gents?"

"Mrs. MacKenzie," one of the crew broke in, "I'm sorry, we all are. I mean, I apologize for our behavior, we shoulda recognized you was a lady an' all."

"I'll survive. Thank you for your contrition Sir. Frederic, *please*? Just a *little* of your time?" Fannie pleaded.

Frederic took her roughly by the elbow and led her out of the lounge and into the lobby. Because of the late hour the lobby was congested with guests, so reluctantly Frederic escorted Fannie to his suite. Once inside, Fannie started sobbing.

"Frederic, I miss you. My life is empty; I can't bear to have you avoiding me like this." She watched his reaction, not sure what to say. "It's true, I was upset when I first learned you gave me the Pox, but I love you. I can forgive you for that, let's just work it out and put our life back where it was."

"I don't know that I want my life back where it was Fannie. I like things just the way they are. I have my freedom, you have yours. It works."

"Well it doesn't work for me. I want children; I want a home like my mother, like every young lady wants. Maybe you shouldn't travel so much Dear, if you didn't travel we could have a real life together."

"To be honest Fannie, I don't think I want that sort of a life together. You need to learn how to pleasure me; you have no idea how to please a man. Why can't you be more like your sister? Lelia's ready to be ridden bareback anytime I make the suggestion. She enjoys men, enjoys life. You need to take a few lessons from her. Then I'll talk about coming back. In the meantime, leave me alone. You embarrass me in front of my friends. Just leave me alone!"

Fannie was dumbstruck. What did he say? What did he say about Lelia? She must have heard it wrong

"What?" Fannie asked with a catch in her breath, suddenly sickened.

"Be more like your sister. She knows how to please a man, and does a damn good job of it." Frederic poured himself a brandy, not offering anything to his astonished wife.

The arguing continued and the looser the liquor made Freddie, the more hostile he got. He gave Fannie a sound pounding, leaving marks on her face and arms. What else could he do? She was crying uncontrollably and wouldn't stop that incessant racket. She got in a few licks of her own that felt like little butterfly wings brushing his face, there was so little force behind her swings.

A clearly defeated Fannie ultimately escaped the hell she walked into, slamming the door of Frederic's suite as she rushed out in tears. Discreetly slipping into the powder room in the lobby, she tried to make herself

222

presentable before securing separate accommodations for herself at Reception. Fannie gathered her bag and stumbled up to her room in a daze, not wanting to be seen.

Back in Dayton Lelia, feeling guilty, caught the last train to Philadelphia, arriving at the Colonnade Hotel late in the evening.

"Is Mrs. Fannie MacKenzie staying here?" she asked the front desk clerk. "I'm her sister; can you give me her room number please?"

"Sorry, Madam, I can't do that," he replied.

"It's okay man, she really is her sister. I'll take responsibility," said a fairly inebriated Freddie crossing over to the desk from the Tap Room.

"Alright sir, I suppose a husband is responsible for his wife. Her room is 537 Madam. I don't have a spare key, you'll have to knock."

"Thank you sir," Lelia turned to Freddie and afraid of the answer to her question asked, "Freddie, have you talked to Fannie? Is she OK? She wasn't herself when she left Dayton and quite frankly I'm worried."

"Yes, we spoke. And we argued and she made a fool of herself in front of my friends. She may look a little worse for wear Lelia, when you see her, but damn it I was protecting myself! She's so "holier than thou" you know."

"What did you say to her Freddie?" Lelia started to

worry about what he may have let slip in the heat of an argument.

"I told her she could learn a few things from you Lelia. You know how to please a man. When she can bed me as well as you then I'll talk about coming back." Freddie started to get fired up again.

"You didn't! How could you tell her about that?!" Lelia's mind was racing trying to figure out how to smooth this over. Rehearsing just what she would say to Fannie, Lelia made her way up to the fifth floor to face her sister.

Lelia knocked on the door of room 537 and a splotchy red-faced sobbing and somewhat battered Fannie stood in the doorway with a shocked expression. She wasn't expecting Lelia. She felt certain Frederic had finally decided to apologize, or so she hoped; and if he were any man at all beg forgiveness for the disease he gave her. She wanted him to hold her in his arms like he once did, and tell her he loved her. But it was Lelia, her betrayer - the whore.

Fannie started lashing out, screaming and hitting her sister with flailing arms to little effect. When Lelia refused to budge until Fannie allowed her to explain, a wild-eyed Fannie in her hysteria ran screaming from the room in her night clothes. She ran the halls looking for Frederic then out the lobby doors onto Chestnut Street. The hour was

224

late and the streets empty. Lelia waited, expecting Fannie to calm down and return to her room. After all, she was in her nightgown for God's sake. When she didn't return after a good length of time Fannie went in search of Freddie, who was still in the Tap Room.

"Freddie, you have to help me look for Fannie before something terrible happens to her," Lelia insisted.

Fannie was wandering around near the Panhandle depot. Fortunately one of the railroad men found her and summoned the police. When officers arrived and tried to question her they found her unresponsive; what could possibly have brought a high-society woman to this part of town in her night clothes? Just as they were ready to take Fannie to the station house Lelia and Freddie drove up. Quickly jumping from the carriage Lelia ran to her sister's side.

"Fannie!" Lelia turned her attention to the uniformed man leading her away. "Constable, this is my sister. Please, sir, please - can I take her back with me? I promise I'll keep close watch over her," Lelia begged.

"I don't know. Who's this gentleman and what happened to the young lady's face?" the officer asked, pointing first to Freddie then to Fannie's bruised and swollen eyes, cheeks and chin.

Freddie was intolerably drunk and of no help to

Lelia whatsoever. But a woman on the streets at this time of night wouldn't have been safe, so Lelia felt it best to drag him along for protection.

"It's her husband. They just had a fight, that's all. I'll take care of everything if you'll just let me have my sister."

The officer agreed and watched Lelia struggle to help the drunken husband and his unresponsive wife into a carriage while managing the horse and buggy all at the same time. "You'd think someone would give me a hand," thought Lelia, anxious to just get the hell out of there and back to some sort of normalcy. Instead the men just stared at the comic scene before them.

Back at the Colonnade Lelia settled Fannie into her room; Frederic returned to the Tap Room to finish the night with his cronies. Lelia felt it was best under the circumstances to get a room of her own and asked the desk clerk to make it as near to her sister's as possible. Lelia was exhausted and prayed that this would all be over in the morning. She needed to make Fannie understand that her affair with Freddie was *before* the wedding.

Morning light didn't bring the slightest improvement to Fannie's fragile condition. In fact, while she was all alone with only her thoughts for company in the dark hotel room, Fannie attempted to take her life. She soaked a sponge in chloroform and lying on her back in the bed sucked on the sponge. She placed a rag over her face and anesthetized herself to the point of not waking up. When Lelia called on her in the morning and found her in this state she immediately sent for the hotel staff physician. Fannie spent the entire day in bed under the doctor's care.

Fannie woke late the following morning, somewhat sluggish but she had her senses back. She refused to see Lelia, wanted no explanations from her. Fannie sought out Frederic but he avoided her at all cost. To add to Lelia's problems Fannie started drinking early in the day so by mid-afternoon she was a belligerent drunk and making a scene again. Hotel management was threatening to call the police and have her thrown in jail but Lelia convinced them to wait until she could contact their brother.

Lelia sent Aaron a telegram from the Western Union office telling him Fannie needed his help urgently; she would explain in more detail when he arrived. Aaron took the next available train to Philadelphia and arrived by early evening the following day. Lelia, and a very reluctant Freddie, met him at the station and explained the situation on the ride back to Chestnut Street, careful not to divulge more than he needed to know.

"Lelia, I need to talk to you alone. I'm very

interested in your opinion on what made Fannie worse, and by worse I mean suicidal. As for you Man, I'll have a conversation with you later." Aaron, obviously irritated, fingered his buggy whip, toying with the thought of using it on this hooligan's "pretty" face. Freddie was actually relieved not to be included in the discussion, although he wasn't thrilled with Aaron's dismissive tone.

Aaron searched the hotel and it was late evening by the time he found a forlorn Fannie in the Tap Room standing at the bar hoping Frederic would walk in. She was wearing a long gown covered with crystal beads and seed pearls, long gloves and a hat smothered in netting and feathers. From her position in the subdued light her bruises were barely visible. Aaron gently approached his sister and tried to convince her to return with him to Evergreen. She didn't go peacefully but he was able to get her on the train.

The trip back to Hamilton was horrendous for Aaron. He booked a sleeper car to keep Fannie away from the rest of the passengers but he had to restrain her to keep her there. She screamed, she fought, she yelled obscenities the entire trip. It was the longest train ride of his life, or so he thought at the time.

Stuart was already waiting at the platform for Aaron and Fannie when they arrived. "I brought extra blankets for Mrs. MacKenzie sir. We had a bit of snow last night and the air is chilled."

"Thank you, Stuart, Mrs. MacKenzie isn't feeling well and the fleece may warm her mood as it comforts her body. Well, let's hope anyway."

The air was crisp and a light snow continued to fall adding to the sparkly crystalline layer already covering the landscape. The ride back to Evergreen was refreshing, cleansing Aaron thought. Fannie was so bundled up only her nose could be seen peeking out. Tightly wrapped in furs and coverlets she looked like a little stowaway fox. Aaron prayed the ride would work to calm Fannie's mood, recalling the hellacious train ride. In fact, he was hoping it would help his own mood because he was ready to kill Fred, and maybe Lelia too, for what he was putting the whole family through. Aaron resented always being the caretaker, the one everyone called for help. That is unless they wanted money, then it was Father. They all knew better than to ask Aaron for money. "A fool and his money are soon parted" - Aaron's credo, because he was related to a family of fools. The Cavanaughs would be paupers if not for Aaron and his business savvy. No, it was Father they begged for money and he would never turn them down. And it was Aaron who had to make up for the wastefulness of the girls and their men. Well, after his "conversation" with Fred, hopefully the rogue knows he'll never see a penny. Aaron looked down at his knuckles, still bruised and slightly swollen. He wasn't much of a fighter but neither was Fred unless he was beating up a woman. Aaron was satisfied that he walked away the victor from that encounter.

Aaron's wandering thoughts and Fannie's silence made the ride to Evergreen seem short and Stuart was pulling into the drive before Aaron realized it. Father was waiting on the porch, anxious to see his baby girl. When Fannie emerged from the layers of blankets and he saw her face Father grabbed her, hugging her tightly. No one but Aaron saw the tears spring from his eyes.

Fannie callously loosened Father's grip and walked past him into the house with Stuart following behind with her bag.

"Aaron, I wish I could have gone myself. I should have been the one to go get her," Father said.

"You haven't been well enough for a trip like that. Besides, you would have killed the bastard and then I'd have to figure out how to get you out of jail. Don't fret about it, this was best; I just gave him a warning," Aaron assured him. "Let's go in, I'll tell you the whole story after everyone's in bed.

Father propped Fannie in his own overstuffed chair

by the fire, encasing her up to her chin with covers to make her cozy. The new cook Bridget, a cousin Aaron sent for from County Donegal in the old country, brought Fannie a luscious tray of food to the parlor. Fannie, peeking out of her cocoon, ate nothing and couldn't be coaxed. She was exhausted herself from the tirade on the train, not sleeping a wink for several nights except for the chloroform incident. She sat staring at the fire without uttering a word until she fell asleep. Aaron carried her up to the bedroom that hadn't changed since she was a girl, surprised at how little she weighed. Her troubles with Fred had taken its toll and she appeared much too thin to Aaron. He only hoped that he was able to care for her with Ella in Washington and Lelia away; Lelia would be more trouble than help anyway. He gently placed her on the bed careful not to wake her, removed her shoes and gently placed the quilts over her clothes. What she needed now was a restful night and Aaron was banking on her getting many of those at Evergreen where she was loved and could be cared for.

Aaron had never been so wrong. True, Fannie did sleep through the night *and* the next day, but once rested she was a terror. That woman wasn't right; everyone agreed she must have been in the throes of a nervous breakdown. The Cavanaugh men weren't equipped to handle her sensitive nature. Father was in a quandary, if

only Mother were alive. Aaron had no choice but to take
her to the Oxford Retreat, which served as a sanitarium for
people with "nervous disorders." They were equipped to
handle problems like Fannie's.

Aaron personally drove his sister to the sanitarium,
leaving Stuart behind with Father. Aaron spoke to her
gently and treated her with kindness, trying to calm her
fears. He didn't want her to feel abandoned by her family
but he didn't know what else to do.

Fannie had only the clothes she packed for
Philadelphia, hardly appropriate for her new arrangement.
Aaron promised he would send for her personal things from
Chicago as soon as he got back; it would help her settle in
if she had the comfort of her own belongings.

They made their way through the ample grounds, a
little stream winding along the road. Aaron pulled up to a
building known as The Pines. Adjoining it was a small
structure called Cook Place which the Doctor used as his
residence. It was a tranquil and inviting setting giving
Aaron high hopes that Fannie would get along nicely here.
The Oxford Retreat was a sanitarium for both men and
women but The Pines was an annex dedicated to women's
"nervous disorders". Unlike other asylums this one did not
house the destitute or criminal; it was strictly for nervous
and mental diseases and addictions. Aaron paid a heavy

price for Fannie to stay there. His information about the quality of care came from a pamphlet that depicted a serene homelike atmosphere and individual care.

"Fannie, I'll be back in a week to see you. I'll bring Willie and Father with me, would you like that?"

"I want to go home, don't make me stay here Aaron. Please! Just let me go home, I'm fine! I'll be good!" Fannie was pleading with desperation, pulling against Aaron with all her might.

"Honey, it cost a little extra but I made sure you'll have a suite, a beautiful little apartment. You'll be happy here; it's just for a little while. We'll be up to see you on Sunday, I promise." Aaron struggled to get her from the carriage into the main building. Finally, two men dressed in white uniforms came out to help him.

"We'll take her from here sir. It will be easier on Mrs. MacKenzie if you just leave quickly," one said. "Just leave the signed commitment papers with us and we'll see that everything is taken care of."

"Aaron, Aaron!" Fannie screamed, struggling helplessly against the orderlies. "Please, Aaron, don't leave me here!" As difficult as it was, Aaron walked back to the carriage and drove out the way he came in. He could hear Fannie's cries all the way down the lane. He convinced himself again that this was best for her.

Chapter 29

Oxford, Ohio – 1875

Fannie, who was already taking mercury for the syphilis, was given an opium derivative to calm her nerves. Her treatment included cold water soaks for long periods of time in a special tub that constricted her movements. She hated being at the Pines, she felt doped and manipulated. She often saw women with linen jackets that completely covered the arms and hands and were belted behind the back so they couldn't move. The nurse on duty patiently explained that the jackets were used so the ladies wouldn't hurt themselves, it was for their protection. Fannie also heard stories from some of the residents about an underground tunnel that led from The Pines to the doctor's house. In a secret room there women had electricity shot into their heads, and sometimes the Doc removed parts of the brain. She was frightened beyond imagination every minute of the day. She wasn't like the others, she lamented; her only problem was despair over her cheating husband, what woman wouldn't be upset? Everything would be fine when Frederic came back to her, she really didn't belong here. She would never forgive Aaron for this.

Aaron, always true to his word, brought Father and Willie to the Retreat the following Sunday.

"Aaron, get me out of here. Get me out of here, I mean it! Father, please help me, I'm frightened here. I need to go home." Fannie begged without shame.

Father and Willie kissed her and left immediately for a walk around the grounds. It was more than they could bear to see Fannie like this. They stayed out in the cold winter weather rather than face Fannie again, and met Aaron at the carriage when it was time to leave. Aaron was steely in his resolve. There were professionals at the Retreat; they knew better than anyone how to help Fannie. He tried to turn a deaf ear to Fannie's weeping and begging, but had to cut his visit much shorter than anticipated because of her constant whining.

Aaron's visits were less frequent and Father and Willie never did return to the Retreat. Lelia, on the other hand, tried regularly to see Fannie but the mere mention of her name sent Fannie into hysterics. It would take hours for the staff to calm her down, even when subdued with heavy doses of morphine. The outcome was always the same, but Lelia continued to visit faithfully.

It was Lelia that contacted Freddie with the news that Aaron had committed Fannie to an asylum, but Freddie didn't care. "She's a lunatic," he said. "She belongs there."

Every week on returning from the retreat Lelia would write Freddie a letter telling him how Fannie was doing and that she constantly asked for him.

"Freddie, you're the only one who can get her out. You would have to take it to court, but I could do all the work. My sister Ella's husband is a lawyer. All you would have to do is sign the release papers. You owe her at least that much, come on Freddie, help her; help me. Won't you help me? Please!" Lelia wrote.

When Fannie heard that Frederic was taking her commitment to court she was filled with hope again. She knew all along that he would come for her. Her daydreams were filled with images of a happy life with Frederic, raising their children, maybe a home in the country. Fannie had a generous annuity from Father; she had plenty of money to buy a homestead. When Frederic came to pick her up she would share her ideas. Everything would be wonderful again.

Fannie was released from the Oxford Retreat only eight weeks after entering, but Frederic didn't show to pick her up. In fact, no one came for her with the exception of Lelia who Fannie refused to see. Feeling she had no one who cared about her and all alone, she hired a driver to take her to the train depot. Hopes dashed, she headed back to

Chicago with an ample supply of morphine to stabilize her moods.

"I can't go back to the house," she thought,"not without Frederic." Fannie was unable to bear the thought of living alone in the home she once shared with her beloved. She would be reminded daily of better times and how hopeless her life had become.

Fannie took a suite at the Palmer House Hotel and sent the chambermaid for her gowns and personal items. She would never step foot in that house again, not without Frederic. Even though her heart wasn't in it she would try to get on with her life, go to parties, the theater. "No, not the theater, it would be too humiliating to run into Frederic's friends," she thought. Fannie created a new life for herself in her hotel apartment. An unhappy life made bearable by a morphine stupor.

Chapter 30

Hamilton, Ohio – 2003

Our first Ghost Walk was such a huge success as a fundraiser that the historic district decided to continue the event every fall. It garnered a great deal of publicity in surrounding newspapers and coverage on local television stations. It was a good feeling for those of us who put so much effort and research into the project. But I wanted more; I was driven to learn everything possible about the souls who shared my house. And the truth of the matter is that just because the Ghost Walk was over for another year didn't mean the hauntings stopped.

Aidan and I faithfully attended the Spiritualist church every Sunday, rarely missing. I had to prove to myself that this communication was real and not something I conjured up in my mind. I enjoyed the regular church service and continued to be uncomfortable with the readings. One cold winter Sunday I drummed up enough courage to register for a mediumship class.

The class didn't teach me how to communicate with ghosts, but I did learn the difference between a medium and a psychic. A medium communicates with those who have passed over, and a psychic gets impressions from extra-sensory perception but doesn't get his information directly from Spirit. I learned the different types of spirit guides and how they help us through our lives; about my chakras and how to meditate. But for the life of me I couldn't communicate with Spirit. Our instructor explained that it was an ability everyone could develop with practice.

Well, I thought to myself, I should be able to get plenty of practice at my house. Completing this class gave me an understanding of Spiritualism and the ability to meditate but I wasn't any closer to having a two-way conversation with my other-worldly house guests. I wondered if they heard me the way I hear them. I was frustrated trying to bridge the gap.

Spring came early. My class in mediumship ended just about the time the daffodils pushed their way through my newly thawed garden beds. The crocuses and daffodils are a cause for celebration for me, an end to gloomy indoor activities and the beginning of spring projects, gardening and walks through the park. Neighbors we infrequently see through the winter walk by our garden gate daily and stop to visit.

With the warm weather our lives move outdoors and the hauntings move from the forefront to the recesses of our minds. That is until one of our spring projects reminded me they never leave, I just notice them less.

This particular spring Aidan hired a contractor to totally gut and renovate one of the second-floor bathrooms. The bathrooms were very rundown and still contained all the original caste iron plumbing. We wanted and desperately needed to change the half bath into a fully modernized bathroom. The project was huge and Gene, our contractor, spent weeks swinging his sledge hammer to remove the eight inches of cement under the tiled floors and the plaster and lathe walls. Demolition was monumental and I thought I would never see the second floor without a coating of construction dust.

After work one night Aidan picked his way through cement powder, nails, broken tile and the small bits of wood to talk with Gene about the progress and just see how the demolition was going.

"Hey, man, how's it goin', looks like you're making a lot of headway."

"Good, good. I expect to be through with the cleanup of all these materials soon; I'd say you should have your house back to normal in another week or so. Then it's a matter of building instead of tearing down."

"You're the boss here, Gene. We just appreciate you working us in; I know what your schedule's like."

"I gotta tell ya man, something weird happened to me today. I'm hardly believing it myself so you're probably goin' to think I'm nuts," Gene said as he wiped his brow and leaned his sledge hammer against the skeleton of a wall.

"Don't worry about it; I've seen my share of weird here," Aiden laughed.

"I was resting for a minute, you know how dirty this job is and hard labor; so I was resting on the sledge handle, taking a breather, when I felt someone behind me."

"No kidding," Aidan said, knowing that Gene was about to describe the type of encounter that we had grown accustomed to.

"Yeah, and I knew for certain I was the only one in the house, that it was too early for you or Erin to be home from work. I turned around and someone really *was* there, standing right where you are in the doorway," Gene said, feeling foolish and watching to see Aidan's reaction.

"Really? What did this person look like?"

"He was a young man; mustache and a funny haircut in an old fashioned suit with a vest. I don't know, he wasn't there long. He just smiled and gave me a nod, like a nod of approval for what I was doing. I don't think I imagined it, but it *was* hot and I was exhausted."

"I believe you, I really do. What happened then,

did he disappear or something?"

"No, he just walked down the hall towards the back of the house. I followed him into the hallway; he turned like he was going into the back bedroom so he was hidden for just a second because of the way the hall turns at the end. By the time I got down there he was gone; not in the hallway and not in the bedroom." Gene said.

"You're not afraid, are you?" Aidan asked. "I need to make sure you'll finish the job."

"Hell no, I'm not afraid. It's just weird. I'm not going to tell anyone except you, people will think I've been drinking again."

"It'll be our secret Gene. But if it's any consolation we have experiences like this too. We may not see them as clearly as you did," Aidan emphasized, "but they let us know they're here."

The bathroom when finally finished was gorgeous, the most beautiful Victorian bathroom I'd ever seen; dark wood paneling with antique tiles and fixtures. Gene did an amazing job. Aidan went back on his word to him just a smidgen; he did tell *me* about Gene's encounter trying to remember every detail. It convinced me that I needed to get back to mediumship training because *I* wanted to experience what Gene had. I wanted to meet the man and definitely the lady on the stairs. I wouldn't make that happen by tending my garden.

I contacted Reverend Joan by replying to one of the many emails I received from her since she gave me a reading. She didn't have any formal classes coming up, but she agreed to give me an intensive private class over a weekend. She lived over five hundred miles from our town so it would definitely involve a weekend trip. Aidan, God bless him, said he would go with me and sit in the hotel room while I took my class.

Reverend Joan taught me not only how to meditate properly but how to use divining rods, how to sense the presence of others without seeing them, how to raise my vibration level and most importantly, how to communicate with my Spirit guides. I was determined to make this work; if this were really possible I should be just as able to contact Spirit as anyone.

"You know, I'm a trance medium Erin; one of few who communicate with Spirit using a trumpet. Could I interest you and maybe Aiden in a séance? I have a special room in my house that I use for just that purpose."

Reverend Joan was a petite soft-spoken person who had been a practicing Spiritualist for many years. I knew she was also a trance medium but I never dreamed she would offer to include us in one of her séances.

"I'm honored that you would ask me. I'm not sure

how Aiden would feel about that though, I'll have to ask him. Maybe another time would be better."

"I understand; another time then."

Aidan picked me up at the end of the second day, and we stood for a long while talking to Joan and her husband on many subjects: life on "The Hill" as she called her country home; traveling around the country to the psychic fairs; and Spiritualism in general. Then the topic of Rev. Joan's séances came up.

"You know, there really is nothing to fear," she said in her quiet voice while looking directly at Aiden. "We always control the session, and I surround us with a white light of love."

"I think I would freak out if something happened," Aiden said.

"No you wouldn't Honey," I assured him.

"How do you know what I'd do Erin? It sounds like a bit more than I care to experience."

I knew better than to push the séance idea. It was better to present it to Aiden in a less threatening way; and at just the right time. This wasn't it.

Reverend Joan said to call her if we wanted to contact spirit. When we were ready she would come to the house to perform the séance in our own home. I was excited at the prospect. What better way to get answers about the lady or speak to the man who appeared on the second floor?

Chapter 31

Evergreen – 1890

"Aaron, I want to see Father. Where is he?"

"Lelia, where the hell does all your money go? Why did I have to wire train fare for you to get back from Chicago. I don't know why you were there in the first place, trying to make things worse than you already have?" barked Aaron.

"I have expenses Aaron. It's hard for me to make do with the little bit Father gives me. And to answer your question I had to talk to Fannie, it was of the utmost importance." Lelia was indignant. The money wasn't Aaron's business anyway, it was between her and Father.

"Well why the hell would you go to Chicago if you knew you didn't have enough money to get back?!" Aaron had no patience for his idiot sister who didn't have the sense she was born with. There was just something about Lelia that set Aaron off every time he saw her.

"Not that it's any of your beeswax Mr. Smarty, but I thought after I talked to Fannie I could spend a little time with her in Chicago and she would buy my return ticket. As it turned out, I couldn't get past that stupid hotel staff, so I never did get to see her. Where's Father? I need to talk to him."

"No more money for you Lelia. You'll just have to live on your allowance; Father's not going to give you any more. Go on home. He bought you a house; you get an allowance, that's all you get. Father's napping and I'm not going to let you bother him."

"O-o-o-o-o!" Lelia was furious with Aaron. She stomped out of the house making enough noise to "wake the dead", a phrase Mother often used when referring to Lelia's tantrums. She unhitched the buggy and gave her horse a bit too much whip, driving recklessly down the road to make a point. Aaron was ignoring her anyway. Once she slammed the door he went on to other things.

Evergreen 1892

Lelia didn't return to Evergreen again until Fannie's funeral. Father was in a drunken stupor and Aaron was in the foulest of moods. It was a beautiful summer-like day with flowers growing everywhere and the birds singing. The sun was warm on her back as she followed the pall-bearers to the family section of the cemetery where Fannie would join Mother and the oldest of the Cavanaugh girls, Mary Marie, who died in childbirth when Edgar was born. The day was perfect in every way except that she was burying her sister; saying goodbye for the last time. Lelia was consumed by guilt for not having cleared her conscience before Fannie's death. She hadn't been given the chance to explain her relationship with Freddie. Lelia hoped that Fannie was able to read in her heart what she wasn't allowed to tell her sister in person. Lelia hoped Fannie was finally happy.

Chapter 32

Hamilton, Ohio – 2004

Reverend Joan was in the area for the spring
Psychic Fair and called to see if we were ready to take her
up on her offer of a séance. Joan had been practicing
physical mediumship in this way for fifteen years, the last
ten of which she had been uncommonly successful.

"What do you think Aidan? Should we try this?" I
asked.

"Sounds like something we could do as a Sashay
maybe," he replied. Aiden still wasn't sure how he felt
about this. "We could kill two birds with one stone; I know
the gang would really be into it."

"No, not a sashay. We have to take this seriously if
we want results, it's not a parlor game. Are you up for a
private séance? Just you, me and Joan?"

"OK, OK. I'm with you. No need to get so upset.
It'll be just the three of us and whoever else happens to
show up," he said sarcastically, "– from the world of spirit,
I mean. No neighbors, I promise."

"I'm sorry Honey; I didn't mean to jump you. I just

really want to find out what's going on." To myself I thought he must think I'm nuts, with all this psychic stuff I put us through; he puts up with so much from me.

I returned Joan's call and invited her to dinner that Saturday hoping we would be lucky enough afterwards to make contact with Aaron or the Lady. I had no idea what to expect, this was new to me.

It was a warm spring evening so Aidan tossed steaks on the grill and we had a leisurely picnic in the yard. Not a lot blooming yet, just early daffodils, a tulip here and there - mostly the dreaded dandelions, but things were greening up nicely. Aidan cleaned up the grill and dishes while Joan and I talked about how the séance would proceed.

"Before we start, I found this obituary for Fannie Cavanaugh I want you to read. This is who I most want to contact tonight, if at all possible. I have so many questions for her, and the information in this news article is all I know about her." I removed the clipping, which I had shared with only Aiden, from its plastic protector and handed it to Reverend Joan. She read it in silence.

TOOK HER OWN LIFE

A Very Sensational Suicide at Chicago, Ills.

A Story of Unusual Interest

The undying love of a woman for one of the sterner sex finally results in self-destruction – the suicide makes a will leaving her property to a chambermaid who had been kind to her.

Chicago, Ills, April 22 – Chicago is greatly excited over the announcement of a highly sensational suicide which occurred some time between 10 p.m. and 10 a.m. It is that of Mrs. Fannie MacKenzie, wife of Frederic MacKenzie, formerly of this city, and who is now in New York, the manager of Fay Templeton. Mrs. MacKenzie was discovered in her apartments at the Palmer House hotel at 10 o'clock Sunday morning, lying in a

251

comatose condition and at the threshold of death. Everything indicated poison by morphine. Doctors were summoned and pronounced the care hopeless and at 11 o'clock the beautiful woman was a corpse. It was soon discovered that she had taken five grains of morphine purchased Saturday in this vicinity. She had settled all her debts and had stated that she was going to leave the city for a few days. She left a letter stating her intention of committing suicide, directing how she should be laid out, and where interred. She requested that no notice be sent of her death to her parents or friends.

A Sadly Interesting Story

The story of Mrs. MacKenzie's life is a sadly interesting one. She was a daughter of W. H. Cavanaugh, of Hamilton, Ohio, who is a millionaire and a man of high standing. She was also the full cousin of Governor Cavanaugh and the sister of the

252

wife of Congressman Byron, of the Seventh Ohio district. Five years ago she married Fred MacKenzie in New York, and about three years ago she came to Chicago, where MacKenzie was located. MacKenzie is a handsome, bright and stylish fellow. Their life here was one of continued wrangling and unhappiness, Mrs. MacKenzie accusing her husband of cruelty and neglect.

Left Property to a Chambermaid

MacKenzie thereupon left her and went to Philadelphia, to which place she followed him, creating a sensation in the Colonnade hotel, where she found him. There she attempted self-destruction by putting a sponge wetted with chloral in her mouth and a handkerchief over her face. She was rescued after hours of hard work. She then went to Ohio with her family, who made an unsuccessful attempt to place her in a private asylum for mental treatment. A few months ago she came back to Chicago and had been living at the hotel ever since. MacKenzie obtained a divorce from her in the court here one week ago. It is believed she hoped throughout her claims of neglect and cruelty in the courts that her actions would bring MacKenzie back to her, for she was hopelessly infatuated with him, and her love was apparently wholly unrequited. Mrs. MacKenzie was a petite blond a superb dresser, and one of the most stylish women ever seen in this city. Mrs. MacKenzie made a will Saturday, leaving her property in Hamilton, Ohio to Maggie McPhee, a chambermaid of the Palmer House hotel who had been kind to her.

"We'll see what happens dear, I really have no control at all over who comes through, if anyone. It's possible that we'll sit here for hours and no one comes through."

Aiden came into the house and started cleaning up while Joan and I spent a few minutes going over the guidelines.

"We need a room where all light can be eliminated," Joan said. "It doesn't have to be a large area since it's just the three of us, and we'll want to put black-out drapes or blankets over all doors and windows."

"Do you need a table?" I asked.

"No, that's not necessary. The trumpet can be placed on the floor. Now remember Erin, no one touches the trumpet. It's a sacred instrument only to be handled by its owner. Does Aidan know that? I should probably have a little talk with him anyway so he knows what to expect. After we get the room ready we'll go over all this once more. Don't be frightened, there really isn't anything to be afraid of. I do this all the time, and we'll surround ourselves with the white light of protection."

"I'm not afraid, just excited I guess; maybe a little anxious about talking to a ghost."

We decided on Aidan's office because it had only one window and a door to the hallway. It wasn't the least bit difficult to block all sources of light. We were reminded to join hands and not to break the circle until told to do so. After a brief review of session protocol and a prayer of protection, Joan began.

"If there is anyone in spirit here with us, please speak."

We sat in dark silence for what seemed like a very long time with no results. I stared into the blackness of the room until pinpoints of light exploded in my eyes. Did the total lack of visual stimulation bring on the fireworks? Is that what it's like to be blind? I mean, do they see the colored lights like I experienced or was my imagination overly-sensitive in the blacked-out stuffy office? My mind was wandering; I tried to refocus.

"Aaron, if you're here, please talk to me," I whispered nervously hoping, but also definitely afraid, he would answer. Aidan sat silently; trying to be supportive he gave my hand a gentle squeeze in the dark.

Slowly the trumpet rose from the floor. I couldn't see it but I could sense it. There was a cool breeze wafting off my right cheek, and then the stuffy room became suddenly cold causing me to shiver. I know I must have squeezed Aidan's hand a bit too hard because he gently tried to loosen my grip. Joan began to make an irritating noise in her throat, like she was trying to clear a frog.

A soft low voice that sounded more like a bad recording said, "Quit bothering me." I couldn't tell if it came from Joan or the trumpet. In the dark it was hardly distinguishable.

"I'm sorry," I said in a hushed tone, "What did you say?"

"Quit bothering me. Stop with all the questions, stay out of my life." The voice was soft and I had to listen carefully to understand. Fortunately Aidan had put a wireless microphone in the room and a recorder on the other side of the wall. Hopefully anything I missed would be captured on the recorder so we could listen to it later.

"Aaron, is it you?"

"Who did you expect? It's my house." The voice seemed to be moving around the room, one minute in my right ear then in my left, above me, in front of me. My breath was catching in my throat; I couldn't feel Aidan's or Joan's hands in mine anymore. Did we break the circle?

Struggling to talk I sputtered, "Aaron, I'm on *your* side. What happened to you was wrong. Is the lady on the stairs Fannie? Do you know the lady?"

The room was silent again. I could feel warmth slowly creep up my body from my feet to my throat forcing a little bile into my dry mouth. I could feel my face flushing, and I longed to hear more of Aaron's words but none came. Joan started making little noises in her throat, or as she called it her instrument, once again. I don't know how long we sat there in the dark. Aidan hadn't uttered a word the entire time and in the blackness I wondered if he

257

was even there. As the room warmed up the feeling came back to my hands and I could feel his hand still gently holding mine.

"We thank you Spirit, and we give thanks to the Lord God Creator for wrapping us in his protective power, Amen." said Joan in a hoarse voice; soft and raspy but definitely Joan's. "You may open your eyes," she said.

Shaking off the numbness we waited for Joan to instruct us to get up and remove the blankets from the door and window. The sun had set and the first stars of the evening were winking in a cloudless sky. We moved from the office into the pub to check the recorder and discuss what we thought happened.

"Can you tell us what you felt, what you thought?" I asked Joan.

"I really can't remember anything past the prayer for protection," she said. "That's usually the way it works. I completely leave my body when they come in; go to my "place of peace" until called back by impulse.

"Aidan, did you hear what happened," I asked, "or was it just in my head?" I turned to watch my husband as he fiddled with the recording device.

"I definitely heard it. I don't know if what I heard is the same thing you did, but I did hear something. At first it sounded like a buzzing bee, but then I began to hear a low voice and eventually words."

He pressed the play button on the digital tape recorder and the three of us listened to a buzzing bee floating in and out of a sea of static white noise.

"Well, that doesn't help at all," I grumbled.

"Not a problem, Honey. Let's compare and make notes while it's still fresh in our minds." Aidan said, always the pragmatist.

Aidan and I sat at the large table in the pub for the next two hours talking and making notes. Joan was exhausted first from the séance, but on top of that she had put in a full day of readings at the Psychic Fair. She left us to our debriefing and went back to her hotel room.

That night my dreams were consumed with episodes from Aaron's life. All through the night I would wake myself up and wrap my arms around Aidan, hugging him to make sure I was awake, only to fall asleep to dream once again of the dysfunctional family who haunted my house.

Aaron

Chapter 33

Hamilton, Ohio – 1894

After Fannie was committed to the Oxford Retreat Father, the Cavanaugh patriarch, began his decline. He began drinking an uncommon amount and could be found publicly intoxicated at least three or four days out of the week. He harbored tremendous guilt; guilt for not going to Philadelphia with Aaron to bring her home, guilt because he didn't visit her at the asylum. He couldn't bear to see his baby girl in that place. It wasn't that he didn't want to see her; he just couldn't tolerate the thought of her being locked up there, even if it was for her own good. He felt helpless. When Fannie was released by Writ of Habeas Corpus and returned to Chicago, Father instructed Aaron to hire a Pinkerton detective to keep an eye on her. He would never allow that worthless husband of hers to touch her again.

True, it was the asylum that triggered his dementia but Fannie's death had a more profound effect on Father.

Instead of drowning his sorrows a few days a week his drinking was constant. The night Aaron returned with Fannie's remains from Chicago the old man was passed out drunk on the couch. This drunken stupor lasted from the burial to - well, it never ended. It was worse than Mother's passing. He drank beer all day at the Brewery then came back to the homestead and sipped Irish whiskey until he fell asleep. He could be heard sobbing through the night and when he woke he took to drink again to forget his night terrors. His health was failing and with each day that passed he looked to be more and more a frail little man.

Just as he had done for Ella, Lelia, and Fannie, Father bought Aaron a house in the city. With the exception of Lelia whose house was in Dayton, their houses were similar in size and all located in what was considered a very prestigious area, an area where great industrialists of the period built elaborate homes lining both sides of the street, in close proximity to their places of business. The surrounding neighborhoods consisted of smaller framed houses built for laborers who worked in their mills, foundries, ice reservoirs and factories. This tree-lined boulevard with large brick mansions of the town's wealthiest citizens earned the name Millionaire's Row in its heyday.

During Fannie's short life she and Frederic rarely

came home to Hamilton or used Fannie's house located there. Fred traveled extensively and Fannie stayed either in Chicago or with Lelia in Dayton. Ella and Samuel Byron's home was across the street from Aaron's, but after Samuel was elected to Congress they too spent little time in Hamilton, living mostly in Washington with the children. Aaron lived in a palatial brick home, maintaining it with the same attention to detail as his dress. Father often said that Aaron ought to be married he had such a fine home, but Aaron had far too many family obligations to add a wife to the mix.

The summer after Fannie's burial Aaron would drive daily to the homestead to pick up his father and bring him to town. If Aaron didn't look after him the old man would brood and sleep at the house all day, it was best to keep him busy and away from the liquor as much as possible.

It was already mid-morning when Aaron walked into the large parlor at Evergreen and found his father lying on the divan curled up with his back to the room. It took a bit of doing but Aaron roused him and got him into a sitting position.

"Pa, why don't you come with me today to the ice houses? I have to stop by the bank then drop off payrolls. It will do you good to get out and see people, it's a beautiful day."

"What the hell are you doing?" Father growled.
"Leave me be, I was taking a little nap."

"Where's Willie? Who's looking after you?" Aaron
asked as he wet a cloth at the basin and wiped Father's
face.

"How should I know man!" Pa growled. "Probably
in the barn. I don't need nobody looking after me, I'm a
grown man. What are you doing here anyway Aaron?"
Most people would steer clear of Father when he was
drinking heavily; everyone that is except Aaron. His father
could be a scary man when he'd been indulging himself
with liquor, which began early in the day, but Aaron knew
how to handle the old man and took his grumblings in
stride.

"I need your help today, Pa. Why don't you come
with me to the ice ponds? I have to take care of the
payrolls and the men are anxious to see you. They love it
when you hang out with them; it makes them feel less
common. And Mr. Hessler at the bank asks about you
every time I go in there. Now let's put some decent clothes
on and get out of here. Some fresh air will do you good."

Against his father's wishes Aaron firmly led him
through the house and out the door. He helped him into the
buggy then ran quickly to the other side, jumped up and

slid into the seat next to him. Taking the reins Aaron eased
the horse and carriage down the lane to the road into town.
A bumpy ride and Father would be too sick to manage the
day. Aaron was always considerate of his father; he felt all
the others selfishly went off to live their lives and expected
Aaron to take care of everything. He accepted the
responsibility because, well, what else could he do? Those
selfish girls thought of no one but themselves and Willie
helped but Aaron couldn't put this burden on him. He was
too young. Aaron was the oldest and he accepted the role
of head of household. They rode along quietly for a few
minutes.

"Aaron, if I had a good horse I could come into the
city anytime I want. I could come to see you and drop by
the ponds. Stop by and see my friends in town. I'm not
needed at the farm anymore and I have nothing to do.
What happened to my horse?"

"He's not a safe horse for you to ride Pop. I put him
out to pasture. He makes a great stud and there's more
money using him that way. I come to get you every day,
don't I? If you don't get into town it's because you don't
want to go."

"I'm not dead, damn it, and I'm not an invalid. I
can ride a horse Aaron. You make me feel like an old man
when you say things like that, I need some freedom."

"I'm sorry Pa; I didn't mean to hurt your feelings. I just don't want anything to happen to you. Even I have a hard time staying on that sorrel; he has a mind of his own, just like you. He's hard to handle. If you want to come into town on your own I'll get you a gentle Morgan that can pull your carriage, and I'll find you a driver. You can come and go as you please. I know just the horse, I saw him at auction last week."

"Don't need no driver," Father mumbled under his breath. "You'd think I have one foot in the grave the way everybody treats me," he said a bit louder to make sure Aaron heard him.

"That's not it, believe me. We all just care about you and want you around as long as possible."

"No one cares but you and Willie. Ella and Lelia been nothin' but trouble for me, and my baby Fannie is gone." Father eventually settled down and went through the motions of Aaron's errands for the rest of the day. Aaron treated him to lunch at his favorite restaurant; they visited the Big Reservoir north of town and stopped by the bank. The old man enjoyed hanging out with the workers at the ice houses. He missed the musty smell of the straw that was used to store the blocks of ice in the deep pits, the coolness of the storage houses and the camaraderie among the men. Since he took Aaron as a partner several years before in the ice business, he didn't feel the need to worry about any of the daily operations. Aaron knew how to make money and the ice houses became extremely profitable after their partnership formed. But the old man missed the involvement; with Aaron in charge it only added to his feelings of being useless, helpless.

By the end of the day the old man was in great spirits. Aaron took him back to Evergreen and stayed for dinner. It was nightfall when Aaron finally headed back to town, to his house on Millionaire's Row. Aaron was proud of his home; it was the only thing that he truly owned. Sure, he spent a lot of time at the farm and homestead, but this was his alone. That sense of ownership, where everything in the house was his doing, it made him feel good.

Later in the week Aaron returned to the stockyards to ask about the nine-year-old Morgan he had seen at auction. Good, it was still available. On closer inspection Aaron decided it was a dependable horse, a good one for his father and one Pa could handle if he had to. Aaron bought the animal, and tying it to the back of his carriage headed out to the small reservoir near Evergreen to see about a driver. He wanted someone trustworthy and sought out Augie Plinkton, one of the laborers. Aaron offered him far more than the two dollars a week he made cutting, storing and loading ice on wagons. All he had to do was be available to drive old Mr. Cavanaugh wherever he wanted to go. Not only was the pay better, and certainly less physical than working with ice, but he would live at Evergreen so he would always be there if needed. This was a once in a lifetime opportunity for a young single chap like Augie.

"Sure Mr. Cavanaugh, I'll bring the old gentleman to town and keep a good eye on him too," Augie said.

"You can start tomorrow. I'll come by at the end of your shift today and we'll pick up your belongings and take them to the homestead tonight. We'll get you settled and introduce you to the family and staff." In Aaron's opinion Augie would have the right disposition to put up with his father's temperament and he was satisfied with his choice.

Later that evening Aaron, pleased with himself and the results of the day, drove Augie to Evergreen with the new horse trotting behind. Father actually took it better than Aaron expected. His hope was that the old man wouldn't scare the boy out of taking the job. It was midsummer and still light by the time they arrived. Father carefully looked over horse and man like they came from the same mare. The horse wasn't what he had wanted and neither was the boy, but it did give him some independence so he was willing to compromise.

"I don't need a driver, boy. But if this is all I can get I'll take you as part of the bargain," said the surly old man, almost nose to nose with young Augie trying to intimidate him.

Augie, nearly reeling from the smell of the old sot, felt he would definitely be earning his dollars. "Don't worry Mr. Cavanaugh sir; I'll stay out of your way. You won't even know I'm around."

"Humph!" Father turned without saying anything more and stumbled over to his couch and bottle. Aaron and Willie introduced the new driver to the house staff and farm hands who helped him settle in. They discreetly filled the young man in on everything he would ever want to know about the Cavanaugh clan and a few things he didn't.

Aaron stayed for dinner with Willie and his father before leaving for Dayton Street and the comfort of his own home.

Augie's job as driver started right away. Father, testing his new found freedom, was up early morning, dressed and ready for town. Augie hitched up the Morgan and picked up his charge at the front of the house.

The first stop was Commerce Bank where Mr. Cavanaugh checked on his accounts. They ate lunch at the restaurant he owned before driving past each of his properties to have a look-see, making sure his tenants were taking care of things. Mr. Cavanaugh owned a considerable amount of real estate. He stopped by his lawyers to ask about pending litigation on people he was suing for non-payment of notes; then lastly on to the Malt House and Brewery, his saloon, right across from the courthouse. While the old man spent his afternoon in the saloon Augie waited dutifully in the carriage across the street, sometimes sitting on the courthouse lawn as he waited for what seemed like forever. As dusk crept in, the old man stumbled out. Augie would drive him back to Evergreen in silence, where he would help him into the house and parlor. His job done for another day. The following day they would wake to repeat the same routine, and the next day and the next and so on. It rarely deviated. On Fridays they would visit the post office where the old man would try to send money through the post to Fannie.

"Sir, Mrs. MacKenzie passed away," the postmaster gently reminded the old man.

"Yeah, humph, forgot," Father said sadly. Every Friday found Augie waiting outside in the buggy while the old gentleman went into the post office once again to send money to his dead daughter.

Chapter 34

Hamilton, Ohio – 2004

I absent-mindedly pushed off with my right foot in the wicker swing in the gazebo and looked through the trial documentation, making notes on old man Cavanaugh.

"Hey Neighbor, what's happening? Need some light refreshment?" Jackie came through the gate of our shared picket fence with a wide-mouthed Miller Lite in each hand.

"Well, of course. How can I turn it down when it's already here?"

"What are you up to lady?" Jackie plopped down on the seat opposite the swing and removed the twist-off tops from the two beers. "I saw you sittin' over here all alone, looked like you could use some company."

I put my notebook aside and turned my thoughts elsewhere, enjoying simple conversation that involved transplanting perennials, tending the gardens in the community park, local gossip; you know, fun things. We spent quite a while in idle chatter, in fact Jackie went home for a couple more beers so we relaxed and talked for almost an hour.

"I better take off, the boys are waiting for lunch and I've already stayed too long. What are you working on there? More about that old man?" Jackie got up from the bench then sat back down.

"Just taking a few notes. Looks like he suffered epileptic fits, they found him all over town, passed out from his "affliction" as they call it in the papers. It also talks about severe dementia. Long after his daughter died he couldn't remember she was dead; asked the same questions over and over about his finances and property – basically forgot things. I suppose when they found him dead in his carriage it was just old age or something."

"I don't know Erin, from what I've heard you tell me I'll bet he was the town drunk. An extremely rich town drunk, but you don't pass out from epilepsy. Seizures only last seconds. That's my gut feeling for what it's worth. I think when they found him passed out he was just shit-faced."

"I still have a stack of news articles I haven't had the time to read thoroughly, so the truth is probably in there somewhere," I said. "It gets kind of boring reading about all the settlements, debts and receipts. I've been skipping over the boring parts and need to go back over it so I don't miss anything. But I would never doubt your gut, so you're probably right. I just can't back it up with facts right now."

"All this research and the books full of notes you're taking, is it worth it?"

"It is; it definitely is! I couldn't make this stuff up if I tried! And what's fascinating is the real history of this town isn't the "official history." It makes me wonder if they're trying to sweep all this under the rug, you know what I mean? That's what keeps me going, getting to the truth."

"Well kiddo, I really do have to go this time. Let me know when the book comes out; it would be an interesting read." Jackie headed back through the garden gate tossing the empties into the recycling bin on her way to the house.

"See ya later." I picked up my notebook and entered a reminder to look into the alcoholism angle; he did in fact own a brewery along with everything else.

Chapter 35

Evergreen 1893

Aaron stopped by Evergreen every day, sometimes to help with the livestock, usually to go over the books and in general just to make sure everything was as it should be with the family and farm. One afternoon as the summer was nearing an end Aaron noticed his father's carriage not in the drive and Augie at the house.

"Augie, where's Mr. Cavanaugh? Aren't you supposed to be with him at all times?" Aaron snapped.

"Yes Sir, I take the old gentleman into town every day. We have the same routine every single day and I serve him faithfully. He's rowdy when we leave in the morning and has a snoot full, pardon me Sir but you know he does, when we come back in the evening. This morning I came to the door to pick him up like I do every day, and he hit me with his cane! Said he 'don't need no damn driver', his words exact Sir. I didn't know what to do; he wouldn't let me in the carriage, kept hitting me."

"I told Augie to let him go Aaron," explained Willie. "Pa insisted he was a man and wouldn't be treated like he couldn't take care of himself; he'd been taking care of everybody for thirty-odd years. It's not Augie's fault."

"We'll let him try it a few days and see how he handles it," Aaron said. "I don't want to take his dignity away, but if it seems unsafe it'll have to stop. If he drinks too much I want you to go get him Augie. Just keep an eye on him, you know his routine."

The new arrangement didn't work out at all. Augie would walk into town knowing the old man would be too drunk to drive home. Mr. Cavanaugh fought him when he showed up at the saloon to pick him up. Augie politely, careful not to embarrass him, folded him into the carriage and listened to his abuse all the way home. Sometimes Mr. Cavanaugh would buy things then forget to take his purchases, causing Augie to go about town picking up all the forgotten items.

Early one fall evening as Aaron drove his carriage from the small reservoir to the homestead he saw Lelia walking along the road from the canal. Aaron pretended not to see her, there was no way in hell he would offer her a ride; if he did he would be forced to listen to her foolishness for longer than he cared to. She rarely came to visit anyway, he wondered what she wanted from Pa this time; money most surely. He didn't feel the least bit bad when his horse kicked up dirt, peppering his sister as he

274

sped by. He pulled up to the house, gave the reigns to one of the hands and walked with a sense of purpose through the front door.

"How are you Mary? Is my father home yet?" Aaron asked.

"Yes Mr. Cavanaugh, he's lying in the big room, taking a little nap before dinner." Mary Montgomery had been with the family almost since Mother died. She was loyal to the Cavanaugh men and was treated with respect by Father, Aaron and always by Willie who was kind to everyone. Both Aaron and Father could be ornery and were never ones to be crossed, but if they liked you there wasn't a thing they wouldn't do for you. And Mary was well liked, the old gentleman often taking her into his confidence. It was Mary who convinced her own sister to manage Aaron's house in the city against everyone's warning. Two of a kind they were, hardworking and trustworthy.

Aaron dutifully wiped his feet at the door. "I believe I saw my sister Lelia walking from the boats, Mary, you can probably expect she'll be here for dinner. Tell Bridget I'll take my dinner in the library; I think I'll work on the accounts while my sister is here," he said handing her his hat and topcoat.

Aaron strode into the large parlor where Father was

275

lying in his usual spot, on the couch with his back to the room. Aaron called his name as he walked over to the well-worn upholstered divan and the shrunken figure that lay there. "Pa, it's almost time for dinner. Are you awake?" Aaron gave him a gentle nudge.

"I'm awake. I was just about to get up and turn the lamp up. It's getting dark earlier these days. Tell me about your day Son, things okay at the ponds? The earlier dusk tells me you'll need to bring back the cutters soon; it'll be time to harvest the ice before you know it."

"The day was great, Pa. I'll tell you all about it later; we signed a sales contract with a new distributor in Cincinnati. He said he remembers you from the time you were a Deputy Sheriff, his name is Grover Smith, they call him Smitty."

"Can't say as I remember him," said Father. He sat up trying to get his bearings while Aaron turned up the gas lamp.

"Well he remembers you and it helped us get the deal. See, you're working even when you're not working. I saw Lelia walking out this way Pa. I told Mrs. Montgomery she'll probably stay for dinner. I'll just take mine in the library and get some work done."

"She was walking? Why didn't you give her a ride?"

Aaron gave his father a look and said, "You know I can't stand the sight of her, that girl is more than I can bear. She's probably going to ask you for something; it's the only reason she visits. Her selfish ways and 'poor me' stories only work to turn my stomach."

"Don't worry boy, she won't get anything extra from me. I spend enough on her, inasmuch as she keeps that lazy good-for-nothing Jarvis fella at Dayton."

"Who would that be Pa - Jarvis?" asked Aaron.

"Some damn artist that says he was injured serving the Union so he can't work. That dumb daughter of mine supports the shiftless skunk with the money I give her. I'm not giving her a dime this time; she'll have to make do with her allowance."

"Don't work yourself up, Pa. I just wanted to let you know she'll probably be here over dinner and want to eat with you and Willie." Aaron supported his father's shaky frame and helped him walk to the dining room where Mrs. Montgomery was already setting the table.

Lelia, winded from her walk, let herself in the front door about thirty minutes behind Aaron. "Hello, everybody."

"Lelia, for cryin' out loud, why don't you knock like a civilized human being instead of barging into someone's home?" barked Father.

277

"Why Father? This is my home too," cooed Lelia. Aaron immediately knew she needed something and had the audacity to ask for it, so he made his exit without a word. He could hear Lelia's annoying whiney voice as he made his way down the hall to the library where he hoped to find some peace. Mrs. Montgomery followed him with a steaming hot Shepherd's Pie.

"Why does Aaron treat me like that? He's terrible to me and I don't deserve it."

"Lelia you get on everyone's nerves here. We always know there's going to be trouble when we see you at the door; you *always* stir up trouble," Father told her.

"It's not so," Lelia pretended to be hurt. She sat down to the dinner table with Father, then Willie who came in from the fields. Patiently, Father waited for Lelia to reveal the true reason for her visit.

"Hey, Willie, how's my favorite brother?"

"Fine Sis, same as always. Nothin' much changes with me." Willie said, half-smiling.

As the men were concentrating on their food, Lelia's mind was visibly working on a way to phrase her next question. "Pa," said Lelia, "you know the wedding rings that Aaron took off Fannie? The ones he took in Chicago?"

"Girl, I don't want to be talkin' about that. Don't

278

go bringing that up again." Lelia's constant nagging over Fannie's diamond rings was a sore spot with Father.

"But Pa …"

"End of discussion, kiddo. If you've got something to say to Aaron, say it yourself. Now let me eat in peace, if you can't do that then leave the table."

Lelia was silent for the rest of the meal. Reluctantly she sought Aaron in the library and cowering like a dog sneaked in to talk to him. She was hoping Father would intercede for her. Aaron was never nice to her and for the life of her Lelia couldn't understand why.

"Aaron, could I trouble you for a minute?" Lelia said softly, as though if she spoke quietly she wouldn't be annoying her brother. She didn't want to face his anger.

"What is it Lelia?" Aaron snarled.

"Aaron I don't want to make you mad, but you know I should be entitled to those rings…"

"That again! What's wrong with you woman? You aren't getting Fannie's rings!" Aaron boomed.

"Aaron, what are *you* going to do with them? You can't *wear* them. I should get them; I helped Freddie pick them out, why I practically bought those rings for her! They should be mine." Fannie forgot her conciliatory tone and was getting a bit angry herself as she defended her position.

279

"Get out! Get the hell out of the library, out of the house. I don't want to see you and I never want to have this discussion again! Got it?"

"You're a dirty low-lived grave robber Aaron! Those rings aren't yours. If they didn't go to the grave with Fannie they should be mine!" Lelia cried.

"Get out or I'm going to drag you out myself," Aaron demanded, causing Lelia to turn tail and run out of the library and into the dining room.

"Pa, you should hear the way Aaron talks to me! He told me to get out of the house, that I'm not welcome here."

"Lelia," Father replied indifferently, "If Aaron doesn't want you here then maybe you better leave."

Now Lelia was really hurt. She had no ride, she came all the way from Dayton to visit Father and Willie; Aaron threw her out of the house which was just as much hers as anybody's and Pa sided with Aaron! She was sobbing as she walked carrying her little overnight bag down the lane and into town. All the harsh words, the way she was mistreated, just the total injustice of it all played over and over in her head as she walked. The canal boat back to Dayton wouldn't leave again until tomorrow. Lelia had planned to spend the night at Evergreen so now she had to figure out where she could stay until morning. Walking along the streets in the growing darkness Lelia wondered if her sister Ella was back in town, maybe she could stay the night with her. Walking along the canal she turned onto Dayton Street and peered through the house windows. She wondered about the families that lived there. Were they happy? Did they love each other? Or were they just as miserable as she was? Lelia created a story in her mind about each family as she stole glances into their parlors and dining rooms. She didn't find anger and hatred in those windows, she found laughing and caring and music; or at least in her imagination she did.

Once on Dayton Street it was a short walk to Ella's house. Lelia saw a carriage tied to the hitching post and breathed a sigh of relief. She knocked at the door and one of the servants answered.

"Yes ma'am?" the woman asked.

"Is Mrs. Byron home? I'm her sister Lelia and ..."

"Who is it Anna?" Lelia could hear her sister's voice from down the hall.

"Why Lelia, I wasn't expecting you," Ella said sprinting down the hall from the kitchen toward the door. "Come in for a minute."

"Ella, can I stay the night here?" Lelia pleaded.

"I can't keep you Lelia, unless you sleep on the floor. I have company tonight; I have no place to put you."

"I wanted to stay at Pa's tonight but Aaron threw me out. I can't get a boat back to Dayton until morning Ellie; I have nowhere else to go."

"I don't know why the two of you can't get along. I suppose you can sleep on the floor in one of the girls' rooms Lelia, but Samuel has important guests tonight, so you need to stay out of the way. Why don't you take your things up to Mary's room and clean yourself up, you're a dirty dusty mess."

"Thanks Ellie, I'll be out early in the morning, I promise." Now Lelia really felt unwanted and rejected; it's a good thing she had some of her "nerve elixir" along. She brought it with her thinking she may need it after talking to Aaron, their encounters were never pleasant; but she wasn't expecting to be snubbed by her entire family. Willie wasn't so bad. Lelia really missed Mother; she wouldn't be treated this way if Mother was still around.

Chapter 36

Hamilton, Ohio – 1893

With the first frost, a sign that winter was just around the corner, Aaron began spending much more of his day at the reservoirs and ice houses and less time at the homestead. Winter, naturally, was their busiest season; he relied on a long cold winter to replenish his inventory. Harvesting began after an extended freeze with the removal of snow and soft ice from the surface of the reservoirs. Horse-drawn plows and men with saws cut the ice in two by four foot blocks, making it possible to guide the cakes with long pikes through the water to the loading areas. Laborers would then haul the blocks to the ice houses where they were stored about twelve feet underground and insulated with straw and sawdust. In years of prolonged freeze ice was cut not only from the Cavanaugh's privately owned reservoirs but also from the Great Miami River, the Miami-Erie Canal and the network of waterways that formed the Hydraulic.

Aaron looked forward to the warm months of summer when he made a good profit distributing ice to local breweries, meat-packers and dairies that depended heavily on his product. Distribution was less time-consuming and labor intensive than the cutting season, giving Aaron more time to spend with Father and Willie at the family farm and Evergreen. In a good year money was abundant and Father and Aaron would discuss how to best invest their profits.

Now that winter was approaching Aaron would move Father and Willie to his house in town where he was better able to care for them. He didn't have time to worry about Pa making the ride from the country into the city in bad weather. Aaron's place was considerable in size, large enough to comfortably accommodate his father, brother, Augie and Mrs. Montgomery in addition to his own small house staff.

Father liked Aaron's house well-enough but it wasn't home to him. He didn't look forward to winters, they made him feel displaced. It was, after all, Aaron's house and Father respected that. He felt like he couldn't be himself or do the things he wouldn't think twice about at Evergreen, like drinking and napping on the couch whenever he felt like it. He wasn't comfortable drinking in Aaron's house, not that Aaron abstained in the least himself. They shared the occasional glass of good port after dinner, but that was the extent of his drinking at

Aaron's. His escape was to meet the boys at the saloon to argue over politics or business or the price of feed. Sometimes they would move the conversation over to the Malt House where they were certain to engage a few *new* points of view.

In the winter months Augie had to drive his charge everywhere, and Father absolutely hated it. He wasn't a child; Augie's constant surveillance aggravated the life out of the old man, made him feel as though he had no control over his own comings and goings; had to answer to Augie who was just a child himself in Father's eyes.

The day came when Father saw an opportunity to escape Augie and eagerly chanced it.

Feathery flakes of snow drifted lazily down, swirling through the air before settling on two or three inches of already packed white down. Twilight slowly ushered out the wintry afternoon as Father bundled up and headed out to the carriage house to hitch his horse to the buggy. He had every intention of declaring his independence; he was taking himself to his saloon where he knew he would find good company, then who knows where. Augie, spotting him, quickly grabbed his coat from the hall tree on the way out the door and ran down the walk after him.

"Mr. Cavanaugh, sir! Wait! Mr. Cavanaugh, wait for me!" Augie cried, chasing the old man to the carriage house.

"Augie, quit followin' me! I told you, I don't need no damn driver! When I wear a standing collar and wear my hair parted in the middle and become a dude, *then I'll have a driver*!" The cantankerous Mr. Cavanaugh lashed out at Augie with the whip reserved for his horse then raced out into the street, the carriage barely missing the shocked young guardian. "You nitwit," the old man said under his breath, snapping the whip.

"Lordy, I'm in trouble now," mumbled Augie as he walked swiftly back to the house. He dressed warmly then walked the few blocks to town to track down the old man. He checked the regular haunts within walking distance. He finally found him in the Malt House and Brewery. Augie was freezing from traipsing down every street in town through several inches of snow. When he approached Mr. Cavanaugh in the noisy bar the old gent offered him a brew.

"Gave you the slip there, didn't I boy?" He was feeling in a pretty good mood by the time Augie found him. "I just needed to warm these tired old bones. We're heading over to my saloon now, come with us Augie."

"No need to worry about that Sir, I'll be right

behind you," it was all he could do to hide his irritation. A couple of beers weren't going to make up for the thrashing he took from the old man's buggy whip.

"Drinks all around! Drinks on the house!" Father bellowed at the top of his voice as he and a small crowd from the Malt House stumbled noisily into his own establishment a few doors down.

One beer for warmth before facing a light snowstorm and Augie walked outside to locate the horse and carriage. He would bundle up and wait for Mr. Cavanaugh there until it was time to take him home. Augie waited and waited but there was no sign of the old gent. He started to worry when the dinner hour came and went; they would both catch trouble for sure. Augie thought he should be easy to find, searching first the saloon then back to the Malt House; Augie couldn't spot him anywhere. Turning the corner at the court house, there he was; lying face down in the snow. There was no telling how long he had been lying there, but Augie thought certainly not for long. One would think the cold snow in his face and his cold wet clothes would have sobered him up pretty quick. Augie helped the old man up and practically carried him back to the buggy. He was hard to handle, like carrying a hundred and fifty pounds of soft taffy. He poured the shriveled old guy in the carriage and bundled him up with the warm dry blankets Augie had used to warm himself. Augie sprinted around the front of the horse and before he could get to his seat saw the darndest site he'd ever seen. The old man, in slow motion, fell forward hitting his head on the dash rail of the carriage. He hit with such force that a comb fell from his front pocket and flew into the street all the way under the horse's front hooves. Augie ran to get him and leaped into the carriage to catch him before the old coot went the way of the comb. Once Augie set him right he saw a large red mark and a knot the size of a goose egg. He'd probably lose his job over this one. Augie just hoped he could get back on at an ice house, since the Cavanaugh's owned every one in the area.

"What's your job?!" Aaron yelled at Augie. "What the hell were you doing boy? What is your job?!" He emphasized each word like Augie was some kind of imbecile that couldn't understand English.

"I'm his driver, sir." Augie replied meekly, head down.

"Not just a driver! It's your job to take care of him; do you think this is taking care of him? Did you take care of him tonight?" Aaron was furious. While he was railing at the trembling young Augie, Mary and Stuart tried to get the drenched old guy up to his room and into some dry clothes. Walking up the steps between them, Father's knees crumpled; barely conscious, he was unable to help himself at all.

"I'm sorry, sir. This job is more difficult than you realize, much harder than cutting ice. He sneaks out, he's abusive – he beat me with his buggy whip tonight when I tried to stop him. I'm not making excuses, I thought I could handle it but I guess I can't"

"We'll talk about it in the morning," Aaron said and took the stairs two at a time, up to his father's room to try and make things right. Stuart had already dressed Father in dry bedclothes by the time Aaron reached the bedroom. Mary was down in the kitchen making a hot supper for the poor shivering old gentleman, having taken the back stairs to give young Augie some privacy with Aaron. Aaron dressed his father's head-wound with some salve and a gauze bandage. "I'll stay with him Stuart. He feels like he's running a fever." Aaron sat at his father's side for most of the night.

The basement floor of the Dayton Street house was a spacious area with seven rooms and a large fireplace. It was reserved as servants' quarters because it was sufficiently apart from the main house. A private entrance led to the carriage house in the back. Mrs. Montgomery kept a small room at the back of the main house near the kitchen; she was the only staff to occupy the main house.

Stuart carefully descended the steep stairs to their apartments below, anxious to find Augie. Concerned about the lad he wanted to see how he was doing and get his story. He found Augie warming himself by the modest fire, only a small blaze being required since the lower level stayed naturally warm in winter and cool in summer.

"Yer soakin' wet yerself, boy," Stuart said to the young man.

"It's not like I don't try my best, you know. I tried to stop him. I waited all night in the cold for him. I practically carried him from the post office to the carriage in heavy snow. I don't think he knows how hard it is to manage the old man," Augie said, "I'm not just making excuses."

"He knows son, he knows." Stuart poured him a bowl of hot stew; the old man wasn't the only one to miss his dinner.

"Do you think he'll let me go?"

"I honestly don't know. Aaron's kind of funny about his father, they're real close; Aaron takes care of him like no one else can, and his father has a great affection for Aaron. Bein' the strong men they are sometimes they come off as threatening, but they're good men. I know

Aaron understands your trials, he's just madder-than-a-wet-hen right now and what I would do is just keep my distance 'til he calms down. See what he says then."

Aaron didn't bother talking to Augie in the morning. He spent the night in his father's room because the shriveled old man was running a high fever and shivering with chills. He remembered his dear mother who died during the last epidemic and thought his father showed the same symptoms of influenza. Aaron was worried beyond words; his sole focus was sending for the doctor. During the interminable wait Aaron asked Mary to make Pa a garlic and camphor poultice for his chest, to ease his breathing. No, Aaron didn't give Augie a single thought; he walked right by him without a word and out the door. He'd find that damned doctor himself, he couldn't wait any longer.

Father was sick in bed for several weeks. By the end of the ice harvest in early February he was just getting around the house without too much trouble. Recuperation was a forced "drying out" for Father, who was unable to slip out for a drink or two. Nothing was ever said to Augie again about the incident but the young man, trying to show his worth, spent his days nursing Mr. Cavanaugh back to health.

Father grew stronger with every day that passed, showing signs of getting back to his ornery old self; itching to get out and about now that the weather was warming. Before Aaron left the house for work in the mornings he methodically inspected each room, verifying that all doors and windows were locked. He insisted they stay locked while he was away - for Pa's safety. Aaron had the only key, but the servants could leave by their private entrance on the lower level. Will was back at Evergreen minding the stock and getting ready for spring planting, so it was just the servants and Father staying in the house.

"The old man's getting antsy," said Mary, "it's gonna be dreadfully hard to keep him indoors."

"Maybe you can help me keep an eye on him, Mary. He's a slippery old devil. I'd have to be as sneaky as he is to know what he's up to," said Augie.

"No problem, dear, we'll *all* help keep an eye on him."

The entire staff remained diligent looking out for Father; but one night the wily old gent managed to sneak out the basement window without being seen. Panic set in, settling over the entire house staff like an oppressive storm-cloud; the dinner hour had come and gone, but still no sign of him. Augie looked in all the regular places but he was nowhere to be found.

Aaron was running late at the auction in Sandusky, so he wasn't home when Mr. Pearson rang the front bell.

"Good evening folks. I found old Bill here out by the Hydraulic; he fell and nearly tumbled in and drowned himself. This isn't the first time I've had to pick him up off the ground, you know. Anyway, I brought him home. I'm not sure where his horse is, must have run off; if I see him I'll bring him to you." Mr. Pearson helped his disoriented charge into the house where Stuart and Augie immediately took over. Mrs. Montgomery thanked him profusely and tipped him with some change from the kitchen jar for his troubles. The three of them cleaned Mr. Cavanaugh, fed him and took him to bed. Of course they would have to tell Aaron what happened, but at least he would be spared seeing his father's condition or hearing the gruesome details. It was that night that Mrs. Montgomery took to hiding Father's boots.

Chapter 37

Hamilton, Ohio – 1894

A luxuriant green lawn, sweet smells from the wild honeysuckle and a warm breeze greeted Bill Cavanaugh as he stepped out on the porch after struggling with the heavy entry door of his son's Dayton Street house. It was a beautiful spring morning and old Bill was planning to hitch his horse to the small buggy for a ride around town. He walked unsteadily out to the carriage house, using his cane for support. His hip was giving him fits since his fall by the hydraulic and the stiffness caused him to limp slightly. Spring meant that Bill would be going back to the farm soon, and that put him in a *very* good mood. He appreciated Aaron's hospitality, didn't mind *too* much staying at Aaron's house in the city; but he longed for the comfort and freedom he enjoyed every single day at Evergreen.

Augie was helping out at the icehouse for a few days and this was the old man's chance to get out on his own. His itinerary rarely changed; he would go by the Post Office for his mail and maybe send some money to Fannie

– no, wait; there was something about Fannie – he wouldn't send money. After checking in with the bank to keep tabs on his accounts he would go by his lawyer's office to make sure those scalawags were following up on his collections. It seemed half the county owed old Bill money. After lunch at Keppler's Restaurant he would spend the afternoon with the boys at the brewery. He had his day planned to a "T", just like yesterday, just like everyday. There was nothing wrong with him, not at all. He couldn't understand why everyone fussed over him all the time; he was perfectly capable of taking care of himself.

His errands behind him, Bill pushed wearily through the heavy brewery doors greeting familiar faces as he walked along the paneled corridor. Usually after downing a delicious meal at his favorite restaurant, he was ready for a pint (or two) of iced unfiltered ale to slake his thirst and take the edge off.

"Hey Duff, how'd you get past the missus to come down here?" Bill teased.

"She don't run my life, I'm my own man. I go where I want to go whenever I want, and I want to spend my afternoons here." Duffy replied, flustered by the old man's teasing.

"Don't pay him no mind, Bill, his wife thinks he's going to a job every day when he comes here," Jackson chided.

"You gotta be kiddin' me!" Bill coughed and laughed from his belly. "How do you get away with that? What does she say when you don't come home with yer pay?"

"She thinks I'm working for you, you chintzy bastard! I tell her you didn't make the payroll again!" Duffy chortled.

"Give my friends here more of what they're drinking," Bill shouted to the bartender, then snaking through the room he shared stories and drinks with nearly everyone in the bar, checking back occasionally to make sure Duffy and Jackson had full glasses.

As the crowd started to thin around the dinner hour, Bill left his friends and headed out to his buggy with a snoot-full. Staggering down the street alongside the courthouse looking for his good-for-nothing nag, Bill was convinced that stupid horse of his had a mind of its own and moved the carriage just to confuse him. He fell a couple times, once on the lawn, once in the road. The townspeople were familiar with the sight of the old man wandering drunk through the streets. Someone helped him to his feet and sent him on his way. Bill brushed the dust off and walked over to the side of the road to relieve himself. While slouched there in the ecstasy of the

moment, grateful he at least didn't piss his pants, Bill
spotted his buggy.

"Damn horse," he swore under his breath. By some
miracle a blind-drunk Bill Cavanaugh unhitched the horse
and managed to crawl into the buggy before passing out.
The horse walked into the road with Bill wobbling back
and forth in the seat, trying to stay upright as he floated in
and out of consciousness. No one paid attention as the
horse ambled down High Street to Fifth and turned at the
canal, his passenger drooping and the reins dragging in the
dirt. It was a sight everyone had seen before, and not one
was willing to face the wrath of Bill Cavanaugh for trying
to help.

That particular Friday Aaron was working later than
usual at the Big Reservoir when word came that Father was
found dead near the canal, only a couple blocks from
Aaron's house. One of the Evergreen farmhands rode at
breakneck speed to find Aaron with the news and sent him
to the hospital immediately. Willie was already on his way
and Aaron was to meet him as soon as he could get there.

Aaron was too late to see his father alive. It would
be years before he quit blaming himself for not taking
better care of Pa. He ran into the lobby of the hospital with
shirt-sleeves rolled up and axle grease on his hands and

upper arms; he had been fixing one of the ice-wagons when the farmhand rode up and didn't take the time to wash.

"Where is he Willie?" Aaron asked breathlessly. Aaron was in the midst of a full-blown panic attack. His breath wouldn't come to him, partially because of rushing to the hospital, but mostly because he was so anxious about Pa that his chest was constricting. Fastidious Aaron didn't even care that he wasn't presentable, his disheveled look the least of his worries; he needed to see Pa. Aaron stood face to face with his brother trying to slow his pulse rate, taking deep breaths to counter the hyper-ventilating. Aaron had learned over the years how to handle these attacks and he worked hard at gaining control. "Where have they taken him?"

Willie tearfully replied, "The medical examiner has him Aaron, he's dead. He was dead already when they picked him up."

Aaron was overcome with grief at the loss of his father. His partner, his trusted friend since he was a small boy was gone. He was his father's shadow from the time Aaron was four-years old. In later years, before Pa ruined his health with drink after Fannie's death, wasn't it Pa that became Aaron's shadow? His constant companion? Aaron wondered what was left to lose. Stuart was already on his way to the farm to fetch the wagon. How many times will

Aaron take the people he loved home to Evergreen in the back of that wagon?

In the dark blanket of a moonless midnight Aaron and Willie followed the open wagon back to Evergreen. As happens so often in spring the night air chilled to freezing. The brothers, eyes ahead and quiet in their thoughts, shivered in the clear cool of the night; it would be the chill of the night to blame if ever they were asked to explain their tremors. The lonely duo took their father home for the final time.

Mrs. Montgomery was waiting for the men with a pot of hot tea mellowed with a bit of Irish whiskey. The boys gently carried their father to the big parlor where he would rest until arrangements were made to place him beside Mother. The big parlor, Father's favorite room; a big room for a giant of a man, he would prefer resting once more in the parlor before being laid to rest at the foot of the family marker in Greenwood, sleeping for eternity with Mother, Mary and Fannie.

Thoughtful Mrs. Montgomery had already sent a wire to Ella in Washington and Lelia in Dayton about the passing of their father. It was Ellie who arrived first, taking the earliest train out of Washington leaving Samuel and the children behind, arriving Evergreen late morning. But, where was Lelia? Mrs. Montgomery expected she would be the first to get there, coming only from Dayton. If she didn't show by nightfall she'd send one of the hands to bring her home. It was Mrs. Montgomery who wrote the obituary for the paper, faithful Mary Montgomery who in her own grief took care of the family first.

Death of W.H.H. Cavanaugh

William H. H. Cavanaugh, an old, prominent and highly respected resident of this county was found dead early last evening when his horse and buggy were discovered wandering along the tracks by the canal in a careless manner; the lines dropped allowing the horse to take its own course. Slumped over the seat was Mr. William Cavanaugh Sr., well-known and successful landowner, farmer and businessman. The hospital on notification from a passerby who said he was in need of attention, sent an ambulance to retrieve him but he was beyond saving by the time he reached the hospital.

The cause of death is undetermined but Mr. Cavanaugh had been ill for many months. It is believed that he died of general debility incident to his advanced years.

Mr. Cavanaugh's ancestors came from Ireland and moved to this county many years ago becoming active in government and the pursuit of statehood. Burial services will be privately held at his beautiful country estate with a Christian burial immediately following at Greenwood Cemetery.

Chapter 38

Dayton, Ohio – 1894

The wire arrived at Samuel Street by daybreak on Saturday finding only Jarvis at home to receive it. He left Lelia at Sam Hing's Chinese laundry the night before; too delirious on opium to do more than flop on one of the dirty flea-infested mattresses in the back room set out for overnight patrons.

Hing's laundry, the antithesis of the Shanghai dens adorned with brocade draperies and velvet lounges, was a dive with dirty shades at the windows and a few mats on the floor. Cheap lamps and bamboo pipes decorated the converted wash room, but opium dreams transported the smokers to a place beyond the here and now.

It was Jarvis who introduced Lelia to opium. For him it helped to create more brilliant and exciting art, but then he knew what he was doing and could control it. Lelia, on the other hand, that girl was going to be addicted if she didn't learn to limit her visits to the Chinaman. Already she was a slow-moving wraith who looked like the living dead. She didn't eat right and was nothing more than skin and bones.

He cautiously walked through the secret back door at the laundry and searched the gloomy flophouse for Lelia. She was sprawled across a mattress in the back corner, her limp form half on the floor and her twisted skirt hiked up around her waist. Sam was tending the room, occasionally helping to hold a tilted pipe at just the right angle above the lamp. Jarvis made his way to Lelia's flop, careful not to step on the drug-induced dreamers in various stages of ecstasy. He was in a rush to get her home, sober and cleaned up before taking her to Evergreen, although maybe just a bit of that euphoria could help after he breaks the news about her father. He gathered Lelia in his arms and tried to bring her around.

"It's Jarvis, Baby; you got a wire early morning saying your father died last night." He decided the best approach was to just come right out with it. Lelia stirred but didn't grasp a word he was saying. Jarvis whispered, "I'll take care of you, don't you worry. I'll take you home, clean you up. I'll take good care of you. You need to snap out of this and take the boat to Hamilton. They're expecting you."

Jarvis sent word to Aaron that he would bring Lelia home first thing in the morning. She had been sick, but she would definitely be there in the morning.

Aaron couldn't have cared less whether Lelia showed for the funeral or not. He was glad Ellie was there, but even if she wasn't he wouldn't really have minded. Aaron had his personal grief to deal with and had no desire to take care of the girls. He knew they would make this all about them and he wasn't in the right frame of mind to listen to their prattle.

Sunday afternoon Reverend Daily performed a dignified service in the formal parlor for Father. Only the family, servants and farmhands attended but still the parlor was full. Father's friends and long-time business associates were invited to the graveside service; the parlor reserved for those closest to him.

Unsure if the fickle spring weather would cooperate, Aaron rented a black lacquered funeral carriage pulled by a team of well-mannered perfectly groomed black Clydesdales. The carriage would wind through town before taking Father to his final resting place alongside Mother. Aaron stood close to his father staring through the glass at the flower-covered casket, waiting for family and friends as they jostled for a place in line. His father deserved a dignified sendoff, and Aaron made sure it would be nothing less. Noticing that now everyone was waiting on him he reluctantly left his father's side, stepped to the back of the hearse and mounted his best horse. He and Willie would follow the hearse on horseback, Ellie and Lelia in a carriage driven by Stuart behind them and an extensive line of buggies, carts and buckboards yet behind the girls.

The long death march reverently wound its way from Evergreen to the cemetery where the family and household staff were joined by as many as a hundred local citizen's who shared a story or a brew with the old man over the years. The mourners enjoyed a warm breeze as the sun darted about the puffy white clouds, leaving them one minute in shadow and the next in light. Reverend Daily read the twenty-third psalm and related it to the many green pastures that had been so much a part of the deceased's life on the farm. The pastor's eulogy became a distant drone in Aaron's ears, words on the edge of hearing that he couldn't quite understand. His mind a blank, he focused on the warmth of the sun's rays when they broke through the clouds. Lelia, standing behind the Cavanaugh boys with her sister Ellie, also was not paying attention to the service. Her thoughts were on china, silver and crystal; those items that belonged to Mother that should be hers now, and how she could get them away from her controlling brother who wouldn't bother to give her the time of day.

When the casket was slowly lowered into the gaping hole, Aaron and Willie, hats in hands, were the first to walk up and release a handful of dirt ceremoniously into the open grave. Just at that moment the sun peeked through an opening in the clouds, and a lone shaft of light shone on Aaron's uncovered head. "It must be an omen," he thought, "certainly a sign of better times to come." An omen? Possibly... but misread. None of them would see good times ever again.

Lelia spent the night at Ella's house, no longer feeling welcome at Evergreen. In fact, Lelia spent the next three week's with Ella talking about the brothers and how they ended up with just about the entire family fortune. It didn't seem fair to the girls that Aaron should have the bulk of the cash, investments and real estate.

"Everything should be split equally, don't you think Ellie?" It didn't require an ounce of effort on Lelia's part to convince Ellie that Aaron was the golden boy here. Ellie's husband Samuel was partner in a highly respected law firm *and* the old man's lawyer; he'd know what to do.

"I'll wire Samuel Lee to make certain, but I think you're right about this. We need an impartial administrator to evenly divide Pa's estate." Ellie said.

Pa died a millionaire; everyone was entitled to a fair share. Lelia to more than her measly allowance and plain little house; and as for Ellie, well, it took a lot of money to keep house and entertain for her husband the congressman.

Before returning to Dayton from the funeral Lelia met with Ellie's stepson Edgar. As the sole heir to Mary Cavanaugh, the eldest sister and Samuel Lee's first wife who died in childbirth, it was agreed that he also should be granted a portion of Pa's estate. Edgar, a clerk in his father Samuel's law office, filed a petition in the courts requesting adjudication of Bill Cavanaugh's considerable assets. They gave no thought to how that decision could come back to haunt them, the resulting lawsuits causing an irreparable chasm splitting the family. The decade-long litigation that followed would be the ruination of one of the wealthiest and renowned families in the state of Ohio.

Chapter 39

Hamilton, Ohio – 2005

During the winter months, in particular around the holidays, I became more involved with housekeeping chores and less with research. Christmas is a festive time in the historic district and involves an abundance of Victorian decorations, Christmas Walks for those seeking traditional celebrations, and more parties than one could possibly attend. A peace settled over our house through the holidays, at least as far as Aaron was concerned. If the Cavanaugh's were around I was just too busy to notice. The cold days of January, on the other hand, were a different story.

I woke early and in an attempt to let Aidan sleep for another hour, carried my cosmetics to the bathroom to get ready for work. Fresh from a shower I stood before the mirror and skillfully worked the blow-dryer and brush through my hair. The large mirror covered the entire wall allowing a clear view of the bathroom and even the semi-dark hallway beyond. Several minutes passed as I routinely stepped through my ritual of brushing teeth, styling hair, applying makeup. In the mirror I noticed a shadow move past the door. Thinking I must have wakened Aidan I called out to him.

"Is that you Honey? Sorry I woke you, I was trying to let you sleep awhile."

There was no answer, so I stepped into the hall and looked towards the kitchen where I thought he must be starting coffee. Noticing all the lights were off at that end of the hallway I turned to my right to check for a light beneath the bedroom door. All was dark.

"That's odd, I know I saw him." My skin started to pucker into gooseflesh and the tightening in my stomach that had been missing for months returned.

I went back to applying my makeup in the mirror, this time with an eye on the shadows beyond the bathroom. A man, yes definitely a man, walked past the door going the opposite direction towards the bedroom, or possibly the stairs to the parlor. I couldn't make out features since only the soft glow from the bathroom illuminated the corridor.

"Aidan?"

No answer, I dropped my makeup brush and moved swiftly to the hall. He was gone.

I told myself it was my imagination and went back to the task of grooming and dressing for the busy day ahead of me. Aidan had the day off work. My plan was to quietly sneak out so he could enjoy a few more hours of sleep, or at least until the sun came through the windows to wake him.

Grabbing my coat and purse I quietly opened the door to the landing and stepped to the other side, gently closing it again.

"Odd", I thought. "Usually the stairs are well lit from the neighbor's floodlights glaring through the windows." It was unusual for the house to be pitch-black like this.

Not wanting to fall down the steps I stood motionless trying to get my bearings. Suddenly I was airborne, it all happened so fast!

CRACK! "Ohhh God, owww, ow..." One minute I was on the landing and the very next sensation was the cracking sound in my head and the pain as I flew into the brick wall opposite me.

"uh, mmm, Aidan!" I thought I was screaming but only a whisper came out. I was in so much pain and too dizzy to stand up.

"Aidan!" This time a little louder but he still couldn't hear me through the hall and bedroom doors. I tried to crawl up the three steps to the second story hall but I wasn't able to lift myself, falling back to the floor when I tried to raise my head. Ready to give up I heard the door open.

"What the hell's going on? What's the racket?" Aidan asked before seeing me sprawled on the floor. "What happened? Are you alright?"

"I don't know," I whispered, still not able to get a good breath. "I went from standing to flying"

"That's ridiculous; you must have slipped off the step."

I knew I hadn't but I didn't care what he thought, I was in pain and couldn't move. "I need help, just help me up. Please."

He carried me up the short flight of stairs and lay me down on the carpet where I rested until I could stand. I was dizzy, the way you feel when you have a bad ear infection and lose your equilibrium; the extreme nausea made me feel I was about to vomit, but the sensation passed.

"I heard my head crack. Do you think I should go to the doctor?"

"Don't be silly. If you cracked your skull you wouldn't be sitting here talking to me. It'll wear off. You need to be more careful going down these steps. Turn the hall light on before you go down. There's so much light coming from the office next door I don't know how you couldn't see to begin with. You need to pay attention to what you're doing and quit walking around in a fog."

It wasn't worth going into it with him. I *was* paying attention, trying to see the stairs in the black stairwell. I was standing nowhere near the steps. I didn't have the energy to explain and he wouldn't believe me anyway.

"I'm going on to work then," I said, starting carefully down the stairs. "I'll see you tonight."

"Be careful, you want me to help you down?"

"No, Aiden, I'm fine. I'll see you at dinner." Too little too late.

Well, I wasn't fine. That mysterious flight into a brick wall left me with a concussion and I spent the night vomiting profusely, only to face the morning with a migraine. Work was out of the question the following day; fortunately it was a Friday and I had the weekend to recuperate. It took a couple of weeks for the dizzy spells to leave, and a couple months to tell Aidan that I thought I was pushed by the figure in the hallway that morning.

The curious incident on the stairs motivated me to resurrect my investigation of the Cavanaugh's after a four-month hiatus. I pulled out all the research papers accumulated over the years and began reading once again about the "Trial of the Century" and the antics of this dysfunctional family.

I poured through news articles that smacked of

sensationalism, analyzed boring details about the estate and read in disbelief the unrighteous testimonies of indignant relatives, all greedily fighting over everything from mansions to teaspoons.

My files had grown to bursting; it took several months to reconcile all the facts of the year-long trial and ten-year settlement. As incredible as it seemed to me, Aaron and Willie ended up with nothing. How could that happen? There must be more to this, something I missed. I went to the Department of County Records and with the help of a clerk found the trial transcripts. Making as many copies as I could, I stuffed my satchel with the disposition and real estate records before walking home to verify what earlier research had suggested.

I analyzed the minutia from the trial transcripts, making a database that tracked clocks and pictures mixed in with large parcels of real estate and promissory notes. It was true; Lelia, Ella and Edgar got everything. Aaron even lost his house, our house.

Well, that explains why Aaron seemed to drop from the city directory, I thought. But what happened to him after the trial?

I returned to the Internet research, expanding it to include areas outside of the county. Certainly there must be an obituary, some census to tell me where he went after losing everything. I left inquiries on every genealogy forum I could find. I expanded my query to include the entire state. Often, if you search on your subject's relatives you will find mention of the person you are looking for, sending you in a completely new direction - so I searched on Edgar hoping I would find a reference to the trial where he prosecuted his Uncle Aaron.

What happened to the money; the land; the Cavanaugh's?

Chapter 40

Hamilton, Ohio – 1895

Aaron confidently strode through the heavy wooden doors of the County Courthouse; it was packed, every seat filled with curious spectators and even the walls were lined with gawkers jockeying for position.

The two sisters were sitting in the front row, directly behind the counsel for the plaintiffs. At first glance you wouldn't know they were sisters. The older woman appeared to be the younger and wore a soft ivory silk blouse under a dove-gray cashmere walking suit. A broach adorned her collar giving her a very proper look. Her hair was pulled loosely up, framing her face in soft tendrils.

The younger sister, on the other hand, had a very angular aspect to her bony frame. Her housedress was clean and neatly pressed but showed obvious signs of wear. Her sunken eyes were blackened from her lack of sleep and drug abuse, her hair matted but neatly tied at the nape of her neck. The stress of the trial made the lines on her forehead all the more pronounced.

Edgar had not yet arrived and the table nearest the jury was already occupied by Samuel Lee and several other lawyers and clerks from his law office. The adjacent defendant's table looked empty by comparison with only Aaron, Willie and a single attorney.

"All rise and give your attention; the honorable Judge Moynihan of the Butler County Court of Common Pleas presiding."

The hushed murmuring of the crowded courtroom grew suddenly noisy as spectators, jurors and participants rose to their feet following protocol. Willie took the opportunity to glance over at his sisters. How did it come to this, the family airing their dirty laundry in this public forum for the entire county to see? His sisters did not acknowledge his gaze.

"This Court is now in session. Please be seated"

Another long day in a string of long days in court began. Witness after witness was called attesting to the mental instability of Bill Cavanaugh, telling stories of a drunken, broken old man who asked the same questions day after day, receiving the same repetitive answers each time he asked; a man who lost his buggy so many times that the family hired Augie Plinkton to follow the old man and keep him safe; a once vibrant congressman, rancher and businessman who could no longer care for himself.

Lelia squirmed in her seat, today was her day to take the stand. Still, after all these years, she was intimidated by her brother and dreaded facing him from the stand. She would be too nervous to speak her mind, she just knew it. The familiar feeling of nausea that settled in her stomach whenever she had to face Aaron caused her breath to catch.

"And when I greeted him on the street he took his cane to me! Whacking me on the head in broad daylight right there in front of the whole town! Everyone in town is my witness," Mr. Staley testified. "And when I questioned him about *why* he was striking me, it was for a debt that I paid off years before! He was crazy as a bedbug if you ask me, downright crazy. He ain't been right since that daughter of his died."

Dan Staley stepped down and Lelia noticed that Samuel Lee gave her a nod. Was she ready?

"Hand on the Bible Miss Cavanaugh," the bailiff said.

"Mrs. Foster," Lelia corrected. Aaron rolled his eyes and said something under his breath to his counsel.

"Mrs. Foster, do you swear to tell the whole truth and only the truth so help you God?" the bailiff asked.

"I most certainly do."

A vise gripped Lelia's heart and her vocal chords

317

allowed only a whisper to escape. Lelia tried to mentally control her involuntary reaction to her brother. During the hours of testimony the judge had to continually remind her to speak up; what seemed like a shout in her head could barely be heard past the court recorder.

Avoiding Aaron's glare, Lelia spouted a litany of transgressions Aaron committed against her, and testified about all the times that Aaron manipulated her father and kept them apart; she explained how she felt Aaron weaseled his way into the family fortune not allowing Father to give anything to the girls, keeping everything for himself and Willie.

Later that afternoon Aaron took his lawyer aside after the day's proceedings.

"Lelia perjured herself. She's not married, never has been. She only says that because of her bastard daughter, a daughter she gave up for adoption because she's too selfish to care for anyone but herself."

"Aaron," his lawyer cautioned, "if I bring that up in court – and by the way, the judge won't see that as relevant to the case anyway – they're going to drag your illegitimate children into this. We don't want that."

"I'd like to see them prove it…"

"Let's take the high road here, our goal should be to prove that your father wanted you to take over the business, that when he gave you and Willie money and property he was of sound mind; that he felt you earned and deserved it."

"I just can't stand the sight of that bitch," Aaron growled.

"Let it go. Your anger has no place in the courtroom." Then Aaron and his lawyer walked off in different directions. Willie and Aaron stopped at Keppler's for an early dinner followed by a few drinks at a bar on Court Street before returning home.

Pushing through the heavy oak doors with glass clouded from years of grime and into the smoky environs of the local tavern, Aaron spotted a larger-than-life character holding his own court in the back corner. He sent Willie to the bar to wait for him then pushed his way through the crowd to the table of Bob Toucka, owner of this establishment and many more along Fifth Street in Newport, Kentucky. The men surrounding him quickly dispersed allowing the two to conduct a little private business.

Bob Toucka was a dangerous gangster, accused of many murders but convicted of none. Sitting with him was his common-law-wife Lucia, noticeable not only because of her flashy dress but more obviously by the absence of any other women in the bar.

"Go powder your nose Lucia; give me about fifteen minutes with this guy." Then turning to Aaron as she walked away, "I got what you asked for friend." The pot-bellied mobster passed a flannel bag, containing something a bit larger than his pudgy hand, to Aaron who in turn palmed a wad of bills into Bob Toucka's other hand.

"You know I'm here for you Aaron. Your gramps and mine were close friends when they worked together in the sheriff's office. I'll help you any way I can. Just let me know what you need."

"I know Bob, and I appreciate it. I wouldn't bother you if it wasn't important."

"One hand washes the other, right pal? Now I'll be expecting that delivery early in the morning – I got a fresh batch of lager coming in tomorrow and I need that ice pronto!" Bob took a deep draw on his stubby stogie and exhaled a choking cloud of smoke. Fastidious Aaron, who was weary from his day in court, did his best not to show his disdain for the nasty habit.

Reassuring Mr. Toucka that his delivery would arrive as soon as the bar opened in the morning, Aaron hid the package under his coat, scooped up Willie at the end of the bar forcing him to gulp down the remainder of his pint, and the brothers walked without a word to the house. It would be another grueling day in court tomorrow for sure, and Aaron had some things to take care of before bed.

Lelia, Ellie and Samuel Lee were spending the days during the trial at Evergreen. After a long day in the courtroom and several hours in the law office preparing for the next day, Samuel Lee, tired and hungry, climbed wearily into his buggy and headed for the family homestead. He was within a mile of home when there was a buzz in his left ear. The horse reared up on his back legs and the entire rig was in danger of tipping over.

"What in Hell?" Samuel barked; then another loud report as a second bullet whizzed by his carriage. The horse took off running and it was all Samuel could do to hold on until the horse slowed to a trot.

It was late when Aaron walked in the front door. He went straight to the kitchen and placed his Remington single action revolver on the table. Taking a kit of alcohol, oil and a cleaning chamois from the cabinet, he spent the next half hour cleaning his gun. Willie walked in, and not saying a word about the gun asked Aaron if he'd like a cup of Irish coffee. The two sat at the kitchen table in silence, sipping the mellow mixture.

Next morning the bailiff struggled to quiet

spectators crowding the gallery; anticipation of Aaron's testimony was an irresistible draw and the excitement was palpable.

"Permission to approach the bench," Samuel Lee blurted loudly in an attempt to be heard over the din.

"Quiet in the courtroom," the judge warned. "You may approach,"
In the sidebar conversation Samuel Lee lost control, "That lunatic tried to kill me! Arrest him!"

"Calm down counselor, is that something you can prove?"

"It was Aaron – that bastard! - I know it was!"

"I'll issue a warning to scare him, but unless you can prove it Samuel, there really isn't anything I can do about it," the judge whispered.

"Mr. Cavanaugh. It has been brought to the attention of the court that you allegedly threatened the life of the Honorable Samuel L. Byron last evening with gunshot as he was returning home to his farm. What do you have to say about that charge?"

Aaron, careful to maintain his composure, categorically denied the stories of threats saying the accuser was the guilty one, guilty of lies.

Judge Moynihan forgot himself, became excited, and pointing his finger at the defendant said, "Is it not true

322

Mr. Cavanaugh that you have been prowling around the Byron farm at night like a chicken thief?"

"No sir I have not," was the response.

The counsel for the defense objected to the terms applied to his client.

The judge then stood and pointing his finger at Mr. Cavanaugh said, "Why I could tell things here about you that would send you to the pen! You're as low as the dirtiest son-of-a-bitch in all of Hamilton."

The sympathies of those in the court-room were materially turned to the defendant as a result of the heated language used by the magistrate. Aaron remained very cool and gentlemanly.

Counsel for the defense then jumped up and asserted that if he were of a mind to he could also tell things that would bring the blush of shame to Mr. Byron's face.

After a short recess to smooth ruffled feathers, court continued for the remainder of that day and several more with Aaron's testimony. Aaron remained calm, controlled and bitter. All the bad things that had come out in court about his father, Willie and himself were nothing compared to the retaliation in store for those who opposed him. They had yet to see the wrath of Aaron Cavanaugh.

The "Trial of the Century" dragged on for more than a year. The outcome didn't favor the Cavanaugh boys, but then how could they compete against the team of lawyers Samuel Lee brought to prosecute them? They were outnumbered. The irony is that Edgar, a plaintiff with his stepmother and aunt, was appointed executor by the court. No better example of "putting a fox in charge of the henhouse" to use Aaron's words.

The doorknocker loudly struck the plate several times, signaling Stuart to the front of the house where he opened the heavy parlor door to an apologetic county sheriff.

"Is Mr. Cavanaugh here son?" he asked.

"Yes sir, I'll get him for…"

"It's okay Stuart; I'll take care of it from here," Aaron interrupted, descending the stairway silently before stepping into the foyer.

"Aaron, I'm really sorry, but I've been ordered to evict you. You need to get your things moved out right away, today even."

"I can't, I have no where to go – WE have nowhere to go."

"I'm so sorry, I asked for more time so you could find a place to live, but Edgar refused. Said this place is his now, not yours. He wants you out now. We're going to have to put your things on the street if you have nowhere to go with them."

For the first time in memory Aaron was defeated. Stuart discreetly watched from the parlor and couldn't believe the scene playing out in the next room. Aaron appeared more overcome than when Fannie died.

"What does he expect me to do without warning? Ellie and Samuel Lee are living at Evergreen now, where can I go?"

"You can stay with me an' the missus until you find a place," the sheriff offered. But Aaron just walked out, paying no mind to Willie, Stuart or the house staff; just walked out. And by nightfall every possession he owned in the world was stacked at the street, the house was dark and padlocked.

Chapter 41

Hamilton, Ohio – 2005

"Mother-Father God, surround me with the pure white light of God's love. Protect me and all those I may contact, both in this world and the world of spirit. Amen"

Before trying to contact the world of spirit I was taught to always say a prayer of protection, a valuable lesson I learned first from Reverend Ann and then Joan.

Sitting in a relaxed position I took deep breaths from the diaphragm, in and count to ten, slowly exhale; deep breath in, hold it, count to ten then exhale. I did this at least five times to put my mind and body in a relaxed state.

I systematically released the tension in my toes, my feet, my ankles, concentrating on each body part until they felt heavy and totally relaxed. Slowly moving up I calmly told my calves, my knees, my thighs to relax; then my pelvis, diaphragm, chest, arms, and hands, relax, relax until all those body parts are un-flexed and asleep. I focused on my neck willing it to release all tension, then the jaw, ears and eyes; slackened, my lower jaw dropped, my eyes remained closed until my whole body was completely at ease. When breathing deeply after my body is stress-free and at peace, I went to my happy place to meet my spirit guides.

*In my happy place I'm floating in a crystal clear pool in a mountaintop meadow. The sun warms and relaxes me while the cool faint breeze takes away the sting of the sun and causes the loose strands of my hair to lightly tease my face and neck. There is utter silence except for the sound of the gentle breeze rushing by my ears. I can hear the faraway call of a raven to his mate flying high above, and the drone of the bees as they skip from one sweet wildflower to the next. In the distance I hear and recognize the shriek of a red-tailed hawk **kee**-eeeee-arr. The sun is warm on my face and I open my eyes to an azure blue sky reaching to all four corners of the earth. The high winds change the shapes of the infrequent cotton ball clouds, tossing them around the nearly empty blue expanse of sky. I can see a distant pair of hawks circling miles above, riding the currents higher and higher, then swooping down to ride them up to the heavens again. I close my eyes and focus on the warm sun, the soft breeze tossing my hair, caressing my face ever so gently, and the chirp of the mountain bluebird intermixed with the shriek of the playful hawks. I float in the cool artesian pool, absorbed in these* sensations and wait to be joined by my spirit guide. I can hear the call of the hawks getting closer, closer, lower and lower as they ride the winds of time.

My master-teacher guide joins me; a Mandan Indian, his name is Soaring-Hawk.

"Why do you seek me child?"

"I want to meet Aaron."

"He lives with you, you have met him."

Remembering to be specific with my request I rephrase my words, "I want to talk to Aaron."

"I can intercede for you. Take my hand."

I look around as we walk side-by-side through the meadow, but I don't see Aaron anywhere. Gradually a bright light appears before me, growing more luminous as we get closer.

"Aaron asks why you continually bother him," Soaring-Hawk tells me.

"Tell him I'm on his side, I want to tell his side of the story."

"He says he doesn't need you, he's happy the way things are. Leave him alone."

"Ask him, who is the lady on the stairs, is it Fannie?"

"No. He says to quit digging into the Cavanaugh family business. It's not your concern, let him be. He'll *give you what you want - just quit pestering him."*

"But... I don't understand. I have so many questions. I..."

"He has nothing more to say Child. He's fading away. Is there anything more you need from me?"

"No thank you, Master-Teacher."

Slowly I brought myself back, became aware of my surroundings, opened my eyes, took a deep breath and moved in the chair. I was so extremely relaxed it felt like I was waking from a full eight hours of sleep, although according to the clock I'd only been meditating for fifteen minutes.

Slowly my thoughts returned to the present, I swiveled my office chair around and rose. What I wanted were answers but he didn't even give me a chance to ask my questions. I set about to straighten my very messy office; organized my bills throwing away the many credit card offers that covered my desk. Stooping down to gather the books that came from Amazon earlier in the week, the ones I tossed to the floor until I had more time to look at them, I noticed something shiny barely out of reach; it caught the sun in just the right way. Thinking it must be change I bent down to get it with the intention of throwing it in the paper clip tray where I collect all the stray items I don't know what to do with. Getting closer to the sparkly object that I assumed was a nickel or a dime, it turned out to be a ring, a small platinum or white gold ring with six little diamonds; a very nice piece of costume jewelry, even though tarnished and in desperate need of a cleaning.

"Where the heck did that come from," I thought to myself. "I know I've never seen it before. I'll bet Aidan bought it to add to my antique collection." Now I was faced with the dilemma of whether to tell him I found it, or put it somewhere he could find it without realizing I had seen it already. The truth is always the best.

I slowly walked through the house on a hunt for my husband; he could be anywhere. We really must buy a set of walkie-talkies.

"Aidan, did you drop this ring in my office?" I found him on the third floor working on a small leak in the roof. Holding out my hand I showed him what I found on the floor of my office.

"Sorry, Sweetie, what'd you say," he said as he climbed down the ladder.

"Did you drop this in my office? I found it in the dust-bunnies behind my desk."

"Don't tell me you were cleaning that office," he said in mock surprise. He took a closer look. "No – nope, I've never seen it before. I'm sure this house has lots of hidden treasures."

"You're kidding, right? If I've never seen it and you've never seen it, how did it get there?"

"I don't know Babe, but it wasn't me. Maybe it was yours and you just forgot about it."

"You don't just forget about a ring like this," I muttered under my breath. Aidan climbed back up the ladder and I headed down to the second floor.

I couldn't wait to apply some jewelry cleaner so I took the ring to the bathroom and soaked it in the pink compound for a while, checking every few minutes to make sure I didn't damage it. I'd heard you aren't supposed to use this solvent on costume jewelry. After soaking it for almost ten minutes I took the tiny brush to the stones trying to clean the settings as gently as possible. The result was remarkable; after rinsing it with cold water I had in the palm of my hand the most stunning ring I'd ever seen. It was unbelievably beautiful, but so tiny I couldn't begin to fit it even on my pinky finger. Who in the world had a finger so small; it must be a child's ring. But it wasn't the kind of ring you would expect a child to wear; it resembled an infinitesimally petite cocktail ring.

I hid the little treasure in my jewelry armoire until I could find its rightful owner; maybe someone dropped it at one of Aidan's parties. I had my own suspicions about just whose ring it was, but I dared not say. I had to keep so much to myself, careful even about what I shared with my husband.

Chapter 42

Hamilton, Ohio - October 23, 1897

"Mother, you sure you don't want to go to the theater with us?" Mary asked.

"No Honey, I promised to drop some food by church for the banquet on Sunday and to be honest I'm feeling a bit under the weather." Ellie was understating her condition by a mile; she was sicker than she could remember being for a long time. Her excuse about going to church was a little white lie. Ellie just wanted to get the kids out of the house so she could get up to her bed and collapse. Samuel was in Washington until the end of the week so she would have the house to herself. She just wanted to be alone and get some rest until she felt better.

"Ok then, but if you're not feeling up to it don't worry about church," Mary said, "I'll take the food by in the morning."

Mary made some tea for her mother before leaving the house with her sisters to see George Bernard Shaw's play *You Never Can Tell,* a four-act play presented by the local theater group. As soon as the girls were out the door

Ellie pulled herself up from the table, knocking her tea to the floor in the process. She crawled up the steps to the bedroom she shared with Samuel and barely made it to the bed without fainting.

Lying in the bed fully clothed Ellie gasped for air. She didn't know which was worse, the severe cramps in her abdomen and bowels or the shortness of breath that sent her into a panic as she tried to breathe. She had made a mistake, she should have told the girls; should have sent for a doctor. Her mind flew in all directions as she lay there getting weaker and weaker.

"They say your life passes before you as you die," she thought, "I wonder if I'm dying. I think I must be dying." Mercifully she faded in and out of consciousness, intermittently sparing her of the pain in her lungs from lack of oxygen. "I need to sleep now, need to sleep." Ellie muttered a small prayer as she slowly expired, fully clothed, curled up in a ball on the bed she shared with her husband for so many years.

Mary quietly opened her mother's bedroom door, not wanting to wake her. Concerned that she felt ill earlier in the evening and frightened by the mess in the kitchen from the tea, Mary had a feeling she should look in on her mother – just in case she needed anything.

"Mom," Mary whispered. "Mom, are you alright? Do you need help getting out of those clothes?" Mary walked quietly over to the small bundle curled up in the center of the bed. As she approached she fought an eerie feeling. She gently nudged her mother but all the heat was gone from her body and the stiffness had already begun to take over. Mary broke into a sob and ran from the room for her sisters, who at the late hour were already preparing for bed.

Mary sent one of the house staff to fetch Edgar; he'd know what to do. With their father in Washington and the girls in shock over their young mother who was dead for no apparent reason, they didn't know what else to do but send for their brother.

Dayton February 7, 1898

Lelia cuddled up under a warm blanket on the couch of her little house on Samuel Street. The winter cold just chilled her to the bone. Jarvis was out looking for work again, he was willing to do anything for a few dollars; just enough to heat the house and put some food on the table would do. Lelia's opium habit was eating away the meager savings they had and their situation was bordering on desperate.

"Damn that Aaron. Now that Father and Mother are both dead there's no money coming in at all. It's been four years since the trial, where's my share of the settlement?" Lelia asked herself. "Edgar is the executor of the family fortune, you wouldn't think it would take four years to figure how who gets what."

Lelia pulled the blanket around herself a little more tightly. There was no food in the house, she was miserably cold and there was no money to escape at Sam Hing's. "God, I wish Jarvis would get home with some good news, I could sure use a taste of the dragon."

Lelia dozed on the couch, occasionally opening her heavy eyes just a slit to see if Jarvis had come in then drifted off to sleep again. The sun was disappearing in the cold winter sky and as it slipped below the horizon the room was enveloped in total darkness. Lelia opened her eyes, just a bit. She thought she heard someone come in; maybe there would be dinner tonight.

There was a soft glow just beyond her reach, and in her dreamy state she imagined the Chinaman was holding the bamboo pipe just so, and the familiar sweet hazelnut smell of the ambrosia's vapors wafted through her lungs. Oh sweet poppy, carry me away, far away.

Jarvis came home to a cold dark house. It was late and he had no luck finding work. He was tired and hungry; he couldn't believe Lelia didn't even bother to wait up for him. He lit the small gas lamp and walked over to the couch where Lelia lay bundled like she was wrapped in a shroud.

"Lelia," he touched her withered blanketed frame. "Baby, come on. Let's go to bed."

"Damn," he thought. "Where'd she get the drug?" He thought he smelled opium when he opened the door; it's hard to disguise the distinct smell. He tried to gently rouse her from her stupor, only to realize it was too late.

Chapter 43

Hamilton, Ohio - August 1901

Aaron stumbled out of the house on Fourth Street where he rented a sleeping room. He was falling-down drunk and it was only midday. On his way to the liquor store to get another bottle of Old Barbee Bourbon – Pa's favorite and now his, he saw a familiar carriage.

"Eh Eddy boy, what're you doin' down here? Slumming it today?" Aaron was hungry for a fight with the man who took everything he owned; including his house and all that was in it. The thought of him living in the house Pa gave *him*, using and defiling everything that ever meant anything to him - well it was just too much.

"Come down here you big coward."

"No Aaron, you're sloppy drunk and out of control. I'm not crazy enough to humor you."

"Well, I do believe that is my carriage; AND my horse!" Aaron shouted. People were starting to gather around the sight of a disheveled and dirty drunk in the street confronting a fine young gentleman passing through Second Ward.

338

"Get down before I pull you down!"

Before Aaron could get his hands on his nephew and wail the living tar out him, a constable rode up to see what the ruckus was about. He knew Aaron personally from the Malt House and tried to diffuse the situation.

"Come on Aaron; let me take you where you need to go before you get yourself in more trouble than you can get out of. I don't want to have to arrest you."

"Let's break it up here folks, there's nothing to see," and with that the crowd began to disperse. "Edgar, move along and get about your business. I don't want any trouble here. I don't know what you're doing in this part of town anyway. Go on, get out of here."

"Come on Aaron, I'll get you back to your room. You don't look in any condition to be doing much of anything."

"Nossir! I'm headed for the liquor store over on High Street. I'm out o' whisky…"

"Mr. Cavanaugh, don't make me take you in. You have a snoot-full already and you just need to sleep it off. It's to your room, or to a jail cell; your call."

The constable tied up his horse and walked Aaron up to his sleeping room and put him to bed. Aaron was so drunk he fell asleep within minutes.

Edgar Byron, in the years following the trial, settled nicely into Aaron's house, situated directly across from his father and step-mother's house. Just two short years after his step-mother Ella died of undetermined causes, his father passed away with a mysterious illness of his own. Now it was Edgar's spinster sister Mary who occupied the beautiful Italianate home across the street, while Edgar lived a lavish lifestyle in his uncle's stately townhome with all its trappings.

Edgar's victory in the courtroom boosted the young man's stature and his name became familiar to everyone in the county. Riding the wave of his success in the courtroom, he ran for County Treasurer – why not? The world and all its wealth was within his grasp. With the publicity generated by the trial, now was the time to take advantage of his new-found fame. The name recognition alone made it an easy win, not to mention all the money that was mostly his now with the passing of his aunt and step-mother. He barely had to campaign. Edgar Byron was a man of stature in the eyes of the small community.

The young County Treasurer was an attractive man in his late thirties, the most eligible bachelor in all of Hamilton some would say. Life couldn't be better.

His background as a litigator and recent two-year term as County Treasurer positioned him perfectly for a run as state representative in the coming elections. A bit anxious about his meeting with the regional Republican Party leaders later that afternoon, Edgar woke earlier than usual to allow plenty of time to get to his meeting in Cincinnati and back before nightfall.

"Angela, I can't find the suit I need for my meeting today. Have you seen the gray linen just back from the cleaners?" Angela was his new housemaid, just over from Ireland. She was still learning the ropes; the house and her new benefactor.

"No sir, but how about the lovely black silk? You look so fine in that one sir."

"I need the gray one; it's my 'Power Suit', if you know what I mean. This is an important meeting; it could launch my political career. That particular suit gives me confidence."

"I'll check the spare bedrooms sir, it must be here somewhere."

Angela found the suit; it was actually in Edgar's own armoire but hanging at the back. She helped him on with the vest, then jacket and straightened his watch fob.

"You look so handsome sir; you'll impress those fellas for sure you will."

Edgar stood taller, feeling even prouder of himself, if that was possible. He gathered the papers he needed for the meeting and slipped them into his leather portfolio and strode out to his glistening carriage. Aaron had good taste, and he had no qualms at all taking over his many possessions – including his horse and carriage.

It was around 10 o'clock in the morning on a hot, sticky summer day when Edgar Byron pulled his carriage up to a way-station on the canal to water his horse and to use the privy. The outdoor toilets at these stations were little more than an ash pit with a wooden seat if you were lucky, but at least there was privacy in the small enclosure. Better to relieve himself while he had the opportunity than hold it until he reached his destination; he had to stop for the horse anyway. Employing a trick he learned as a child he breathed through his mouth instead of his nose; it staved off the disgusting stench of the public toilet.

Walking the narrow path behind the station to the outhouse, his head was down as he watched his step through the low-lying brush.

"Oh-h-h," he moaned in a deep guttural tone. There was an explosion at the base of Edgar's head. His first thought was he had a stroke and grabbed the back of his head at the point of pain. He felt so woozy. He brought his hand to his side to grab something solid for support. It was then he noticed the blood, a lot of blood, dripping from his fingers. His eyes rolled back at the sight and he slumped into a faint where he stood. Half-conscious he felt a cloth slip over his head and heard muffled voices. Helpless, he lay still and let the distant voices do what they would; he was powerless to lift a finger against them.

"Grab his feet, I'll get his shoulders."

Two men dressed in dark non-descript clothing carried the limp body to Edgar's carriage, dumped him behind the seat then drove south to the Kentucky border.

Edgar regained consciousness. The stale air inside the flannel bag that covered his head was stifling hot and it was difficult to breathe, but that became less of a bother as the pounding in his head overpowered all other feeling. He tried to plot an escape from his predicament. He was wedged quite tightly behind the seat. But even if he could manage to jump off the wagon his hands and feet were bound behind him, so outrunning his abductors was out of the question.

Deep in thought planning his escape, Edgar didn't notice the carriage come to a stop. In the midst of working to loosen the ropes around his wrists he was roughly grabbed by the shoulders and yanked out of the back of his own carriage. He had no sense of time, didn't know how long he had been unconscious or bumped along behind the seat. His only sense was of the throbbing in his head that consumed his thoughts and kept him from thinking clearly. Fortunately for him, he floated in and out of consciousness, and when he was out he suffered no pain.

One minute Edgar was shrouded in a velvety blackness, a void where he was deprived of all feeling, then a feeling of flying – free as a bird.

Splash!

Cold. So cold it took his breath away. The flannel bag no longer hindered his sight. Eyes stinging all Edgar could see was murky darkness, felt a fast current pulling at him but something was dragging him down; down through the rushing brown water. He struggled to hold his breath, not wanting to swallow the muddy liquid that enveloped him as though he were in his mother's womb, but his lungs were burning. Fighting the weight of whatever was pulling him down was futile. Enough was enough. He relaxed all his muscles, swaying in the current like the eelgrass that grew along the river bottom, and breathed in the silt-filled river water. His thoughts wandered, then no thoughts, then deep sleep. Life left his earthly body; cold, quiet, a new source of food for the carp that gathered at the river bottom.

The sheriff vigorously slammed the ornate

doorknocker several times, but there was no answer. He was about to knock on the large oak door with his fist when it opened wide. A lovely young lady in black uniform and a crisp white apron stood in its stead and addressed him.

"Good morning sir, how may I help you?" Angela asked in her practiced voice.

"I'm here to see Mr. Byron, is he in?"

"No sir, he went to a business meeting in Cincinnati and hasn't returned home yet."

When Edgar Byron didn't show for work the morning after his meeting, and then the next, his office staff became worried. He wouldn't miss the debriefing he scheduled with the local party officials after his visit with the Republican leadership. That was two days ago. His secretary sent for the sheriff who was now making the rounds and interviewing associates. He started his search at the young man's residence.

"Have you heard from him Miss? It seems no one in his office has been able to contact him and they are beginning to worry."

"I haven't sir, but you might want to check with his sister. She lives across the street, third house from the corner. He may have told her his plans. I'm simply his new domestic and he wouldn't share those things with me."

"Thanks young lady. I'll check with Ms. Byron and

see where that leads me."

When the sheriff left Mary Byron's house he had no more of an idea where Edgar might be than when he started his investigation. He decided his best bet was to check in on Aaron Cavanaugh. If his disappearance involved any foul-play then Aaron could be a really good place to start.

The sheriff found Aaron sitting on the stoop of his Fourth Street boarding house, hiding his drink of choice in a common brown paper bag.

"Hey Aaron, starting kind of early aren't you?"

"Don't know what you're talking about."

"I really don't care if you ruin your life Aaron; I'm here to ask about your nephew. Have you seen him?"

"Not since your man pulled me off him when the fool came down here to gloat in my carriage."

"Well, that leads to why I'm here. He's been missing for several days and yours was the first name that popped into my head. Did you do anything to hurt him or make him disappear?"

"Nope, wish I could take credit for that but no. What happens to all my money? My house? Do I get it back?"

"Not unless he's put you in his will- and then only if he's found dead or goes missing for five years."

"Damn weasel…"

"Aaron, if you hear anything I want you to let me know right away. We have everybody out looking for him, and I mean everywhere. Will you do that?"

"Sure, if I don't kill him myself first." Aaron knew more than he was letting on, the sheriff could feel it. He had spiraled into a hopeless situation in recent years and no one knew *what* he was capable of. The sheriff knew one thing though; he didn't stay sober enough to do much of anything anymore.

"Thanks Aaron. See ya around." The sheriff mounted his horse and continued his search while Aaron went back to doing what he was doing.

Edgar Byron was nowhere to be found. The last anyone knew he was leaving for an important meeting in Cincinnati, but after checking with the party-leaders there, the authorities learned he never arrived. Deputies followed the road he most likely took along the canal but discovered nothing.

"How the hell could there be no trace?" the sheriff exploded, and loudly, to his deputies. "We should be able to find the carriage – the horse for God's sake!"

"There's nothing sheriff. We interviewed at every station on the canal between Hamilton and Cincinnati. No one has seen him. There's no trace of him along the road, questioned the locals all along the probable route – nothing. No one has seen him."

"This doesn't make sense. Wire all his relatives, he can't just disappear."

But he did. Edgar's sister in California said there was a plan for him to visit in the fall after the elections. But the last letter she received from him gave no indication that it would be sooner. The other sisters could give no clues to his whereabouts. The search continued for months, then a year. There was no sign of young Edgar Byron, richest and most promising young man in the county.

On August 9th 1902, the anniversary of his disappearance, the following news article appeared in the *Columbus Dispatch*. At that point in time none of his family had heard from him. In fact, there was no trace of him ever after that fateful day; that day which by all accounts should have been the launching of his career on the state and national political stage.

Hamilton, O.
Man is Still Missing

Mr. Edgar C. Byron, 34, of Hamilton, O., has been strangely missing since Aug. 9 of last year

when he left home
ostensibly to make a
business trip to
Cincinnati. No trace of
him has been found by
relatives who have
instituted a nation-wide
search.

He is the oldest son of Samuel Lee Byron, a former congressman from the Third Ohio District, and a grandson of William H. Cavanaugh. He served for a term as Treasurer of Butler County.

Epilogue

Hamilton, Ohio – 2008

"It's really hard to say goodbye to this place. We put so much of ourselves into restoring it." Aiden stacked the last moving box into the back of the U-Haul van. "It's amazing how much you accumulate over the years. Where in the world will we put all this 'stuff' in the new house? It's only a fraction of the size of this place."

"Yard sale," I answered. "Yard sale, Craigslist and EBay. Whatever is left – Goodwill."

"Remind me, Erin, why did we sell this again?"

"It's just too much house for only two people. With the kids grown and gone there's no need for this much house honey."

"I'm gonna miss this pub," Aiden remarked as he looked longingly at the cavernous party room that was home to so many good times for him.

"Well, one last goodbye Sweetie. Unless the new owners invite us to one of their Sashay's, or whatever they decide to call it now, we won't be seeing the inside of this place again. We need to get moving before they show up to move in. I'll tell you this; I'm sure looking forward to a much smaller place to clean."

We passed the new occupants on the Fifth Street tracks hauling a trailer of their precious belongings. New owners, new look. I wondered if they would experience the past lives that we did in that grand old house. Well, it was theirs now; time for new memories, for them AND us.

HAMILTON 2009

The new young couple, with four children all under the age of ten, had settled comfortably into the Dayton Street house and they were beginning to make renovations of their own. Their taste was splashy modern and would be considered by some to be incongruous with the nineteenth century architecture. While removing some non-loadbearing walls in the basement they discovered all kinds of things used for filler: large old chunks of coal, newspaper, metal objects. As debris came falling down during demolition an envelope glided across the room, landing on an old table in the corner. The new lady of the house walked over to the table, picked up the envelope, and pulled out a yellowed dog-eared news article from The Daily Republican.

WATERY GRAVEYARD FOUND AT BASE OF CINCINNATI BRIDGE

Joint Investigation Illustrates Cooperative Efforts of Two Fine Local Police Departments

Cincinnati police received a tip from a Newport dock worker who led them to an area off the Ohio River Suspension Bridge. Several bodies were found along the bottom near one of the center piers, among them the body of the young clerk, Richard Chasteen. Chasteen was killed in December, 1889, as he was about to be called to testify at the trial of Bob Toucka, southwestern Ohio's most notorious gangster, and one of his thugs from the Newport Kentucky waterfront. Toucka was indicted in the murder of Pete Daniels, a College Hill marshal and is a suspect also for the Daniels murder. The death of Mr. Daniels left the prosecution powerless to proceed and with the loss of the only witness all charges were dropped.

Seven men were recovered from the river in varying degrees of decomposition, most unidentifiable and weighed down by concrete blocks indicating a gang-style execution. Mr. Toucka, who owns several bars in Hamilton. O and Newport, Kentucky, remains the primary suspect in these drowning's but as of this printing has yet to be charged due to a lack of evidence. Hamilton City Police along with the Butler County Sheriff's Department were called in to help with the investigation and the identification of the unknown victims.

Written across the top of the article, in barely legible script, was a note that read "One hand washes the other"